The Bloodline

Jessica Mayer

For Samantha,

A sibling is an eternal grounding link.

Thank you for being mine.

Front cover image by Ava Bourne

ISBN: 979-8-218-62485-9

Chapter One

Crystal chandeliers, fancy ballroom dances, golden champagne, and elegant clothing paired with an enormous home that can only be described as a dream is all anyone ever sees. That's all the DuVonet's are to anyone.

No one sees the bruises effectively covered with makeup, or the blood that pours from the wounds on my body that never seem to heal. No one sees the silent tears, or hears the screams of the children when they're all that's left in their big, empty home.

No one sees anything but perfection. And why would they see anything else? The DuVonet's have appearances to keep, and people to please. They have certain expectations to exceed, and can't afford to fail to meet a single one.

Why would anyone see what happens to the children when the guests leave?

Why would anyone care?

Would anyone care?

I often ask myself that question. Any time I think I'm strong enough to tell anyone the truth about the esteemed DuVonet family, about who we really are, what our lives are truly like. I think I know deep in my heart that I'll never truly be strong enough, and I know somewhere within me that no one will care. I wish I could find the strength to defy them, if not for my sake, then for my siblings.

But I'm weak.

I'm far too weak to do a damn thing about it. Maybe there's nothing I can do. Maybe there is. Maybe I should stop causing a scene, sit down, and play the goddamn piano, exactly like he wants, making sure to not miss a single note. Maybe that will make my life easier. Maybe that's how I survive long enough to get out of this house.

Atticus DuVonet. Aged seventeen. The oldest child of Sebastian and Elizabeth DuVonet. The greatest disgrace to the admirable DuVonet family name. The child that never should have been born. The child that received the brunt of Sebastian DuVonet's abuse.

Pardon, Sebastian DuVonet's "alternative parenting methods", as he'd like to call them. What he believes is somehow best for us, and is supposed to make us stronger people. I think it only makes us silent punching bags.

Just once, I'd like to turn things back on him. Make him understand what he's doing. Make him see the damage he's causing. Somehow, I'd like to get inside his head, and make him see the true results of everything he's done to us throughout our entire lives.

But I say nothing. I do nothing. I can only silently accept the fact that I can't change the things happening around me. There isn't a single thing I can do. So I sit at the piano and hope that my fingers don't betray me as I press the keys without even thinking about my actions. Almost as if it's some kind of self preservation, ignoring the world around me, like I'm floating inside my own mind.

"Wrong!" My father screamed as the back of his hand collided with my cheek. I had already been playing for two hours, with my face growing hotter, and stinging more with each passing moment. Somehow, even if I played every single note exactly correct, it was wrong in his eyes.

My father was an ugly man, in every sense of the word. He had a nose that resembled a knife and had hair the color of crusted battery acid. There was no soul found in his dark eyes, and his figure caused him to tower over me. I might have been tall myself, but he still found a way to shadow me. Maybe he merely wanted me to think he was bigger than me. I don't really know.

I said nothing to him. I rarely ever let him hear my voice. I can't help but wonder if he's convinced that I simply don't know how to speak. Maybe he thinks I'm stupid, and that his screaming and acts of violence will magically make me smarter. I wonder if he ever once thought about the things he did.

"Get the hell out of my sight," He gruffly said. I remained silent as I walked through the house that never felt like home, to the room that I never slept in, holding the tears in my eyes, refusing to let them fall. No one needed to know that I was capable of crying. No one needed to see the eldest brother be anything but the strong soldier he painted himself to be.

If I had the chance to do so, I remained in my bedroom constantly. I didn't see a point in ever leaving it. There was nothing for me on the other side of these four walls.

Nothing I could openly have, anyway.

A quiet knock came at my door, and I held the oxygen inside my lungs as it slowly pushed open, revealing my brother Alastair on the opposite side.

Alastair and I may have been twins, but our appearances could not have been more different. He had light blonde hair that seemed to hold the breath of an angel within it, and my hair was darker than midnight. His eyes were shadowed with a murky brown color, and mine beamed with a shade of blue that seemed to give a youthful feeling, only I didn't ever feel youthful. I felt like by the age of seventeen, I'd lived a full life already.

Our build was the same, both of us being tall and skinny men, but we shared no other commonalities. Alastair never really said much, he didn't have to. We simply understood each other, even if we could never really find much to agree on. I think the only thing we ever truly could see eye to eye on is our hatred for our father.

"Are you alright?" He asked as he sat down next to me on my bed. I noticed the way he held his hand to his stomach as he spoke, as if his lungs would eject from his body if he breathed too hard. I didn't have to ask to know exactly what happened to him tonight.

"If you have to ask that question, you already know the answer," I laughed. It was hard, nearly impossible to be able to laugh at anything. But I knew if I didn't laugh eventually about something, no matter how unfunny, I'd lose my sanity.

"How bad was it this time?" He asked after several moments of sitting in silence. Somewhere within him, I think he was hoping that I'd turn to him, and tell him that nothing bad had happened to me tonight. That everything was finally okay, and we didn't have to keep living this life. But I don't think a day like that will ever arrive.

"It's been worse," I said. And it was true. Tonight had been one of the most tame nights of my father's anger. If I didn't know any better, I'd almost say that this was a good day, a happy day.

Except, good days don't exist in the DuVonet family. They never have, and they never will. We aren't that kind of family.

Although my brother understood the things I faced on a daily basis, that didn't make talking to him easy. We both faced our own version of "parenting" from Sebastian, and no matter the overlap between what we dealt with, it wasn't an easy thing to speak about. So most nights, we didn't. We sat together with a mutual understanding of how horrible our lives have become. And even worse, we knew we still had to keep our public image clean, and paint our father as a kind, and caring man, who deeply loves all of his children, and would never even dream of causing them any kind of harm.

I sat in silence with my brother for a long time. We didn't need words to tell each other the exact thoughts running through our heads. We just knew.

After enough time, another quiet knock came at the door, leading my younger sister, Anastasia into my room. Anastasia, aged sixteen, was an outspoken girl, a dangerous quality to have in this home. But somehow, she never seemed to show fear, even when fear would be the very thing to keep her alive.

She wore a harsh expression constantly, contorting her brown eyes into an unfulfilled stare, like there was no life behind her eyes. She kept her long blonde hair in an organized updo, and stood with perfect posture. She appeared most like the image our father tried to protect, and if any outsiders had only seen Anastasia inside this home, they might believe the perfect family story Sebastian has told.

She never spoke to us much, and she often pretended that everything was truly alright, and we really were the perfect family. I think that makes her my father's favorite, which sounds like a horrible thing to be. I wonder how long it will take her to stop attempting to keep those walls up around us, and accept her life for what it really is.

Anastasia could try all she wanted to pretend our family wasn't dysfunctional, and she could try to keep things hidden from me, but I could read that girl like a book, whether she realized it or not. I understood her because I once was her. At one point, I wanted to be the perfect son my father dreamed of, but I gave up that impossible goal a long time ago. It just seems to be taking Anastasia a bit more time.

She sat on the bed next to Alastair without saying a word. The sigh she released as she allowed herself to flop backward onto the bed for a moment of rest communicated more to me than any string of words ever could. She's never experienced my father's wrath like Alastair or I have, and I'm eternally grateful for that. But I think that also means she'll never be able to truly understand us, or really open up to us. She'll think we don't understand. Or maybe, she doesn't understand us. I guess it's hard to say which is which.

"You can talk to us, you know," I offered to my silent sister. I knew she wouldn't really respond to me, but all I could do was open the door to her.

"For what reason? There's nothing you can do," She shot back, sitting upright. Part of me wondered if our family image was finally starting to crumble in her mind, and if she was beginning to see things as they really are.

"It can help to talk about it, Anastasia," Alastair said. He could be quite hypocritical sometimes, himself never even really talking to me about any of the things he went through. But again, it's not like I ever tell him much either. Maybe we're more alike than we thought.

"I don't need a therapy session from you two," She pushed.

"Then why did you come into my room?" I asked. My tone wasn't hostile in any way, at least, I don't think it was. For once, I wanted to truly understand my sister. I wanted her to know she wasn't alone, she had us.

But of course, I knew she'd never listen, not to me at least. Maybe not to anyone at all. I knew there wasn't much I could do, but I had to try.

She looked at me for a few moments, analyzing the features of my face, including the half of my face that still felt like fire. She stared at the redness for a long time, her expression blank. I could tell there was something she wanted to say.

But she didn't speak.

She left the room without another word, closing the door quietly on her way out, again leaving Alastair and I to sit in silence, our only comfort found in not being left completely alone. And maybe that was enough for right now.

"She has to talk to us eventually," My brother finally said. I wonder if he was trying to be optimistic, or if he truly believed that our sister would open up to us one day. She hasn't in the past sixteen years, I doubt she's likely to start soon.

"She doesn't have to, but that doesn't mean that she shouldn't,"

Anastasia is a strong young woman, but even the strongest of soldiers will crumble eventually. I can only hope she knows that we'll be there to pick her back up when she begins to fall apart.

Alastair slowly lowered himself backward, allowing himself to finally lay down. He moved with a tense breath, pain clear in the way he exhaled.

I lifted myself off the bed, crouching down to the floor. I smoothly pulled out the small cooler I kept hidden underneath my bed, removing two small ice packs that smelled like an old hospital from the hidden sanctuary.

I pressed one to my cheek, handing the other to my brother for his injured abdomen. We sat silently together for a while before the door opened in silence once again, this time revealing Annabelle, the youngest DuVonet child, only fourteen, on the other side. Despite his clear pain, Alastair sat up to look at our little sister. I don't think I would ever admit it out loud, but to me, Annabelle felt less like a sister, and more like my own child. Like she was my responsibility to protect, and take care of, like I owe it to her to make her life much better than mine ever could be. Or maybe I feel bad for her, for having to deal with the misfortune of being the child of Sebastian DuVonet.

Her cheeks were red from her tears that couldn't stop escaping her bright blue eyes that looked like they held the innocence of the world within them. Her brown hair began slipping out of the neat braids that she previously wore.

I felt rage building up inside of me, like a fire was burning inside my chest. How could a man ever harm his own children?

Annabelle had learned to keep her tears silent as the rest of us did. She moved to sit between Alastair and I, clinging to me as the quiet pain continued to escape her. I hope she knows that no matter how alone she might feel in this world, she'll always have Alastair and I.

Over the years I've learned that there are no words that can truly bring any comfort. The feeling of comfort doesn't exist to a person who's had their entire right to feel safe in their own home ripped away from them.

And I firmly believe that the only sentence that will ever bring us any peace at all is "Sebastian DuVonet is dead."

"Do you want to talk about it?" I asked, still holding my sobbing sister. She couldn't form words, so she simply shook her head. Her body shook as her tears continued to pour, and all I could do was hold onto her.

"Atticus!" I heard my father's wicked voice scream. I could see the panic spread across Alastair's face, we both knew what our father had planned for me.

I shifted our sister closer to Alastair, and the two stared at me with concern written on their expression. Nothing good ever came from our father summoning one of us.

"I'll be alright, don't worry about me," I said with a small smile. Annabelle had no idea what our father had planned for me, and that was for the best. She didn't need to know all of the things he did to me. She didn't deserve to know how awful things truly are. She's just a kid.

I quickly left the room, racing to the dining room where I knew my father would be waiting for me. I moved in silence, careful to not make eye contact with him as I entered the lavish room.

"The garage, now!" He barked. I didn't know what his reasoning was tonight, but it didn't matter. He thought I deserved to sleep in the cold and dirty garage, so I would. There was nothing I could do to change his mind, or to stop him. All I could do was accept my fate.

I nodded to him in understanding as I moved to the door that led to our unused garage.

I suppose I shouldn't refer to it as unused. It's one of Sebastian's favorite places to punish me. It's used nearly every single night.

The moment I stepped through the door, I was pushed to the ground, landing hard on my elbows as the door was locked behind me. It was pitch black in here, I couldn't even see my hands in front of my face. Darkness was the only thing that surrounded me. I was completely, and totally alone.

Which meant that no one could see me reach for the ice pick I kept hidden in the back of the only cabinet in this filthy storage room. No one would know a single thing that happened to me inside this garage, or the thoughts that screamed inside my head as I spent countless cold nights alone, locked inside.

The cabinet was against the wall, that much I knew, the only struggle was finding the wall in the void that closed in all around me. I stood myself up with only an ounce of struggle, and I felt my way through the darkness, pushing myself in the general direction of the wall. I'd done this so often that a map made of emptiness formed in my head every time I was locked in here.

I found the cabinet after only a few moments, I may have even set a new personal record for my speed. I quietly opened the door that kept my hidden ice pick behind it. I didn't think about anything I was doing, I just did it. It felt like I wasn't in control of my own body. And maybe I wasn't. Maybe Sebastian was.

I removed the ice pick from its secured spot, and rolled my sleeves up with a sense of urgency, feeling every emotion to ever exist run through me all at once. My head felt like it was going to explode, all I could hear was the sound of my heartbeat echoing through my skull.

Before I could even think to stop myself, the ice pick made contact with my right arm in a horizontal pattern, causing blood to begin dripping from my arm. My arm stung as it heated up with my blood pushing onto my forearm. I angled my limb downward to avoid getting any blood on my suit from this evening.

I knew I'd have to clean my own blood off of the floor tonight, but I didn't mind. I felt like I had done what needed to be done.

I wish I could feel in control of myself, in control of my life. For once, I want to do something solely because I want to do it, not because Sebastian tells me to.

But I don't have the freedom of choice. I do what he tells me to do, hoping to get it right for once. But I know deep within me that I'll never do anything right by his standards. I will always be the DuVonet child that never should have been born.

The ground was a familiar cold. I'd slept on this floor so often I don't think I could ever relax if I slept in a bed. I didn't complain, I knew my words would never matter in this house, there was no point in even trying to speak.

The night seemed to move slowly, the seconds feeling like hours, the minutes feeling like days, and the hours feeling like months.

I laid on my back, staring into the empty ceiling that I pictured was the night sky illuminated with stars twinkling brightly as if they were singing to the moon. I thought about my life, how I got here, how I would get out of here.

But above all, I thought about myself. I know sons will often mirror their father, and ultimately become him. But I'm nothing like him. At least I certainly hope I'm not. I don't think I could ever be like him. I think I'd take my own life before I ever did any of the things he's done to us.

I think he hates me the most because I remind him of himself when he was my age. Maybe I just look like he did. I could never be like him, I'd never put my children through what he's done to us. I think I hate the idea of even looking like him. Like it's my divine punishment for even being born, is being cursed to look like my father.

Eventually, the daylight began to provide a small amount of light to the garage, and I made sure to keep my ice pick hidden, using the ounce of illumination to guide me. I knew I didn't sleep, not really, but it didn't even seem to bother me anymore. I think I've gotten used to not sleeping, never being able to relax enough to even attempt to fall asleep.

The door opened and my father stood menacingly in the doorway, staring at me with disappointment clear in the way he presented himself. It wasn't anything particular I had done, he was just disappointed that I existed.

"Inside," He barked. I lifted myself off the ground and began walking back to the house. I felt dead, like I didn't even exist anymore. Maybe I didn't. I guess there really isn't a way to be certain that you're real.

I noticed my siblings sitting at the long wooden table in the dining room with perfect posture, staring at me. I looked to Alastair, noticing his eyes fixed on my wrist, where my white undershirt poked out from my suit jacket sleeve. I glanced at my wrist, searching for the same spot he stared at.

And then I saw it.

I lifted my eyes to make eye contact with my brother, who held fear and pain in his eyes. He had seen the small amount of blood from my arm that got onto my white shirt, and in that moment, I knew he realized everything I tried to keep hidden from him for years.

Well, maybe not everything. I still have some of my secrets.

My father whipped his head to face Alastair, tilting it downwards so as to intimidate him. Alastair stood up silently as he prepared himself for whatever that horrible man was about to say to him.

"Can I trust you worthless fools to go run an errand?" He asked, turning to look at me as well. Alastair and I said nothing, but nodded in response.

"Good," He huffed, handing me a sealed envelope and a piece of paper. The paper had an address written on it. I didn't fully recognize it, and even though it felt somewhat familiar, I didn't bother to question it. I could never remember any addresses, my brain didn't seem to have the capacity for it, I could only ever remember how to walk to places.

"Don't do anything stupid," My mother said. I hadn't heard her voice in so long. It sounded like a dying cat, and she looked like one too. She had hair that was a putrid shade of red, clearly unnatural, and beady blue eyes. She was just as bad as Sebastian. She made herself the victim at any possibility. I never felt bad for her, she loved him and it was clear to see. I could never feel bad for a woman who loved a monster like my father.

Alastair walked toward me with great poise, but I could see in his eyes he was close to breaking down. He held himself together, but I could tell that somewhere within him, he was being pushed closer and closer to the edge.

We walked to the front door together in silence, quickly exiting the house and speed walking out of the gated yard, out of sight of the cameras posted at the face of the house. We got halfway up the street before my brother stopped me, yanking my right arm toward him.

"Alastair," I cautioned him as he rolled my sleeve up to examine my arm. I knew I couldn't stop him, no matter what I said.

"Atticus," He delivered with both an attitude, and fear.

"Stop," I said as he exposed my arm, staring at the countless scars that covered it. I could feel the pain radiating from him. It was clear he didn't know what to do, or what to think.

"How often?" He asked. He couldn't even look at me. I wondered if he was disappointed in me. If he thought less of me for trying to find my own ways to cope, even if they weren't good ideas.

"Alastair,"

"Don't lie to me," He pushed, bringing his head up to face me, tears forming in his eyes. I couldn't even fully read the expression on his face, I couldn't tell what he thought of me.

"We should get this done for Sebastian before he gets too angry with us," I said, pulling my arm back to release myself from his grasp, lowering my sleeve.

"You don't have to hide everything from me! I'm your brother for Christ's sake!" He shouted as I continued walking on the street. I didn't turn around to face him, I couldn't.

"Let's go," I forced. It wasn't a suggestion, and he knew that. He knew if I didn't want to tell him about something, there would be nothing he could do to force me to speak.

He continued to walk alongside me in silence, neither of us even acknowledging our brother standing right beside us.

It was silent the entire way to the address on the small piece of paper. As we approached the house, a wave of panic came rushing over me. I certainly recognized the house, and I felt myself silently praying that my mind had failed me, and I didn't really know this home, that I was wrong, and overly panicked for no real reason.

I walked up to the fabulous oak door, ringing the bell right beside it. After a few moments of standing with my brother silently, the door creaked open. I held my breath, hoping that it wouldn't be exactly who I was expecting on the other side of the door.

Shit. Sebastian knew. He had to have known.

But there's no way he could have found out, all this time, I've been careful.

He doesn't know anything. He never pays enough attention to me to know anything. There's no possible way for Sebastian to know anything.

The door fully opened, and he stood watching me with his gorgeous green eyes, and a half-smile, his brown curls falling onto his face. It wasn't that I didn't want to see him, but more so that I didn't want Alastair to see him.

"Well, Atticus DuVonet, how strange to see you here," He laughed, leaning against the doorframe.

"You know him?" Alastair whispered to me.

"Yes, this is Gabriel Lumone," I said back, not trying to quiet my voice. I tried to stay as calm as I possibly could, but I felt more and more panic setting in with each passing second.

"I'm offended your brother doesn't know who I am," Gabriel said, dramatically waving his hand to his head in shock.

"Do you know why we're here?" Alastair asked. I always forget how blunt he is when our father isn't around.

"You don't?" Gabriel looked at me with suspicion. It was clear he didn't truly know either. I wouldn't have expected him to know anyway. It's not like my father would ever have any reason to engage with him.

"Gabriel, who's at the door?" A woman's voice called from inside the house.

"Atticus and Alastair DuVonet!" He called back as I flashed him the envelope in my hand, right as his mother came to the door.

"Come inside, boys," She said in a sweet voice. Ms. Lumone was an insanely kind woman, she treated every child as if they were her own. She had welcoming chestnut eyes and hair of exactly the same color, and she had the exact same smile as her son.

"We really shouldn't," Alastair began.

"We can stay for a few minutes," I interrupted. Alastair looked at me with confusion written all over his face. He ripped the envelope out of my hand and gave it to Ms. Lumone.

She nodded and went further into the house, exiting from sight. I looked to Gabriel for a moment as my brother pulled me away from the door.

"What the hell are you doing?" He half-whispered and half-yelled at me.

"It's only a few minutes," I whispered back. I knew it was a terrible idea, but I selfishly wanted to spend a few moments with Gabriel.

"You'll get the beating of your life, we both will!" He still whispered.

"Five minutes,"

"How do you know him?" Alastair interrupted me. I felt my heart race. I couldn't tell Alastair, and I knew that much. But he isn't stupid. It wouldn't be hard for him to figure things out on his own.

"What?" Maybe I didn't have to worry about my father knowing, but Alastair knowing could be just as bad.

"How do you know this guy?" Panic raced through me. I knew my brother would never hurt me, not really, but I couldn't risk him knowing. No one can know.

Before I could respond, Ms. Lumone returned to the door, calling for my brother and I.

"Give this to your father for me, dear," She said, handing me a smaller envelope. I knew better than to ask her what this was for, I didn't need to know, and I don't think I really wanted to know either.

"I'm sorry, Ms. Lumone, my brother and I have to go," I quickly said, ending the interaction, speeding away from the door, back to my brother.

"Atticus!" Gabriel called. I froze. Alastair stared at me like he was trying to rip me apart with his mind. I debated between turning around and running for my life. I hesitated. The world around me seemed slow. I finally turned back around to face Gabriel.

"Maybe it won't be as bad as you think," He said. God, it felt like he could read my mind. I'm not totally convinced he can't. He seems to always understand exactly what's going through my head at any point in time.

"It will be. It always will be," I said, grabbing my brother's arm, and leading him back toward the house that haunted my life. I could feel Gabriel's eyes stabbing the back of my head, but I couldn't turn around to face him.

He knew things were bad, but he'll never know how bad they really are. I won't allow him to know. It wasn't something I could even really talk to him about. How do you even tell your boyfriend about the absolute hell you face at home?

Chapter Two

"So who was he?" Alastair began. "Who was he that he would be so worth getting your ass handed to you by Sebastian?" He pushed. I knew he was going to ask, and there would be no avoiding that. But that didn't stop part of me from silently hoping he would never bring this up ever again.

"Shut up," I shot. Alastair stood in front of me, keeping me from walking. I tried to move my steps to go around him, but he pushed my shoulders, causing me to stumble back a few paces. "What the hell?!" I shouted. I felt my anger building up inside of me, boiling like lava in a volcano, ready to erupt. It almost terrified me to think that I might have my fathers temper. And worse, his anger.

"Who was he?" He yelled, shoving me again.

"None of your business!" I grumbled, shoving him right back. I jerked my hands back, hugging them close to my chest. For a moment, I felt exactly like Sebastian, a feeling I never want to experience ever again. I tried to compose myself, but I also knew my brother wasn't going to give up that easily.

My brother lunged at me, trying to hit me. He had a lot of anger inside him, but none of it was truly meant for me. I just happened to be the closest person to him that he knew could easily fight back. And maybe he thought I looked like Sebastian, and this would be the closest he could get to fighting our father.

His closed fist collided with my jaw, and I felt the sour taste of pennies begin to fill my mouth.

"Fight back!" He yelled as small droplets of water began to fall from the sky.

"I'm not hitting you," I said, spitting my blood onto the sidewalk.

"Hit me!" He yelled, taking another swing at me, missing this time. His footing became loose and his stance faltered, his next swing displacing his whole body.

Instead of dodging his attack, I grabbed hold of my brother, pulling him to me. I kept my arms wrapped around his back, keeping him in his place as he sobbed into my shoulder as the rain began to fall harder.

"It's alright," I whispered to him, holding onto his shaking body. I didn't really know what to do, I've never seen my brother like this. This wasn't the sort of thing we really talked about. I suppose we never really talked about much, but certainly not this.

There was something wrong somewhere within my brother, and it was no longer something he could hide. He was always either incredibly angry, or incredibly detached from who he was. And I suppose I understand to a certain extent, but something about Alastair feels so immensely wrong.

I can't make him talk to me, I can't make him do anything. I can hope that he'll find the courage to speak to me, but I wouldn't wager that he will. He isn't the kind to speak up, he never has been, and I doubt that's something that's going to change in the near future.

The rest of the walk home was completely silent, I couldn't even hear Alastair's breathing. Part of me wasn't even sure he was breathing. All I knew was that he somehow was still standing next to me, but he didn't even feel like himself. It felt like I was walking home with a ghost, a cold figure I couldn't quite recognize as my brother, no matter how much he looked like me.

I wish my brother could understand how much I care about him, and I wish he would tell me what's going on with him.

I wonder if he wishes the same of me. I guess I can't exactly expect him to talk about his issues if I won't even talk about mine. I already hide so much from him, and I think he knows that, even if he doesn't admit it.

I led my brother to the front door of our prison, prepared to face Sebastian's wrath for taking so long to return.

Much to my surprise, no one stood on the other side of the door, not a figure, not a single sign that anyone even lived there.

Alastair and I removed our shoes, making a beeline for the stairs. I wasn't surprised to notice my brother following me into my room. He knew we had to talk about what happened today, no matter how much he didn't want to.

We sat on my bed for a while before either one of us spoke up.

"How did you know that boy?" He asked. I can't blame his curiosity, but that simply wasn't a question I could answer. Not safely, at least.

"I've taken piano lessons with him before," I lied, hoping my brother wouldn't press any further.

"It seemed like he knew you pretty well,"

"He's one of the only friends I have," I said, continuing to try to think on my feet. I knew he was only going to ask more and more questions, but at least this gave me somewhere to continue from.

"You've never mentioned him before," He pushed. I could tell he didn't quite believe me, but he couldn't exactly prove I was lying either.

"He was never relevant to the conversation at hand," Panic raced through me, I couldn't keep avoiding Alastair's questions, he'd figure everything out eventually.

"He seems important to you,"

"As I said, he's one of my only friends,"

"Then why have you never mentioned him before? Why do you keep trying to turn the focus away from him?" Alastair asked, getting more and more persistent with every word he threw at me.

"How can you say I'm trying to turn the conversation around, when you won't even acknowledge what the hell happened on our way back here?" I asked, finally turning to look at him.

"Shut up," He spat back, his irritation growing by the second.

"Oh, so it's alright when you do it, but if I do it," I snapped. I knew I probably didn't have much time left in this conversation before he stormed out, but I had as much right to be frustrated as he did.

"Atticus, please. For once in your life, shut the fuck up," Alastair barked. There was no denying it, there was something wrong with my brother, and he wouldn't talk to me about it. There was nothing I could do to get him to speak, but wait and hope.

The silence between us was tense. I could tell Alastair wanted to leave, but at the same time, he didn't want to be alone. I can't say that I blame him, being alone anywhere in this house is a terrifying thought.

"What is going on with you?" I finally asked.

"Don't worry about it," Alastair harshly said.

"You telling me not to worry makes me worry," I said.

"Well, don't. I'm perfectly fine," He said, standing up and leaving my room without giving me another chance to speak. I knew he was lying to me, but there was no way I could prove it. If he didn't want to tell me the truth, he wouldn't, and there was nothing I could do to change that, no matter how badly I may want to.

I care about my brother, more than anything. I care about all of my siblings. Just because I don't say it that often, doesn't mean I don't care about them. But it's hard to remind people that life is worth living when you constantly think about ending yours.

I heard the main door to the house fly open, and immediately the screaming voice of my father followed. I hadn't seen either of my sisters when I got home, I knew they had to be with him.

I practically threw myself down the stairs, rushing to get to them. My father wouldn't do his job and be their protector, and so that responsibility fell on me.

"There's not a single damn good quality about you!" He screamed at Annabelle.

That son of a bitch.

"She's fourteen! What the hell is wrong with you!" I shouted at him before I could even think about what I was saying. I can't even remember the last time I spoke to my father, but I knew that this was the first time in a long time he had heard the sound of my voice. Part of me wondered if I had really said those words aloud, or if I had only thought them.

"What did you just say?" He asked, turning his attention away from my sister. I could see in her eyes that she was pleading with me to stay silent, but I couldn't, I wouldn't. I think Sebastian was surprised that I still had a voice after I had spent such a long time keeping it hidden from him.

"You heard me," I said. I knew what I was doing was a horrible idea, but I couldn't keep myself from calling him out. She's a kid. She doesn't deserve this, no one does.

I almost let my body shut down completely, I knew what was coming, and I knew I couldn't stop it. I had to let it happen. But I'd rather it be me than my sisters. At this point, the only thing I felt anymore was my body hitting the ground after Sebastian shoved me.

He's a coward, that's all he is. He's a shell of a man who couldn't deal with his own failure, so he takes it out on his children, the people he's supposed to love the most in the world, the people he's supposed to be ready to sacrifice anything for.

But as I learned a long time ago, he's ready to sacrifice us for anything.

I try not to think about what's happening to me in the moment, I let my mind wander somewhere else. Usually into the future, a future where I'm happy, and away from him. A future where I don't have to hide who I am, and who I love. A future where I'm finally free for the first time in my life.

And with each strike to the face, I feel that future slip further and further away, until it seems like an impossible hope, something that isn't even worth clinging onto, because I know deep down it will never arrive for me.

I could end everything, I could make this all stop, I could free myself from him. There's a million things I could do to change my entire life right now.

But I can't leave my siblings. I can't leave them here with him all alone. I'd never be able to forgive myself for leaving them trapped here with him.

It surprised me that Alastair never came down the stairs as I expected him to. I don't blame him for staying away, I suppose that if I were him, I'd do the same thing.

At least I think I would.

"Leave him alone!" Anastasia shouted, pulling me out of my own mind.

Shit.

Why couldn't she stay quiet? Why'd she have to say anything? Why did she have to try to get involved?

My father pulled himself off of me, moving toward Anastasia.

Fuck.

I tried to pull myself up, but my joints wouldn't move. I had to lay on the ground, powerless, unable to move or even form words to stop him.

His hand collided with her face, and all I could see through my quickly bruising eyes were the tears streaming down Annabelle's face, and my mother tugging Anastasia's hair toward the stairs. I couldn't do anything to help them. I've never felt more useless in my entire life, knowing that there wasn't a single thing I could do.

The world felt silent. I couldn't hear anything but my own blood flowing. For just a split second, I thought I was dead.

But then I realized that I could never be so lucky.

I stayed on the ground for a long time, I couldn't pull myself up. It felt like I'd been there for hours before two hands grabbed my arms, hoisting me up, draping my left arm over a shoulder to keep me standing.

"You alright?" Alastair's muffled voice asked.

I still couldn't speak, all I could do was groan. I assumed he would take that as his answer.

"Good to know," He said, starting to drag me up the stairs.

He brought me into my room and sat down on my bed with me as gently as he could. The moment he was no longer holding me upright, my body completely collapsed under me, and I let myself fall backward onto the bed.

"That was pretty brutal," Alastair said, his voice still muffled as he moved to grab the ice packs that I kept in the cooler under my bed.

I still could only groan in response.

"What hurts the most?" He asked, holding the two ice packs. I knew I couldn't speak, so I attempted to lift my hands to point to my face. My fingers hadn't even lifted off the mattress before they felt too heavy to hold. I'm sure all I had to do was try a little harder, but I couldn't convince myself to care enough.

I couldn't communicate my biggest problem at the moment with my brother, I could only hope he'd look at my very obvious injuries and see what was causing me the most pain.

He stared at me for a few moments before placing one of the near-frozen solid, hospital-smelling pieces of cloth on my entire face. The cold stung in a way that made me feel at peace with myself.

I don't regret what I did tonight, I've never regretted standing up for my sisters, and I never will.

"You can't help everyone, Atticus. You have to get rid of this hero complex thing. Sometimes there's nothing you can do, and you have to accept that," He said. I feel like he was more so trying to justify his own compliance and silence.

I couldn't speak to him even if I wanted to. I feel like he just doesn't understand me, I don't think any of my siblings really do. They think they know me, but I don't believe they even know a thing about who I really am. Honestly, I don't even think I really know who I am. I think I'm a fraud, a scared little boy hiding in this body, pretending to be this big and mighty protector that I wish I had. I think I force myself to become everything that I wish I had when I was a kid.

I always talk about myself like I'm an artifact, minutes away from death. Then again, I guess people are always mere minutes away from death. You never know what your last moment can be, why not envision everything you do as if it's the last thing you'll ever do?

"Atticus,"

"What?" I asked as the swelling in my jaw had finally gone down enough so that I was able to form words again. It still hurt to push the word out of my mouth, but what choice did I have?

"Were you even listening to anything I just said?" Alastair asked. It was clear to me that he was also off somewhere within his own mind.

"Something about a hero complex,"

"You've been ignoring me for the past twenty minutes? Seriously, Atticus?" He scoffed, like he was personally offended that I couldn't focus on words while being in immense pain.

"Oh, my sincerest apologies for feeling like I was about to die at any moment," I snapped. I don't think I meant to give him such a harsh tone, that was just the way the words flew off my tongue.

"Why do you always have to be like this? You're just as bad as Sebastian is," Alastair said, standing up from my bed. I'd never felt so much strength build up in me so quickly. I grabbed his wrist without even thinking, keeping him from walking away from me.

"Don't you *ever* compare me to him again," I said, looking my brother in the eyes for the first time since he noticed the blood on my sleeve that revealed the scars my arms bore to him.

There was a kind of emptiness behind his eyes, almost as if there was nothing deeper than the surface of him. Like he was a ghost. Like he was already dead.

He didn't bother to say another word to me, he just left me to lay in my pain. I don't blame him for anything, and I hope he realizes that.

In all honesty, I don't think he does. I think he blames himself for everything, even the things so far beyond his control. I think he and I are the same in that way. Always blaming ourselves for even the smallest inconvenience. And always apologizing for everything, even the things that don't need an apology.

I wish talking to him wasn't so complicated. I wish he could read my mind, and understand everything that I wanted to tell him, but was too afraid to put into words. Maybe then I'd have the confidence to speak the truth no matter where I went, or who I was with.

I knew there was absolutely no chance I'd be able to freely move for the rest of the night, meaning I'd have to miss the ballet performance Anastasia has been rehearsing for for months. Not that she even enjoyed ballet anyways, she only did it because our parents told her to.

Still, I would've liked to see her dance. She's always worked hard in ballet, no matter how much she hates it. And she's good. I wonder how much better she would be if she actually enjoyed dancing.

And although I can't be there to support her, I'll finally have time to myself, time to finally feel like I can live a life I'm happy with. And for just two and a half hours, I can feel free. I can't help but feel selfish for trying to enjoy this time. Sitting here, wallowing in my own pain instead of trying to build my strength to be useful to my siblings.

I take my limited time when I can get it, which isn't often. Only when I'm recovering from the beating of a lifetime, and my limbs won't even work well enough to keep me standing for longer than five seconds.

I know Alastair is still here, but the powerful silence that lingered between us, despite being one room apart from each other, made me feel like

I'd be alone forever in this despairing house. He almost never went to see Anastasia dance. I don't know how he always managed to stay away, but I can hardly remember any evenings sitting in the performance hall with my brother. He was just never there.

It's going to be a long night, I can feel it already. A silent two and a half hours, the only sound I'll be able to hear is my own blood rushing through my body and the sound of my brain pounding against my skull, begging to escape.

Am I selfish for feeling glad I finally get a moment away from Sebastian? Is it wrong that for once, I feel like I get a break from responsibility? Is it so immoral of me to want to get away from the life I'm forced to live? I feel like a monster for not wanting to fight against him anymore.

Alastair already thinks I'm exactly like Sebastian, and if I've already hit the point in my life where I've become so similar to him that my own brother compares the two of us, do I even deserve to still live? Am I really just like him? Is it possible that I'm a carbon copy of him? Am I really that bad?

I couldn't stop the thoughts that were building up in my head, and I certainly couldn't stop the tears that came pouring out of my eyes. The one thing I never wanted to be in life was like my father.

I begged for whatever God was out there to make sure I'd never become like him, even if that meant killing me before I had the chance to turn into the man I hated more than anything in this world.

I'm not even sure I believe in God anymore. Not a benevolent God anyways. What kind of "loving" God could sit back and let something like the mess of my entire life happen?

I don't think that I really hold any faith in the belief that there's such a thing as a "higher power". I think I believe that when you're born, you're dealt a stack of cards. And I definitely believe that I got one of the shittiest hands ever dealt.

I didn't want to sleep, I couldn't sleep. I couldn't escape my life, not even in my dreams, something was always there, haunting me, reminding me that I'll never get away from it. Not really, at least. Part of me will always be held back by the way I was brought up. It will always be permanently ingrained into my head, all the hell I've faced in the seventeen years I've been a prisoner to this life.

My entire brain is being programmed to never forget what I've survived. I'll never be able to escape this life, no matter what I do. Something will always be there to remind me, and no amount of fighting against it can stop it. I'm shackled to my life and to my past, and the memories will never go away. And I don't think I'll ever be able to pick up the shattered pieces of who I could have been. I'll never be able to put who I could have been together. I'll never know. And I think that breaks my heart more than anything. The not knowing. And the fact that there's no chance I'll ever know.

Is it wrong for me to mourn who I could have become if my situation was different? I don't even know what kind of chance I would have had. I don't know what I could have done with my life. Half the time I don't even think I know who I am now.

I think I've earned the right to at least miss what my life should have been like. If only I had good parents, if only things had been different.

My life has been filled with the "if only" thoughts and the desire for something different. Maybe if I'd spoken up so many years ago like I always wanted to, things would be different than they are now.

There are billions of different ways for any given situation to end, and I think it breaks my heart to know that there was at least one outcome where I could have avoided everything I've gone through. It hurts to know that I made the wrong decision somewhere down the line, and that's how I ended up here, laying on my bed, unable to move or even process what's going on in this empty house.

Sometimes I remind myself that I was just a kid, there was nothing I could have done differently. I didn't know my life would go like this.

And sometimes, I wish I could go back to little seven-year-old Atticus and hold him. Maybe I'd even lie to him and tell him that things will get better, so that he has the hope to keep going, to see that maybe, just maybe, his life is one worth fighting for.

Seventeen-year-old Atticus doesn't even have that hope anymore. I think that hope died out a long time ago. I don't know when, but it vanished so long ago that not even a sliver of it remains.

Maybe I just like to lie to myself, I don't know anymore.

Alastair still remained silent, I worried about him when he was silent for too long. Even when it was only him and I here, he'd at least hum loud enough so that I could hear him through the wall.

He's always been very musically gifted, much more gifted than I. His talents lie within his voice, which I guess isn't something that our father really cares much about. The only talent he seems to care about is the one he forced into my hands.

I don't even like the piano, but Alastair, he loves to sing. That's something that should be fostered, not a forced enjoyment of an instrument that he makes me play at his parties, like some sort of dancing monkey, so his friends don't see through the lie he makes us all live.

Alastair's voice is truly incredible, and I wish he'd sing more often. I haven't heard him sing in months. Normally he'd sing any chance he'd get, especially when it was just him and I together, but lately he's grown silent.

Maybe I just couldn't hear him over the sound of my heart beating, or my blood pumping, maybe his voice was giving out on him.

I don't know why my mind kept giving me excuses and explanations, when all I would have to do to get my answers was force myself to stand up, and walk into the bedroom right next door. Maybe something within me is trying to tell me something that I'm not quite sure how to understand.

I felt my concern growing with every passing moment, hoping to even hear the sound of his breathing, and still. Nothing. It was strange for me to not hear even a single sound from Alastair, especially in times where we didn't have to remain completely silent.

Not a sound could be heard between the wall. My stomach twisted itself in knots and I couldn't silence the alarm bells ringing in my head. Nothing would drown out the fear I felt building inside of me.

But I still couldn't move.

I still couldn't force myself to even stand up. I couldn't move off of my bed. My head was pounding and my legs felt like they would fall off if I moved even an inch. It felt as if my entire body was being held together by a single thread that threatened to unravel at the drop of a hat.

Is this what it feels like to die? The immobilizing fear of not knowing what's going to happen in the next few moments that could make or break your entire life.

I had already known something was off with Alastair lately, and the deafening silence only solidified my stance in my worry. This wasn't like him, none of this was. I don't know what's happened to my brother, but he simply isn't himself anymore. I don't know who he is, he feels like a stranger to me.

Maybe I'm paranoid over nothing. Maybe he's fine, and I'm simply making a big deal about something that isn't even real. Maybe my mind has become so locked into the idea that I have to save everyone all the time, that it's become impossible for me to distinguish what is real danger, and what's all in my head.

No. He's not fine and I know that. If he was fine, my mind would be able to relax, at least a little bit.

Trying to get my body to move when it's shut down is a damn near impossible task, but I don't have a choice right now. I have to get up. I have to check on him. I have to see that he's okay. If nothing else to put my mind at ease, and to silence the screaming I feel building in my head in fear for my brother.

I think the adrenaline finally started to push itself through my body, because without even thinking about it, my limbs began to slowly move toward my floor, beginning with my left leg, gradually sliding down the side of my bed, and touching my foot to the ground.

I don't think the problem will be getting myself off the bed, I believe it will be the standing that presents an issue.

But that didn't matter right now. I had to push myself through the pain I felt shooting through my body. I couldn't let myself stop now, not when I knew something had to be wrong.

Before I knew it, my second foot had touched the ground. I didn't have any feeling left in my body at this point, none that mattered anyway. I had no choice but to keep moving forward, to keep fighting my way to Alastair.

I didn't even have to think anymore, I just kept pushing myself through the shooting ounces of pain that remained, pure adrenaline kept pushing the aches out of my body, making it easier to stand with each moment.

Eventually, my pain subsided, and I made my way to my bedroom door without an issue. Maybe my body finally went into shock, and once I was able to get to Alastair, and see that he was okay, I would only collapse once again.

His room was right next to mine, not a far journey by any stretch of the word, and yet it still felt insanely difficult, like climbing a mountain in the dead of winter without so much as a scarf to keep warm.

It felt like I was trudging through quicksand trying to get to Alastair, each step starting to prove more difficult than the last, but I had no choice. I had to get to him. It was almost like some sort of instinct was pulling me to him, calling for me to ensure that everything was alright with him.

I don't think things have truly been alright with Alastair in a long time, but of course, I'd never say that to anyone, I'd keep that thought buried in my mind, and I'd let it die with me if I had to.

Alastair would kill me if I ever tried to discuss his personal matters with anyone, and I owed him the respect and privacy to keep my conclusions and thoughts to myself. He didn't deserve to have his issues aired out for the whole world to see. I don't think anyone deserves that, in all honesty. I have my own issues, and he has his. We both can recognize that there isn't something completely right with the other, but that doesn't mean we feel the need to announce it to the whole world.

But at this exact moment in time, I need him to be alright. That's all that matters to me right now, making sure that he's safe. Our own issues and problems with each other are meaningless, they won't matter until I can know with absolute certainty that Alastair's alright.

My steps seemed to carry me with more and more urgency with each passing second, making my steps heavier, and my movements stronger.

I finally reached his door after what felt like a complete cycle of life and death. It was almost as if I was lost in time, like time itself didn't even exist anymore, but lived as a concept only in my mind.

"Alastair?" I knocked. He gave me no response, I still heard no sounds on the other side of the wall.

"Alastair, this isn't funny," Silence.

"Say something, Alastair!" My fear grew larger and larger with every passing second, I couldn't keep standing around doing nothing.

"If you don't say something, I'm coming in!" I warned him. My pulse raced and my entire body felt tense, everything around me seemed to freeze and I could move nothing but my hand.

The handle turned with such a slow movement that even a snail moved faster than it. The door creaked open, sliding on its hinges so slowly that I could feel the milliseconds passing by.

"Alastair?" I called into the apparently vacant room. I saw nothing within it, only the blank walls that matched my own room. There wasn't a hint of individuality or personality anywhere in the room. It was almost like a ghost lived in it.

I moved further into the room, trying to peek around for any signs of my brother, still turning up blank. There wasn't a single hint of him anywhere in this depressing room. It was an empty room that he only seemed to visit, almost like a bleak hotel room. Uniform, bland, and lacking any real value or joy to it.

It's not like he had a joyful life, but there wasn't a single item in the room that could even make him crack a smile.

It made me question if my brother even existed at all. There weren't even any pictures hidden anywhere in the room. It made me feel like he was only real in my mind, and couldn't be found anywhere else. And I guess that's partially true.

The version of him that I've come to know is one that only exists to me. He's presented himself in a different way to everyone he's ever met. And I'm the only person who knows him the way I do.

Out of the corner of my eye, I couldn't help but notice that Alastair had his bathroom door closed, which he never does. Leaving the door open is one of his most unfortunate habits. The sounds of alarms continued to blare through my head, and I still couldn't figure out exactly what it was they were trying to tell me. I still didn't know what to be wary of, or what exactly was wrong with my brother.

I moved to the door, knocking on it out of pure instinct, hoping to hear even the smallest sound responding to me from the other side.

"Alastair?" I asked, listening, trying to hear his breathing on the opposite side. I could hear nothing but the sound of my heart beating in my throat, feeling as if it would choke me out, right on the floor of my brother's bedroom. My chest tightened and the air escaped my lungs, I felt frozen. I felt like nothing I could say or do would matter. I couldn't help but feel like things were already so far beyond saving.

"Are you in there?" I asked again, knocking once more. He still said nothing to me, and my fear only worsened. I felt my heart sink into my stomach as my dread continued to grow. I knew deep within my soul that something was incredibly wrong.

And still, I was terrified to open the door, afraid of what I might find waiting for me on the other side, only hoping that no matter what I found, my brother would be alright. That was the only thing I cared about.

Chapter Three

I opened the door, my heart feeling like it was caught in my throat. Nothing in the world could have possibly prepared me for what I saw on the other side of the door.

I looked on the ground, finally seeing Alastair, his arms split open, and his bright red blood coloring the white tile floor. I couldn't breathe, without even thinking about it, I grabbed every single towel in the bathroom and began wrapping his arms.

"What the hell did you do?" I asked, feeling my tears pour down my face as I continued to wrap the wounds, feeling Alastair fight against me, trying to free himself from my grip. He didn't seem to have any emotion left in him, he didn't cry, he didn't show any regret. He just fought me. He wouldn't stop fighting me, using the little strength he had to thrash against me and try to rip himself away.

"Stop fucking fighting me!" I pushed back.

"Just let me die!" He screamed at me. I wouldn't let his words stop me from preventing him from bleeding out on the bathroom floor. I couldn't. I had to save him.

Fuck what he said about a hero complex.

I can't let my brother die. I refused to let him die, not like this. He's my brother. And despite everything that's ever happened between us, I love him. And I can't live my life without him. I came into this world with him, I can't imagine living in it without him.

"Alastair, I'm begging you to stop fighting me," I said, more tears running down my face. I held the towels to my brother's arms, the red soaking through the formerly white towels. Nothing seemed to stop the bleeding.

"I can't do this, Atticus, please, let me go," He pleaded. I couldn't, I wouldn't. I would not let my brother die on the floor.

"You can, and you will. Please," I said. He just looked at me, and I finally saw some emotion from his hardened face. He seemed sad, he still didn't seem to regret what he'd done, but I think he just didn't want to leave me in this world without him. At least, I hope that's what he was thinking.

He finally stopped fighting against me, and allowed me to save his life. The slices in his arms were so deep that they had to be sealed up, but I knew that I couldn't take him to a hospital, our father would find out, and that would only make everything worse.

But I also knew that Annabelle had a sewing kit in her room. It wouldn't be the most conventional way to resolve Alastair's wounds, but it would work.

At least, I hope it will.

"Stay here, don't move," I said, rushing out of the room to my younger sister's bedroom right down the hallway.

Annabelle's room was as bland as mine and Alastair's. Every room in this house lacked any amount of personality, it was a sad sight to see. I guess that was how Sebastian kept such a tight grip around all of us, we didn't have any sense of self. There was nothing that separated us from the masses.

Because of the emptiness of the room, it wasn't hard to find the sewing kit stashed underneath her bed. Under the bed seemed to be a common hiding place for all of us, and it was always the first place one of us looked if we desperately needed something. I think that was one of the few things that truly united us all. Something we didn't even use words to understand.

I grabbed the kit, running back to Alastair's bathroom, kneeling down next to him. He weakly pulled a lighter out of his pocket, for a reason I didn't really understand. I didn't even know he carried a lighter.

"To clean the needle," He said, seeing my confusion as he handed it to me, knowing the exact idea I had in mind to save his life.

I held the lighter to the tip of the needle for a few moments, hoping it would be enough to keep his wounds from becoming infected. I found the thickest thread possible in Annabelle's kit, hoping that it would be strong enough to close the wounds on his arms.

I managed to thread the needle without too much difficulty, thanks to the fact that my hands had finally stopped shaking long enough for me to even hold onto it.

"This is probably going to hurt," I said, removing the towel from his left arm, staring at the bloody mess waiting for me.

"Can't hurt more than slicing my arms open," Alastair tried to joke.

"That's not funny, Alastair," I said as I began to push the needle through his skin on his left arm.

"You're right, it's not funny, it's hysterical, you just have no sense of humor," He laughed, wincing as the needle made contact with his skin. He has a horrific sense of humor, that much is certain, but if humor is how I can get him to talk about his problems, I have to take what I can get.

"Don't move," I said, never breaking my concentration as I moved the thread in a zigzag pattern across the open wound.

"Don't be mad at me," Alastair said after a few moments of silence, his fingers tapping against his leg.

"Why would I be mad?" I asked, still focused on the final few stitches on the left arm, refusing to make eye contact. I don't know if I can look him in the eyes without bursting into tears.

"Atticus, I tried to kill myself, and you're the one who has to save my life," He said, his eyes piercing into my head.

"So?" I asked, moving the towel off of his right arm and quickly beginning to stitch the wound.

"You shouldn't have to. You shouldn't have to be sitting on the disgusting, bloody bathroom floor stitching your brother's arm back together because he's emotionally stunted, and can't talk about his problems like a normal person," He said, finally taking on a more serious tone. It hurt me to think that he felt he was less-than for wanting to die. It's clear to me that he thinks he's selfish for what he did, but I disagree. I can't say that I blame him for wanting to escape this life, and I don't blame him for thinking this was the only way. He's not the only one in this house who's had these thoughts, he's simply the only one who had the strength to truly act on them.

"You're not the only emotionally stunted person in this family," I said. I didn't think he'd believe any of the things I could say, but I had to at least get the words out there. Maybe they'd mean something to him. But maybe they wouldn't. I don't know if they'd really mean anything to me.

"You don't have to lie to me because you know I'm unstable," He said, staring at my hands as I put his right arm back together.

"I'm not lying to you," I said, focused on his arm. He didn't believe me, and he probably never would. He's always been stubborn like that.

"You can't tell Annabelle or Anastasia about this," He pleaded. He couldn't risk letting our sister's think that he's not as strong as he pretends to be. If I couldn't understand anything else about him, at least I could understand that.

"Why would I do that? They don't need to know any of this happened. It's for the best if they don't know," I said. I'd never share my brother's personal battles with anyone, they're not anyone's business.

"I think we need to talk," He said as I put the last stitch in his arm.

"I agree," I said as I stood up, extending my hands for my brother to grab as well, so that he could finally stand up.

"But how are we supposed to clean this up?" He asked, motioning to the bloody bathroom.

"I'll get some towels and clean it up,"

"Sorry I didn't use the bathtub," He said with a smirk, like he was trying to make another bad joke.

"Don't apologize," I said, cleaning up the already bloody towels off the ground, reaching into the cabinet that was below the sink, grabbing the other towels stashed underneath it, and wiping up the mess as best as I could.

It didn't take as long as Alastair was probably expecting it to, meaning he had less time to prepare for the conversation we both knew we had to have, and could no longer avoid.

"Do you want to start or should I?" He nervously asked.

"What's been going on with you?" I asked first. It was clear that he was nervous and he wouldn't know how to begin. If I didn't ask first, I'd never get an answer out of him.

"What do you mean?" He asked, like he was trying to dodge the question.

"You know what I mean. You're angry all the time, you tried to fight me earlier, you don't talk to me, or anyone. You're here but you're not. Talking to you is like talking to a ghost. I feel like I don't know who you are anymore, and honestly, I don't even think you know either," I said. I think more than anything, I missed my brother. He's an asshole, and I hate him sometimes, but he's my best friend, and there's no one I'd rather get pissed off by, or have to take care of after a difficult night.

"I don't know what's wrong with me," He began, his voice cracking.

"I never said there was something wrong with you, but something is going on that you're not telling me about," I interrupted before he had the chance to rip himself to shreds.

"There is. There's a lot that I haven't told you. And there's a lot I don't think I can keep from you anymore," He began, moving to go sit on his bed as I followed closely behind him, mimicking his actions.

"I figured that much out on my own," I said. Alastair took a deep breath, and held it in his lungs for what felt like forever.

"Things have been getting worse, not just here, but everywhere. So many people expect me to do one thing, and to be someone specific, and it's not me. Everything is stacking on top of everything, I can't do this," He said as tears began to drip from his eyes.

"What are you talking about?" I asked. He still couldn't find his words, I don't think he even fully understood what he was feeling, he certainly couldn't communicate it to me.

"I'm supposed to be the perfect, strong older brother. And I know you obviously don't see me like that, but Anastasia and Annabelle do. And obviously I love them more than anything, but I can't keep doing this. I'm not this strong, defensive brother I pretend to be. Sebastian's becoming worse to everyone, me included. And I didn't want to tell you that because I know you get it so much worse, but it's tearing me apart," He finally released. I understood him perfectly. He had all these expectations dumped on him, and it's not fair. It's not who he is, it never has been, and it never will be. He's never really even had the chance to find out who he is, he's always been told, whether it be directly or indirectly, who he has to be. He's been thrown a mold that he's told he has to contort to fit into, forced to bend and break himself over and over, all to please the people that don't even really matter.

"We all deal with things differently, and just because you think that I have it worse, doesn't mean that the way you feel isn't valid. He still treats you horribly, and it doesn't matter if you think you're better off than me. That doesn't make it any easier on you," I explained. I don't know if he believes anything I say to him, I hope he does. But I can't really be sure. I don't think I'll ever know how much of what I say he believes.

"I don't think I can deal with this for much longer. How the hell do you manage to deal with everything?" He asked. I didn't know how to answer him, I don't think the truth would help him, I think it would only make everything worse. I can't tell if the truth would be worse than a lie. But lying didn't feel like the right thing to do either.

I can't lie to him. He's my brother. He'd know I'm lying anyway. He seems to always know, even if he never says it out loud.

"I let myself go numb a long time ago. Tonight was the first time I really cried in, I don't even know how long. I let my mind go somewhere else. It's not much, but at least then I don't feel like I'm trapped where I am," I said. He deserved to have at least one person in his life tell him the truth, even if it didn't necessarily make him feel better.

"Where do you go?" He asked. He was trying to find his own sanctuary, but he clearly couldn't think of a place that would be safe. That's not something that any of us have ever had. A place to go where we won't be afraid. A place where we feel genuinely safe, and where we know there's not a single person who wants to hurt us. Alastair wanted to find that place for himself, in his own mind or an actual physical place he could visit. In any case, he needed somewhere.

"I like to go into my future most of the time," I said, finally turning to look my brother in the eyes.

"What?"

"I let my mind wander into what I want my future to look like. When I'm out of here, when I can finally," I paused, catching myself before I could reveal the very thing I've kept hidden from Alastair since we were eleven.

"Finally what?" He asked, noticing my hesitation. I never thought Alastair would be one to judge me or tell anyone, but I'm too terrified of what can happen to me to even tell my own brother.

"When I can finally be happy," I said, changing my entire train of thought. He stayed silent for a long time. I don't think Alastair ever really thought about his future. I think he's been too focused on simply surviving in this house to ever worry about what could come next. Maybe he didn't think he even had a future.

"Am I ever there?" He finally asked.

"What?"

"When you go into your future, am I ever there? Do you ever see me there?" He clarified. I guess I never really thought about it. I'd like him to be there, but I think all this time I assumed he'd stop talking to me once he found out the truth about who I am. I think I imagined that whenever we finally got out of here, he'd never want to speak to me again. We'd become strangers that looked alike.

"Of course you are. Why wouldn't you be?" I asked. He seemed surprised that I want to keep him in my life. He looked at me like he believed that after I got out of here, I'd never want to see him again. Maybe he thought he'd be a reminder of the hell of living in this house.

"I don't know. I guess I thought you'd want to put everything about this house and this family behind you. I thought you'd want to pretend we don't exist," He shrugged. I guess I know him better than I thought. I guess we share the same fears too.

"For one, I'd hardly call us a family, we're people who happen to share genetics and live in the same house. And while I do want to put this house in my past, that doesn't mean I want to forget about you and our sisters. I only want to forget about our parents, and everything they put us through," I explained. I could see that my words were finally starting to get through to him. He didn't simply assume I was lying to him. I could tell he genuinely believed the words I spoke to him. Or maybe I'm only trying to make myself feel better.

"You really think we'll get out of here?" He asked, studying the various injuries all over my face. He still didn't think we had any chance of making it out alive. Not that I blame him for thinking so. For the longest time, I'd accepted the fact that I'd probably die inside this house. And I don't know how, but that's not something that I fully believe anymore. I think I finally have hope for the first time in my entire life. At least, I'm going to allow myself to pretend that I do.

"I do. That's not me saying it will be easy, I know it won't. But I do think we'll make it out eventually," I said, giving him a smile.

"I don't know why I did this," He said, his expression hardening. Alastair obviously didn't want to beat around the bush anymore, he had to talk about what caused his actions today. This wasn't something that we could sweep under the rug and pretend it didn't happen.

"It doesn't have to make sense," I said.

"But shouldn't I at least try to make some sense of it? I mean, Christ, Atticus, I sliced my wrists open on the bathroom floor. Obviously I did it for a reason!" He said, his tone angry and distressed.

"You can try if you want, but you still need to realize that not everything makes sense. Think about how much you've been through. It's been piling up and building inside of you for seventeen years. You were going to break eventually. Tonight was your breaking point," I explained, trying to keep him calm.

"But what was the breaking point?" He screamed at me, pushing himself up from the bed, a mistake.

Alastair hadn't accounted for how his blood loss would affect him, and he began to stumble about, nearly falling backward. I had to forcefully push myself up, and grab his hands before he had completely fallen over, and knocked his head on the solid ground. I pulled him back to the bed, forcing him to sit back down.

"You need to calm down,"

"I need to know what the fuck is wrong with me!" He shouted in my face.

"The current issue is the amount of blood you've lost in the past twenty minutes!" I shouted back. I knew yelling back at him wasn't the right decision, but it was the only way I could get him to actually hear the words I was saying, and not brush them off to disappear into his own mind.

"I don't know why I'm like this," He said quietly. I could see that he was fighting the tears that were forming in his eyes. I love my brother, and I hope he understands that. I just don't know how to say that to him.

"Not everything has a reason behind it. Sometimes things end up certain ways. We don't have to like it, but we have to accept it. But you need to realize that who you are is not your fault. It's a result of what you've been through. It's not something that you can control. And the sooner you accept that, the better off you'll be," I think I was telling him the things that I knew I needed to hear. I know if someone would have said these words to me when I needed them the most, it would have made all the difference to me. It still wouldn't have changed my situation, but it would have changed my outlook on life much sooner. I knew if I needed these words, my brother probably did too. Maybe even more than me.

"I can change, can't I?" He asked. I could see nothing but pain deep within his eyes, he didn't want to be hurting all the time, no one did. He didn't deserve this. He deserves to be able to have some amount of peace and genuine happiness in his life. He deserves at least that.

I didn't know how to answer his question. Maybe he could change, but maybe he couldn't. Maybe he would always have to feel this pain that he carried with him like a child carries their comfort blanket. But maybe he'd be able to let it go.

"I don't know. I think if you want to, you can. And if you try, I think you can. But I don't think you can change while trapped in this house," I said. My words felt wrong. I didn't want to give him false hope, but I didn't want to destroy him either.

"So I have to suffer until I make it out of here?" He asked very bluntly. His bluntness will always and forever be the trait that knocks me on my ass like a gut punch. I wouldn't have worded it the way he did, but now any answer I can give him is going to suck.

"I wouldn't say it like that,"

"What other way is there to say it? I'm suffering every single day, Atticus. There's no other way to describe how I feel. Every single day is the same exact feeling, and it refuses to go away. Nothing I can do is going to make it any better. I feel like I'm stuck in the mud here. I don't know what to do, and I feel like I can't say anything about what's going on inside my head, because we're all going through it here. We're all dealing with a shitty situation. Why would I not come right out and say it exactly how it is?" He pushed. I have to admit that I did sometimes admire how blunt he was. When he knew what he felt and what he wanted, he had absolutely no issue with communicating that to whoever he deemed necessary.

"You're right. And I wish I had a better answer that I could give you, but the truth is that I don't. I don't have any magic words to make it all better. I don't have a way to fix our lives and make all of our problems vanish into thin air. I have absolutely nothing that I can do to fix anything," I began, watching the light drain from his eyes.

"Atticus," He started.

"But I can listen. I can be there for you. And that might be all that I can do, but sometimes that's all that you really need. But I can't do anything for you if you stay silent. Just because we all have to deal with shitty things, doesn't mean you have to deal with them alone. You can't let everything bury you so deep into this hole you've built in your mind," I said softly.

"Since when are you a poet?" He laughed, like he was trying to dismiss the severity of the situation.

"How long have you been feeling like this?" I asked, still keeping my tone soft. He hesitated to answer me, which told me everything I needed to know. He's been like this for a long time, and he can't keep it a secret from me anymore.

"A while,"

"How long is a while?"

"Six months," He practically whispered, as if he spoke quietly enough, I wouldn't be able to hear him, and I'd drop the topic altogether.

Alastair may be blunt, but I'm just as stubborn as he is blunt.

"Whispering isn't going to get you out of this conversation, surely you recognize that, right?" I asked.

"Part of me hoped it might," He responded, still utilizing the same soft tone, sounding like he wished he could disappear right into the floor, never to be seen again.

"You should know how I am by now, I don't easily let things go. No matter how hard you may try to fight me on it. You and I both know that there's a lot going on in your head, and we both know that you have to tell someone before it tears you apart," I said. I think I might have been projecting, at least a little bit, but it's almost impossible not to.

"I feel myself slipping away every single day. I don't know who I am anymore. I don't know how to live. I don't know how I'm supposed to find something to keep me happy in this life. I can't keep living like this. I have to escape this one way or another, and I've stopped caring if that way is death. I need to find some way out of this hell, or I don't think I'll be alive for much longer," He paused, I could tell there was more he had to say, but he didn't know the right words yet. I could see Alastair's expression change as he decided to let the words continue to flow out however felt right.

"I think about running out in the middle of the night every night. I think about packing a bag, jumping out the window, and getting the fuck out of here every single night. I don't know what stops me, and I don't know if it'll work for much longer. I have places I could go, I could leave here any random night, and go somewhere else without a second thought, and no one would be able to find me. *I could leave whenever I want*," He finished.

"But it's not that easy," I added. I knew exactly what Alastair was saying, I've had the same thoughts in my mind for years. But something always keeps me chained to this house like a dog chained to its pathetic little wooden shelter in a sad backyard.

"No, it's not. I always thought it would be easy to leave this place. I remember when we were kids, I would think about how I would leave when I was finally old enough. It took me a long time to realize that my age never really mattered, I could leave whenever I wanted. It's just a matter of finding the courage to actually be able to leave. I could've left when I was eight, at least then I could've avoided," He stopped himself. I felt my heart sink into my stomach. Just because we never talked about it, doesn't mean we haven't gone through the same things. Not talking about something doesn't make it go away.

"You couldn't have known," I offered. I knew that wouldn't make any difference to him, but I didn't know what to say anymore. I had to say something, I didn't want him thinking the words he said bounced right off of me, and I didn't care. I know how my brother is, and if I remained silent, he'd never open up to me again.

"I should've left back then though. But I think I stayed for you," He whispered. I think he was afraid that I would blame myself for the horrible things that have happened to him since we were kids. But the truth is, the only person I blame for anything is Sebastian.

"Me?"

"I couldn't leave you. Not here, not then, not ever. No matter how fucking annoying you are, you're still my brother," He laughed, wiping tears from his eyes.

"I'm going to choose to ignore the fact that you called me annoying, because you've been through hell tonight," I joked, finally letting myself smile.

"I don't think I'll ever be able to peacefully leave here until I know you and the girls are out of this shit hole. I can't leave any of you here," He added. It was a nice sentiment, but I believe that if he has a way out of here, he should take it. Just because I'm stuck here, doesn't mean he has to be.

"You don't have to let yourself be stuck here because of us. We'd be alright without you, and we'd be able to join you sooner than you'd think," I said.

Leaving was a scary thought. We all imagined it would be easy, but actually escaping this house for somewhere better was a terrifying idea to ponder. This torment is all we've ever known, I don't think any of us would be able to function in a proper loving home. Anything and everything even remotely similar to my father scares the hell out of me. I think I believe that if I somehow get out of here, he'll come after me. I'll have to watch my back everywhere I go, I'd never be able to really be at peace, always fearing that he's only two steps behind me, lurking around, waiting for the perfect moment to strike me down and ruin everything about who I am, and who I might have built myself up to be.

Sometimes, I even fear that I am him in another body, and the reason I'll never be able to escape him, is because I am him. I don't want to be like him, but something within me makes me feel as though I'll never get away from here, because it's been built into the foundations of who I am, and who I will always be.

I don't know how I would be able to know if I'm like him.

I think I'm afraid to ever build my own family on the simple chance that I could be exactly like my father. I don't think I'll ever have anything close to a normal life, because I'm too terrified of becoming exactly like him.

If I ever become like him, I hope to be shot in the head and buried in a backyard to rot.

"I think I would feel too guilty to leave you all here. I wouldn't know peace if I knew you three were still stuck here, facing everything we've tried to fight against for so long. I wouldn't feel right abandoning you guys here," Alastair said. His willingness to protect others is going to be his downfall one of these days. I guess the same could be said about me.

"If you have an out, you should take it. And I mean it. If you have a chance to get out of here, you have to take it. You can't spend your whole life worrying about everyone else all the time, you'll never actually live that way," I told him. I didn't think he'd listen to me, he never does, but I had to at least try.

Alastair sat silently for a while. He clearly had so much to say, but didn't know where to begin with the countless thoughts that had been building up in his mind for God only knows how long.

"Have you ever thought about the fact that everyone who knows us thinks we hate each other?" He finally asked.

"What?"

"People at school. They think we hate each other because we never talk to each other in public. Granted, we don't talk to each other much in private either, but no one at school has ever seen us interact with each other. And so they believe we hate each other," He shrugged.

"And how do you know that?" I asked. I didn't understand what he was going on about, or what he was trying to say, it was like he was speaking in riddles.

"People are always asking me why I hate my super cool brother Atticus. They think that because we don't talk to each other we automatically hate each other," He laughed. I think he was expecting me to make some sort of comment on being referred to as the cool brother.

"I do think you hate me sometimes," I quietly said. The smile slowly faded off my brother's face.

"Why would you think that?" He asked, looking like his heart shattered into a million pieces.

"Probably for some of the same reasons other people think that. And the fact that you compare me to our father," I confessed. I've never seen my brother's expression switch faster in my entire life, his eyes grew ten sizes, and his lips twisted into a frown that was so wide, I thought it would split his mouth in half.

"Atticus, I didn't mean that. Please tell me you know that I don't see you as even remotely similar to him. You're nothing like him," He apologized. I could see the gears turning in his head, and I think it clicked in his mind that his last words to me were almost a comparison of me to the worst man I'd ever known.

"I understand that you were upset with me, but you have to hold some truth of that in your mind to have ever even said it in the first place, correct?" I didn't want him to feel guilty. But I did want to understand what was really going on deep within his mind.

"No, I don't. I don't know why I said that. I wasn't planning to do this, you know. It just sort of happened. I didn't mean to say that, I think it just kind of happened," He said. Of course, I believed him, but that didn't take away the hurt from what he said. I think those words are going to stick with me for the rest of my life. Even if he didn't believe it, or if he didn't mean it, that didn't mean it didn't still hurt.

"I don't hate you, Atticus, you know that, don't you?" He asked when I didn't respond to his previous statement.

"Sometimes. But other times, it's hard to not feel that way. Maybe if we talked to each other more, I could push those thoughts out of my head completely," I finally said.

I wonder if Alastair thought I hated him. Maybe the cause of our issues with communication had to do with the fact that we've spent a large portion of our lives believing that the other hated us. I know that I've held nothing but love for my brother my entire life, but that doesn't mean that he knew that. I wish it was easier for us to talk about these kinds of things, maybe then we could have avoided most of tonight's events. I never expected talking to my brother would be one of the most difficult things I've had to do in my life, and yet it always is. I wish we could read each other's minds, and instantly understand what the other needs to say. Sometimes we understand each other, but most of the time we get lost in our broken and improper communication.

"Why do all of our problems stem from a lack of communication?" He asked, laughing.

"Because our whole lives we've been conditioned to think that you solve problems with your fists instead of your words," I laughed. We make truly awful jokes sometimes, but it's better than swinging at each other in the street because we don't know how to talk to each other.

"Does this mean we're going to walk around the hallways skipping around with our arms linked together?" He continued laughing. It was nice to hear him laugh again. It's been a long time since I've seen my brother happy, truly happy. Of course, I've seen him fake a smile and pretend to be filled with joy, but I haven't seen genuine happiness from him in a long time.

"Oh, absolutely," I laughed back with him. Our brief happiness was instantly broken at the sound of a car pulling into the driveway.

"They're back already?" Alastair asked me, the blood draining from his face.

"I guess. Just pretend you're asleep, we'll talk at school tomorrow," I said, standing up to leave his room. As I moved closer to the door, I felt my brother grab my arm, preventing me from exiting the room.

"I do love you, Atticus," He said. I don't know that I've ever heard him say those words to me before.

"I love you too, Alastair," I responded without a second thought. He let go of my arm, and I used the little strength I had left in my body to quickly stash Annabelle's sewing kit underneath Alastair's bed, and practically sprint to my bedroom, throwing myself onto the bed, pretending to be asleep.

"What the fuck is wrong with you?!" I heard my father screaming downstairs. Out of pure instinct, I instantly flung myself off the bed, rushing into the hallway, finding Alastair meeting me there. I gave him a look to protest his attempt to help due to his blood loss, but I knew I wouldn't be able to stop him.

The sound of glass shattering and my sister screaming could be heard moments after I entered the hallway, and that alone was enough to send myself and Alastair flying down the stairs.

We stood at the bottom of the stairs, trying to examine the situation, immediately noticing Annabelle in tears and Anastasia standing still with her head down.

"You're an embarrassment!" My mother shouted, slapping Anastasia across the face. I couldn't stop myself from trying to dive forward at her, the only thing that held me back was Alastair. He knew it wouldn't end well for anyone if I tried to intervene. Not that anything that's going to happen tonight will end well anyway. But my intervention would only make everything worse.

Having to simply stand here, and be a silent witness to everything happening in this house destroyed me constantly. I wanted to scream, and cry, and pull my parents away from my sisters, but something always keeps me from acting on these thoughts. It rips me apart having to stand there, and let everything happen. There's so much I can prevent, so much I should prevent, and I don't. It doesn't matter what happens to me as long as it keeps my sisters safe.

"Why the hell are you two down here?!" My father shouted. I didn't know what excuse to give him, the words completely escaped my mind.

"We heard things breaking and thought someone was in the house, Sir," Alastair said quickly, once he realized I could form no words.

"Get out of my sight," He growled. We didn't have a choice but to do what he said, if we didn't, things would only get worse.

Alastair pulled me back up the stairs, he knew I didn't want to move. Everything in me wanted to fight against my brother, but I knew I couldn't. I didn't have any fight left in me today.

I went back into my room, expecting to be abandoned for the rest of the night, but much to my surprise, Alastair followed right behind me.

My brother walked to the center of my room as I shut the door, I could feel my heart pounding in my chest from the pure anxiety of what I knew was happening to my sisters. The moment I turned around to face Alastair, he immediately pulled me close to him, sobbing into my shoulder.

I couldn't cry, my eyes wouldn't allow it. I just stood there, holding my brother. I didn't even attempt to convince him that things would be okay. I didn't even believe that anymore. The sliver of hope I had found earlier was instantly ripped away from me.

We stood together for a long time, it was all we could do. I expected our sisters to come in here at some point, but they never did. Alastair and I stood together for well over an hour before he finally returned to his own bedroom for the evening.

I climbed into my bed, finally being allowed to stay in this room for the first time in a long time. I couldn't even sleep, I only stared at the ceiling, listening to the sound of my heart beating.

I knew I had to go to school in the morning, and I'd have to cover up a majority of my very visible injuries and come up with a lie to defend the others I couldn't hide.

Because God forbid anyone finds out the truth about my parents, and discovers that the "perfect" DuVonet family is a load of shit, and the entire family name is held together by a single string that holds the weight of the world on it, threatening to snap at any given moment.

No one can ever see the truth that lies behind this perfect family. And it's not like anyone would ever believe me anyways. My parents have too many people fooled. No one would ever believe a single word I could say against them. Someone would always have some bullshit excuse that defends them, as if they live with my parents and know what they're like when no one else is around.

Because why would anyone believe that the great Sebastian and Elizabeth DuVonet treat their perfectly behaved children as their own personal punching bags?

Morning came sooner than expected, and much sooner than I was prepared for it. I didn't sleep at all, it was rare that I did sleep.

I was still in severe amounts of pain, but I didn't have a choice but to trudge through it. I moved into my bathroom which was as plain as the rest of my bedroom and lacked any individuality.

I covered the bruises and cuts that covered my arms with some makeup that my mother put in my bathroom long ago, gently moving to cover the bruises along my jawline courtesy of Alastair. I learned how to cover bruises a long time ago, and I've been doing it for as long as I could remember. I knew I didn't have any other choice. The only visible injury I didn't bother to cover was my black eye, I knew I could come up with a believable enough lie for that.

I changed into a plain black sweatshirt and black jeans. They weren't formal clothes, but at least they prevented anyone from seeing the bruises, and it would keep people from asking too many questions.

I went downstairs to be inspected before school to be approved to even leave the house. It was how my parents ensured that no one would ever find out about their sinister behavior.

"What happened to your eye?" My father asked. He knew of course, but he had to know my lie in the event that someone decided to tell the school and call my parents.

"I was playing basketball with Alastair and he accidentally passed the ball too high and it hit me in the face," I said. My father didn't say anything to me, he only nodded, and sent me on my way out the door, where I found my three siblings already waiting for me.

"What's with the eye?" Alastair asked.

"Don't you remember? You hit me in the face with the ball when we were playing basketball," I said. My brother had to know the lie too in the event that he got pulled into the office about my injury.

"I don't understand why we have to lie," Anastasia said as we began on our way to the school all four of us attended.

"What are you talking about? We're not lying," I corrected Anastasia. We had to lie to keep ourselves safe, it was our only option. Telling the truth would only make everything worse.

It wasn't a far walk to the school, it only took about ten minutes. And it was even less time before my sisters took off on their own path, separating from me and Alastair.

"Love you too!" We said in unison, turning to look at each other with disgust. Our moments of synchronization only encourage people to ask us if twin telepathy is real, a question we get asked every time we meet someone new.

"I hate when we do that," Alastair said, moving toward his group of friends.

"I thought we were going to talk to each other at school from now on? Already going back on your word?" I asked, laughing.

"Oh shit, yeah," He joked, walking back toward me.

"Link arms with me," I smirked, my only goal now to embarrass my popular, mysterious brother.

"You're kidding,"

"I've never been more serious in my entire life, Alastair Victor DuVonet," I said, placing my fist on my hip, leaving an open space for my brother to link arms with me.

"You did not just use my full name," He dramatically gasped.

"Oh, but I did," I laughed as my brother linked arms with me. I finally looked straight ahead, noticing Gabriel standing not too far away from me. Part of me hoped Alastair didn't notice him.

"Isn't that the kid from the house the other day?" He asked, motioning in Gabriel's direction.

Shit. Of course, he would notice the only person that I didn't want him to know about. It's like he does things like that on purpose sometimes.

"Oh, yeah, it is," I answered, feeling Alastair pulling me toward him. "Woah, woah, wait, why are we going toward him?" I asked.

"Aren't you guys friends?"

"Well, yeah," I stumbled.

"So let's go say hi," He said, tugging on my arm, trying to pull me closer and closer to Gabriel.

"Don't you have friends?" I asked, my nerves increasing with each passing moment as I knew there would be no getting out of this.

"Why are you so against me knowing this kid?" He asked. It's not that I was against Alastair knowing my boyfriend, it's that I was against him knowing that I'm gay.

I didn't have a chance to stop my brother, he just kept pulling me toward Gabriel. God, why does he always have to be so stubborn?

"Well good morning," Gabriel said. I kept my head down, I didn't want him to see my eye, I knew I wouldn't be able to lie to him, not about this.

"Hey," I said, still keeping my head down.

"Since when are you two best friends?" He asked, surprised to see my brother and I in such close proximity to each other.

"Contrary to popular belief, we don't actually hate each other," Alastair said.

"I'm shocked," Gabriel said with a clearly sarcastic tone.

"As much as I'd love to stick around, I have shit to do this fine morning," Alastair said, letting go of my arm. "Talk to me in fifth period today!" He added as he practically sprinted toward his friends, leaving me to speak to Gabriel on my own.

Chapter Four

"What's the matter with you?" Gabriel asked as soon as Alastair was out of earshot. I knew I couldn't hide the truth from him forever, but I had to try and keep things from him for at least a little while longer.

"It's been a rough twenty-four hours," I said quietly, still refusing to look up at him. I knew there would be no hiding once he saw my eye. He's not stupid. Even if I don't tell him the truth, he'll figure it out on his own with enough time.

"Look at me," He said suspiciously, like he already knew what I was trying to hide.

"Gabriel," I began in protest. Before I could do anything to plead my case, he lightly pushed my chin upward, so that I would look him in the eyes.

"What happened to your eye?" He asked, his eyes growing wide as his concern clearly grew by the second.

"It's nothing, Alastair just sucks at basketball," I said, trying to brush off his concern. I didn't like lying to him, especially not about things like this, but I didn't have a choice. I didn't know how to tell him the truth. It wasn't exactly safe for me to tell him anyway.

"Are you sure that's all it is?" He asked. He didn't believe me, I know he didn't. But it's not like I had the option of telling him everything, at least, not here.

"I mean that's not everything that's happened in the past day, but that's what happened to my eye," I said with a light laugh. Gabriel clearly didn't find my joke funny, as he only stared at my features, clearly noticing the spot on my jaw where I very poorly tried to cover my bruise. Part of me wonders if I did it badly on purpose, as if anyone knowing the truth was going to change my situation.

"Why do you have makeup on your jaw?" He asked. It's not like this is the first time I've had to do this, but this is the first time he's ever asked. I wonder if he was finally beginning to put together the pieces that have been laid out in front of him for so long. He had to know something wasn't right. He wouldn't keep asking questions unless he knew.

"Alastair,"

"Are you going to blame him for everything?" He interrupted me. Of course, he's not going to believe me when I'm actually telling the truth.

"He tried to fight me when we left your house yesterday. He got a good swing on me, and bruised me pretty bad," I explained. I don't think he was quite convinced. Maybe with his growing suspicion, I'll never be able to convince him of anything, unless I tell him whatever conclusions he's already come to.

"Why'd he try to fight you?"

"There's a lot going on with him. He was mad about a lot of things and didn't know what to do, so he attacked me because he knew I could fight back if I had to," I said. I wasn't going to tell him everything that happened with my brother yesterday, he didn't need to know, and it wasn't my place to tell him. Only Alastair can decide who knows about the events of yesterday.

"You know you can tell me if something's going on, right?" He asked. Gabriel cared more than anyone I've ever met, and if he knew the half of what really happened when I went home, he'd make sure I never had to go back. But it isn't that easy. I didn't know how to tell him anything. Maybe I'll tell him everything soon enough. But then again, maybe I won't.

"We should get going," I said, quickly changing the subject. Gabriel didn't try to pry any further, he knew he wouldn't get anywhere if he kept trying to force information out of me. He knew he had to wait, and be patient.

I spent the first half of my day with Gabriel, I was with him constantly from eight in the morning until noon. It's nice to be able to spend so much time with him, considering the fact that I almost never see him outside of school.

"I heard there's a partner write-up for homework in physics," He mentioned in our first hour together.

"I assume we're partners?"

"Obviously. Your house or mine?" He asked. I don't know why the question threw me off so much. My mind instantly raced through all the horrible things that could happen if we did something as simple as work on an assignment at my house. I couldn't subject Gabriel to even being near my father.

"Hello? Earth to Atticus?" He said, waving his hand in front of my eyes. I hadn't even realized how long I'd left his simple question unanswered.

"Your's," I finally uttered.

"I figured," He chuckled, moving his hand to grab mine. I felt myself freeze. I didn't want to tell him I was afraid of the chance of someone who knows my father seeing us. I didn't want him to think I was ashamed or embarrassed of him, that couldn't be further from the truth. I'd scream to the world how in love with him I am if I could.

But I can't. Because I'll die if I do.

I'll admit, I felt safer knowing that Gabriel was right beside me, but that doesn't mean that I felt safe enough to tell anyone the truth.

"Is there actually a write-up, or is that the excuse I'm supposed to tell my father so that I'll have permission to leave the house?" I asked. Gabriel knew Sebastian was strict, but that was all he really knew about my father.

"Maybe a little bit of both," He said with a smile. I didn't mind lying to my father about what I was doing if it meant I got to spend time with Gabriel. Granted, if he ever found out the truth, he'd kill me. But somehow, I never really cared about that. I was relieved to even be able to know Gabe, and to be able to love him.

Even if it meant risking my life on occasion.

My day seemed to move slower when I wasn't with Gabriel, even when I saw my brother, time felt like it slowly ticked by. Maybe it was boredom. Maybe it was dread. Maybe I'll never really know what my emotions are, and I'll always feel like a scarecrow made of straw, hoping to ever understand even a single thing about myself.

"I think the teacher's going to have a heart attack if she sees us actually talking to each other," Alastair said, nudging my shoulder, snapping me out of the thoughts that filled my mind. He seems to be good at pulling me back into reality, even if he doesn't realize it.

"I think everyone's shocked," I smiled. I'll admit, it's nice being able to socialize with my brother, and actually feel like we have some kind of relationship, instead of two soldiers fighting the same war.

"Who's your partner for the physics write-up?" He asked, noticing I wasn't completely mentally there. It was like he kept tugging on the strings to pull me fully back into reality, refusing to let go.

"Gabriel,"

"That kid from this morning?"

"The very same," I said. Alastair gave me a look of rising suspicion. He had to know something was going on, he might not know what, but he has to realize there's something I'm not telling him. He's not an idiot.

Well, not a complete idiot, anyway.

"You guys are working at his house then?" He asked, seemingly trying to pry information out of me, like he was some kind of detective, and I, his prime suspect.

"Well, there's no chance in hell we're going to work at our house," I laughed.

"You know you can talk to me about anything, right?" He asked, studying my face, as if it wasn't identical to his.

"Of course. Why?" I felt the panic rush through me, why would he be asking me these questions? What does he think he's going to gain from interrogating me like this? Especially in such a public place?

"Just saying," He said, looking me up and down, still wearing that stupid look on his face. That stupid look that seems to shoot directly into my soul, like he knows all my deepest, darkest secrets. Like he knows everything there is to possibly know about me, and that he could use my secrets as a weapon against me whenever he pleases. Like I'm completely transparent, vulnerable, on display for everyone in the world to see, for everyone to mock. Degrade. Manipulate. Like I'm some kind of zoo animal, there for everyone else's entertainment, and never given a chance to think for myself.

He knows.

He has to know.

I felt like I couldn't breathe, my throat feeling tighter and tighter with each passing second, the air escaping my lungs, my body constricting in on itself, choking me out as if my own body is trying to kill me in the middle of this stupid fucking classroom.

I can't breathe.

I'm going to pass out.

Am I dying?

This feels a lot like dying.

Snap out of it, Atticus.

Stop panicking.

If you panic, you're going to give everything away.

Stop being fucking stupid.

Just fucking breathe.

"Are you okay?" Alastair finally asked, seeing the red on my face grow, spreading across my entire body. But I couldn't respond, the words didn't exist to me. I couldn't even think clearly. Everything was blurry, I couldn't see, I couldn't do anything.

"Atticus," He said, pushing my shoulders, trying to snap me out of the trance I was so clearly stuck deep within. But still, I could form no words, I sat there, growing redder and redder with each second, filling with panic.

I didn't think. I didn't speak. I stood up, practically sprinting out of the classroom, dashing to the bathroom, nearly collapsing on the cold tile floor. I sat on the ground with my back against the wall for a long time before anyone else came into the disgusting school bathroom.

I could hear three other boys laughing as they walked past me, as I was practically dead on the ground. It wasn't worth it for me to say anything to them, I knew it wouldn't end well. It didn't matter anyway. I couldn't even see their faces, they looked like blurry messes. Maybe it was my vision going out from pure stress.

"Is that the great Atticus DuVonet?" One of them asked, mockingly. I always seem to forget how well-known I am in this shithole. Everywhere I go, everyone seems to know who I am. And it fucking sucks.

I didn't bother to respond, they were going to say and do whatever the hell they wanted. My words didn't matter. They never have, and they never will.

I didn't even know what was going on, I felt all three of them ripping me off the ground, pinning me against the back wall. I still couldn't see their faces, I couldn't process what was going on. I only felt their fists sharply push into my stomach repeatedly, knocking the little air that was left in my body right out, leaving me coughing, sputtering, and struggling for my life. But somehow, this felt like pricking my finger in comparison to the things Sebastian has put me through.

It felt like it went on forever before they finally let me go, dropping me back down to the ground. I don't know what I did to them to deserve that. Maybe they thought it would make them cool, or popular to attack someone well known, the son of a very powerful man.

Maybe I just exist.

Maybe more people than I first thought are exactly like my father, and the fact that I have life still within me is enough justification for people to beat the shit out of me. Maybe there was no reason. Maybe people don't need a reason to be violent. They just are.

I didn't try to get back up, I let myself sit on the cold and unforgiving ground. I think I deserved it. I deserved pain. I didn't deserve to be happy. This is how it's always going to be, and I need to learn to accept that.

"Atticus?" I heard a muffled voice ask. I couldn't tell who it was, and I still couldn't even see clearly. I sat limply on the ground. I didn't even care enough to respond to my name.

"Atticus!" Another voice called, slowly snapping me back to reality. Fuck.

It had to be Gabriel and Alastair. I couldn't be lucky enough for it to only be one of them. Why the hell were they together? Were they talking about me? What did they say? Was this a coincidence? Was this on purpose?

"Dude, what the fuck happened to you?" The voice I knew to be Alastair's asked, as both of the shadowy figures lifted me off the ground, helping me stand upright.

"I got beat up," I quietly shrugged.

"By who?" Gabriel asked, his voice ringing in my ears.

"Don't know," I winced. Did it even matter? What's done is done.

"Why?" Alastair asked, draping my arm around his shoulder. I shrugged, I didn't have any other answer. "You know, I'm getting sick of carrying you after you get beat up," Alastair laughed.

You have to be fucking kidding me. Is he that stupid on purpose or does he have to try?

"What?" Gabriel asked. I didn't even have to look at Alastair's face to know that he realized exactly how badly he fucked up.

"It's just an inside joke," He said, trying to save his ass.

He's not technically wrong.

"That's a pretty shitty joke," Gabriel pushed.

He's not really wrong either.

"Can we please focus on the fact that I'm dying right now," I groaned, trying to shift Gabriel's focus to my injuries rather than a joke about my abuse.

"You're not dying, Atticus," Alastair scoffed.

"I mean he looks like shit," Gabriel said. I could see his shadowy face studying me. Maybe he was wondering if any of these new injuries would leave some kind of scar. What would he think of me then?

"Thank you, that really means a lot to me," I grumbled.

"I think you need to go home early,"

"No!" Alastair and I said together, cutting Gabriel off from finishing his sentence. We couldn't let him even consider the idea, we knew how that would end.

"You're clearly really injured,"

"Doesn't matter," I said, interrupting him once again. I couldn't go home early, I couldn't be there alone with my parents for that long, that would actually kill me. I could survive the rest of the day, I didn't have a choice. I never have a choice.

"What the hell is going on with you today?" Gabriel spazzed. This wasn't like him, but I can't even blame him. He's frustrated that I'm keeping every little thing from him. He knows when I'm lying, he simply picks and chooses when he wants to call me out for it. Apparently, this time, he's decided to call me out constantly.

"Nothing's going on," I said. I knew he wouldn't believe me, but I had to lie to him, what choice did I have? My only alternative is to tell him the truth, and that could be just as bad as telling him a lie.

"Alastair, what happened to his jaw?" Gabriel asked, his tone firm. I didn't have to see his face to know he was glaring into Alastair's soul.

"I punched him in the face yesterday after we left your house," Alastair said sheepishly, like he was embarrassed of what he'd done.

"Why?"

"I was pissed and knew he could fight back if he wanted to," Alastair said. At least maybe now Gabriel would believe me.

"And what happened to his eye?" He continued to press.

"Gabe,"

"I don't want you to answer, Atticus. I want Alastair to answer," He said. I could tell he was getting more and more pissed by the second, but there was nothing I could do. I had to let him keep asking questions, and hope that Alastair wouldn't fuck up.

"Atticus is a klutz and fell down the stairs," He said, clearly taken aback at the question, forgetting the entire story from this morning.

Mother fucker.

Of course, I love my brother, but I guess he really can be the biggest fucking idiot I've ever met. Or, maybe he changed the story on purpose. I guess I'll never actually know.

"Why did you lie to me?" Gabriel said, turning to look at me. He still doesn't know the truth, but he knows that both of us are lying, and that might be just as bad.

"I didn't," I began, but I didn't even know what to say. I couldn't deny that I had lied to him, he caught me in the act. I think that lying again would only make things worse between us.

"What really happened to your eye? And why are you both lying to me?" He asked, his patience wearing thinner and thinner by the second. There was nothing I could say to fix this, Gabriel knew something wasn't right, and now, he's not going to stop until he knows what.

"We're not lying," Alastair offered. It was hopeless at this point, there's no saving ourselves now.

"You're both shit liars," Gabriel pushed, his frustration clearly growing.

"It's worked this long," I whispered to myself.

"What else have you been lying to me about? And for how long?" He asked. Shit. He wasn't supposed to be able to hear me. It's not like I wanted to lie to him about anything, ever.

I didn't have a choice.

I seem to keep justifying my shitty actions by claiming I don't have a choice. Does that make me as bad as my father? I lie about everything to everyone. My own brother still doesn't even know that the boy helping to keep me standing is my boyfriend.

How horrible am I?

All I do is lie to the people I love, about everything.

"Atticus," Gabriel pushed, breaking me from my trance, as his face slowly became clearer and clearer, and I could see the pain etched across his features.

"I don't know what to say," I stuttered. And I guess that was true. I didn't know what to do, everything seemed like the wrong choice.

"How about the *truth*?" He asked, as I noticed the tears beginning to form in his eyes. I know I was hurting him, but I didn't know how to tell him the truth either. I can't tell if the truth would hurt more than a lie.

"It's not that easy," I quietly said.

"Yes, it is," He said, fighting the small droplets of water that were beginning to poke at his eyes.

"Trust us, it's not. It's not an easy thing to tell your friends," Alastair began, trying to somehow fix things.

"That's all I am to you?" Gabriel asked, interrupting my brother's defense.

"Gabriel, please. I'm begging you. Not here, not now," I pleaded. I could feel Alastair's eyes burning a hole in the back of my head, his gaze never leaving me. It felt like he knew all my secrets, like he could see right into my mind and discover everything I'd kept from him for so long.

"He's your brother for God's sake!"

"That doesn't make this any easier!" I shouted, shocked at my own aggression. I don't know what's wrong with me, I've never spoken to him like this.

"Fine. You and I will talk about this after classes today, and I swear to you, Atticus, you better tell me everything, the truth this time. Not some bullshit lies," Gabriel said, clearly pissed off with me. I don't even blame him, I deserve it.

"Sorry to interrupt whatever is going on right now, but what exactly are we supposed to do with you, Atticus?" Alastair asked, sounding embarrassed.

"Leave me here to die on the floor," I sighed.

"Oh, but when I say the same thing, it's a problem?" He laughed. I'll admit, I was surprised to hear him joke about the events of last night, especially in front of someone he hardly knows.

"Yes, that very much was a problem, you were actually about to die," I said defensively.

"Oh, so you admit you're not dying and you're just dramatic?" He asked. It's almost like he tries so hard to be an asshole.

"Alastair, I swear to you that I will break every bone in your body if you say some stupid shit like that again," I pushed back. It was nice to be able to joke around with my brother sometimes, no matter how horrible our jokes were. I don't imagine anyone else appreciated our sense of humor, but did it really matter? At least we could get along.

"Seriously though, can you even stand on your own?" My brother asked.

"Only one way to find out," I said, removing my arms from their shoulders. My balance faltered for a split second, and Gabriel instantly moved to catch me. Not that I needed it, but it was nice to know that no matter how mad he was at me, at least he was still more than willing to catch me if I fell.

"Isn't your teacher looking for you?" Gabriel asked us when my balance had fully returned.

"She saw Atticus run out, and when he hadn't come back after fifteen minutes she sent me after him. Isn't your teacher looking for you?" My brother asked, returning the question.

"Lunch period,"

"How did you both find me? At the same exact time?" I finally asked, still somewhat suspicious of the two.

"Saw each other in the hallway," Alastair began.

"Figured I'd say hello,"

"And then I told him I was sent to look for you,"

"So I tagged along. Not like I had anything better to do," Gabriel finished. The whole situation still felt strange to me. Then again, most things did.

"Right," I said with a tone drenched in suspicion. I don't know why part of me didn't believe them, something in me was constantly suspicious of everything. I wish I didn't think like this, but I do.

"Come on, we need to get back to class," Alastair said, trying to push me forward out of the bathroom.

"Or I could skip the rest of the period," I said. I didn't want to go back to that classroom, and have everyone in there ask me a million questions.

"Atticus, go back to your class," Gabriel said. I still didn't want to, but I would, only because he told me to. I owe him at least that.

"Fine. I'll see you later," I said with a somber tone. I had only taken one step when Gabriel grabbed me, wrapping his arms around me, and pulling me close to him. I don't think I really cared that Alastair was still right next to me. My brother is going to think whatever he wants, and I don't believe there are any words that could change his mind.

I didn't want to let go of Gabriel, but I didn't have a choice. Here, I couldn't cling to him and believe that everything was going to be okay. Not now, not in this place.

Alastair made me leave the bathroom first, walking me back to our classroom. I felt his eyes trying to see into my soul to understand what exactly happened back there. I didn't have an explanation for him, I didn't even have an explanation for myself.

"Is there something you're not telling me?" My brother finally asked me as we entered the boring classroom.

"There's plenty of things I'm not telling you," I said, trying to dodge the question.

"So much for you being all about honesty all of the sudden," He spat as we sat back down.

"I do care about honesty, but I do still respect the fact that you have secrets, and I'm hoping that you respect that I do as well," I said, hoping he wouldn't press the matter further.

"Is there something going on between you and Gabriel?" He asked. My heart stopped. I couldn't even read the expression on my brother's face. I couldn't figure out if he was angry, disgusted, didn't care, or simply didn't understand.

"Why would you ask me that?" I said, feeling the blood drain from my face, hoping my brother wouldn't notice.

"It's only a question. It seems like he might have feelings for you, I just don't know if it's mutual," He began, his expression still blank.

"Does it matter?" I quickly asked, preventing him from even finishing his statement.

"Not really,"

"Then why ask?" I asked coldly, trying to force my brother to drop the subject altogether. I wish he would respect my privacy, as I respect his.

As I expected, it didn't take long for a group of my classmates to come toward me to start asking me a million questions. Part of me was almost relieved, because it forced Alastair's questions that I couldn't even answer to stop.

"Atticus, what happened to your eye?" Some girl asked, trying to move her hand to my face. I quickly pulled my face away from her, keeping her from touching me.

"Basketball injury," I briefly said. This girl clearly had feelings for me, she made no effort to even try to hide it. Not that I cared, but she made me feel weird about it, and it wasn't like she was the only one. Though, I doubt these girls actually liked me as an individual, I think they just liked the prestige that came with my name.

I could hear Alastair trying to hold in his laughter at my current situation. He was clearly getting a lot of enjoyment out of my painfully obvious discomfort.

I'll never understand why the girls at this school always try to flirt with me, and never Alastair. We have the same face, only different colored hair and eyes. And he's definitely more approachable than I am, always being the social butterfly of the family. I go out of my way to avoid speaking to people.

"Oh, poor Atticus!" Alastair said dramatically, grabbing onto my shoulders. I do really wish it was acceptable for me to slap him sometimes. I doubt anyone would really question two brothers fighting with each other though, it happens all the time.

"Must you?" I asked, turning to look at my brother who could no longer conceal his laughter.

"Oh, I must," He said, bursting with enjoyment, reveling in the fact that I didn't know what to do in this situation.

It felt like an eternity before this class finally ended. I wanted to get away from this entire environment. I felt like some kind of dancing circus monkey, with everyone crowding me, like they were all watching me.

The day trudged slowly on, I didn't see anyone I cared to speak to during the rest of my day. Not that it was a long list of names. But that doesn't mean that people didn't try to speak to me, though. I'll never understand why people constantly approach me when I've made it very clear that I don't care to engage with them.

Must be my obviously bubbly personality that makes them so inclined to attempt to become my friend. But it's probably only the fact that my father is rich, and they want his money and prestige from me.

Jokes on them, I don't even see a dime of that money.

"Are you ready to go?" Gabriel asked me in the schoolyard after the last class of the day was long over with.

"I still have to tell my sisters where I'm going," I said, spotting my siblings standing together not far from me, quickly walking toward them.

"Atticus, can you help me rehearse for my next recital when we get home?" Anastasia asked bluntly. I think she takes after Alastair much more than me.

"Not even a hello?" I joked.

"Can you help me or not?" She persisted. A little rude, but I'll allow it, because she had a horrible night yesterday.

"I'm not coming home with you three right now,"

"What? Why not?" Annabelle asked. She didn't like being home if I wasn't there. Not that it happened often, or that I didn't understand why she hated it. She's only a scared kid who needs someone to be there for her when things get rough. I just happened to be that person for her.

"I have a partner assignment to do. I'll be home soon though, alright?" I said, trying to reassure her. She seemed upset with me for this, and turned away, beginning the walk home on her own. I know she'll forgive me at some point, but right now, she needs her moment to be pissed off. And I could understand that.

"We'll see you later. I'll tell Sebastian where you are," Alastair said, rushing after Annabelle, with Anastasia following right behind him.

It hurt me that Annabelle was upset with me, but I understood her pain. She looks at me as her only defense against our parents, a fair feeling. I don't blame her for being upset that I won't be there, even if it's only for a little while.

It didn't take long for Gabriel to come up behind me, lightly grabbing my shoulder. I couldn't avoid this conversation any longer. I owe him the truth, as much as I may not want to tell him. I don't know how he'll react to learning about all the things I've kept hidden from him.

"Let's go," He said, nudging me in the direction of his house. It wasn't a far walk, but the silence made it feel like it was an eternity. I needed to think of what I would say, but somehow, an eternity didn't feel long enough.

His mother was home, as she always is. Sometimes I wonder if she ever leaves this house. I hope she does, I hope a woman as kind as her isn't forced to live like some caged animal.

I didn't speak to her other than a small greeting to be polite, she never really talked that much anyway. I let Gabriel lead me into the gorgeous study that was in his home, the shelves filled with books I'd never even heard of, like this place contains all the knowledge in the world.

"You owe me the truth," He began, sitting down at a long wooden table, urging me to do the same.

"I know," I said shakily, slowly sitting down.

"So what really happened to your eye?" He asked, jumping right into the only question I hadn't figured out how to answer.

"It's complicated," I whispered. I've noticed that I whisper when I don't know what to say, it's like I think that if I'm quiet enough, I could sink into the ground and no one would know, and no one would ask me any more questions. I'd vanish quietly. I guess I'm a lot like my brother in that way. I wonder if it's genetics.

"Is it? Or do you not know how to tell me the truth?"

"Both?"

"What, did someone hit you?" He asked. I felt my heart pound in my chest, threatening to crush my ribs just to burst through.

"Well, yes," I said, feeling the weight of my words crush me like a bug.

"Who?" He asked, concern displayed on his face.

"It's not that simple,"

"Atticus, who hit you?" He asked, noticing the aura of panic growing around me, enclosing me like an animal at the zoo. I felt my hands begin to shake. I wanted to tell him the truth, but I don't know how. I felt tears forming in my eyes, and I tried to fight them away, but I knew I couldn't.

"Atticus,"

"If I tell you the truth, if I tell you anything, you can't tell anyone. Not even Alastair. He can't know that you know," I pleaded.

"How serious is this?" He asked. He no longer seemed concerned, he seemed angry. He has to realize something sinister is going on. I think he knows everything, but he needs me to say the words out loud.

"I need you to promise me you won't say anything. Trust me, telling someone will only make things worse," I urged. I won't tell him anything until he promises me, I can't. And I know he isn't the type to go back on his word.

"Okay, I promise," He said. I knew I still had to rely on the hope that he meant what he said, but he's never let me down before.

I tried to catch my breath, feeling the oxygen get caught in my throat. This was going to be painful, that much I know, but I have to tell him. I think I owe him at least that.

"My black eye, along with many other bruises, was given to me by my father," I finally managed to push out. For the first time in my life, I said out loud what my father was, and the words didn't even feel real.

I sat silently as I watched Gabriel's expression quickly shift through the five stages of grief within a matter of seconds. He didn't know what to say, he merely sat there, staring at my hands that lay on the table. I could see the rage building up deep inside of him.

"How long has this been going on?" He finally asked when he could form words once again.

"My entire life,"

"Does he only hit you?" He asked. He's done much, much more than simply striking me. He's done more than I could ever repeat.

"No,"

"What else has he done?"

"I think it'd be faster to name the things he hasn't done to us," I said. I don't know if he thought it was just me who faced my father's wrath, but I knew I had to at least hint to him how complicated my situation really is.

"Move in here," He said, still staring blankly at my hands.

"What?"

"Live here, you'd be away from him. He wouldn't be able to hurt you here," He continued.

"It really isn't that easy. I can't leave my siblings there, Gabe. That's one thing I absolutely refuse to do. I don't care what I have to go through, I'm not leaving them trapped there, that would only make everything worse for them," I explained.

"They have friends, right? People that could take them in?"

"We're not separating. Not like this," I said firmly. This was one thing I'd stand my ground on.

"But you'd all get out,"

"No, Gabe. Not really. Not alone. We'd never survive on our own. We need each other to survive getting out of that hell. We can't do it alone," I didn't expect him to understand, I only hoped he'll listen to me.

"Then what are you going to do? Just deal with it? Pretend that you're all some perfect family until he kills you one of these days?" He said, his rage boiling over.

"I don't have a choice, Gabe. I don't expect you to understand, but I do expect you to realize that I'm doing the best I can in the shittiest situation possible, and that I'm doing everything I can for myself and my siblings," I said, trying to get him to understand a single word I was saying. I don't know if my words were actually getting through to him, or if he was still so set in the idea that we could simply leave. Before he had a chance to respond, Ms. Lumone entered the room, a beaming smile on her face.

"Atticus, your brother is here. He says your father needs you home for the party tonight," She said softly.

Fuck. I forgot about that.

"We'll talk later," I said, quickly grabbing my belongings and moving toward the door. I didn't want to leave, but I knew I didn't have a choice. I had to show my face at my father's dumb party, or everything would only get worse.

"Alastair doesn't know, does he?" He asked. I knew he was talking about our relationship, he just didn't want to risk saying anything in front of his mother. Not that she'd care, but you never know who someone might tell.

"No, he doesn't. And he's not going to find out, not for a long time," I said, rushing out of the door to go meet my brother.

Chapter Five

"Sorry to have to drag you away," My brother said, leading me back toward our hell-house. Neither one of us cared about our father's latest grand display, but still, we had to be in attendance.

"I forgot about that stupid party tonight. How mad is he?" I asked, trying to determine what I had to prepare myself for. I knew it couldn't be anything too horrific, given the sheer amount of people that would be making their way to our home. Sebastian would have to be on his best behavior for at least a few hours.

"Not as angry as you'd expect. He's actually kind of in a good mood," My brother said. This was a first. I've never seen him enjoy his life, especially not in the company of his children. I find it hard to believe that there's anything that can bring him any amount of joy other than inflicting pain on us.

"Are you sure that's our father?" I asked, laughing.

"I'm still not convinced he even is our father," He said back. Finding out Sebastian isn't our father would be like a dream come true. But that statement remains just that. A dream.

"We could only hope to be so lucky," I said. Luck wasn't something that the DuVonet children had, it never has been, and it never will be.

"Do you even know what this party is for?" Alastair asked, kicking rocks that he found on the sidewalk. It wasn't often that there was a reason for these parties. Usually, it was our father's way of showing everyone how much better he is than them.

"Probably just for Sebastian to boast about how glamorous his life is, and how rich he is," I said, turning to face my brother as we arrived at the gate to the house, walking up to the main door with an overwhelming sense of dread building up deep within ourselves. I hated this house. I hated being here, and I think more than anything, I hated my life.

Opening the door was an act that filled both of us with so much stress and agony, but we had to be here. We'd never survive the rest of the week if we skipped this stupid party.

"And there's my pride and joy now!" My father boasted, as Alastair and I walked through the door, coming toward us and placing his hands on our shoulders.

What the fuck?

"Which one is Atticus and which one is Alastair?" Some man in nice clothing I'd never seen before asked my father.

"The dark-haired one is Atticus and the light-haired one is Alastair," He said as the man moved to shake my hand, and then my brother's.

"You boys have no idea who I am, do you?" The man asked with a laugh. He kind of looked like my father, only evil wasn't blatantly displayed on his face. He looked younger than him too. He was tall, taller than Alastair and I, and his dark hair lay neatly on his head, his dark eyes seemed to have a kind of warmth to them that was absent in my father's eyes.

"No, Sir," I said. I think he was surprised at my formality, I doubt anyone's ever addressed him as Sir.

"I'm your Uncle William," He said with a laugh. I didn't even know my father had any siblings. I've never really pictured him as ever growing up either, I kind of envisioned that he sort of appeared one day as a bitter man with a stick shoved up his ass.

"I didn't know we had any uncles," Alastair said. Again with the detrimental bluntness. I wondered how angry our father would be for this comment.

"You have several, boys. I have four brothers and two sisters. All of them will be here tonight," My father said, smiling. I don't think I've ever seen him smile before, it's horrifying. Like a kind of unnatural facial contortion that I would give anything to never have to see ever again.

"I didn't realize everyone was coming tonight," Uncle William laughed. He almost seemed like he might truly be a good person, it makes me wonder what exactly went wrong with my father. But then again, he could be exactly like my father, and putting on a face in front of us. I wonder if that kind of skill runs in the family.

I wonder if it's been passed down to me.

"Oh yes, they've all been looking forward to finally meeting my incredible children," My father laughed. I knew everything he was saying was absolute bullshit, he's never said a single positive thing about any of us in our entire lives. He's a performer, and he's just putting on another show.

I tried to look at my brother, turning to see Sebastian staring directly at me. He wouldn't do anything in front of his brother, but I couldn't risk him doing something behind closed doors. It was like his eyes were stabbing me over and over again, like he wished he could kill me by just looking at me.

"What happened to your eye, son?" He asked, faking sympathy.

"Oh, Alastair isn't very good at basketball," I laughed, prompting the same reaction from my brother. We knew that was all we could do. Maybe playing along will spare us from some of our father's violence.

"Right, well, boys, you both need to be more careful," My father said, slapping our shoulders. I suppose I shouldn't be surprised that he still has a way of showing his true colors while performing for someone else.

I turned to look at my uncle, noticing he wasn't laughing. Instead, he looked rather concerned. I wonder if he was beginning to piece together what really goes on here when no one else is around. Maybe he already knew, maybe he lived through the same thing. Or maybe he knew his brother well enough to see through his lies.

"Right. Sebastian, when should the rest of our siblings be arriving?" Uncle William asked, looking me up and down, his eyes lingering on my own for a moment too long.

Does he know?

"Any minute now, dear brother," My father replied, noticing the way he looked at me, and more specifically the way he looked at my eye.

With perfect timing, two even younger-looking people entered the house, a man and a woman. The woman looked significantly younger than both my father, and my uncle. Whereas the man looked to be about the same age as William. The woman almost looked like Annabelle, with brown hair like my sister's, and blue eyes that resembled mine. I guess DuVonet genes are incredibly strong, you could definitely tell we're all related.

"Marcus, Mary, good to see you both," My father said with a painfully fake smile. Seeing him smile was genuinely painful to look at, I think it hurt me more than any of the punches I've received.

"Sebastian," Marcus said coldly. I could only assume he was another uncle. One that seemingly didn't like his brother very much. Not that I blame him.

"These are my boys, Atticus and Alastair," He said, motioning to us as he said our names this time. It was almost strange to me that we never knew about our father's siblings, and they had never even seen us in our seventeen years of life.

"Good to know," Mary said. It was clear that neither of them liked my father, and I don't blame them. I don't know their reasoning for their dislike of that awful man. I imagine he was just as awful to them as he was to us. He's not exactly the kind of person to be good to anyone, not unless it somehow benefits him.

"You boys should go get changed before the rest of our guests arrive. And help your sisters finish getting ready," He said, nudging us to go up the stairs and get out of his sight. He knew he could only pretend to like us for so long before his illusion would begin to crumble right in front of him.

We didn't bother to question him, we quickly moved up the stairs, out of his line of sight, and out of earshot, both walking into my room, seeing our sisters already waiting in there for us, sitting on my bed. I guess I shouldn't be surprised they chose my room, it's like everyone sees it as a kind of safety zone.

"What the fuck is going on down there?" Anastasia asked. I'm glad to know all of us are equally confused about what possessed our father to suddenly treat us like people.

"We have no idea," Alastair said, shrugging his shoulders and moving into his room to grab a suit. I doubt we'd really ever find out the truth about why our father acted the way he did. It would have to be one of life's great mysteries.

"Apparently, we have four uncles and two aunts that we knew nothing about," I added, pulling out a suit of my own from my closet.

"We do?" Annabelle asked, as Alastair came back into my room, walking straight to my bathroom to change. I didn't even question it, I knew he didn't want to be back in his bathroom, he didn't want to be in his bedroom at all.

"He can't change in his own bathroom?" Anastasia whispered to me. How could I forget that she knew nothing about the events of last night?

"Don't worry about it," I said, dismissing the questions that I knew were beginning to form within my sister. It wasn't my place to answer any of them, and only Alastair could make the decision to tell anyone about what happened.

"We do. Three of them are here now," Alastair said, walking back into the room as I traded places with him to change my clothes.

I couldn't help but stare at my bruised eye in the mirror. I want to do something to make this hell end, but I'm powerless. No one would believe me anyway. Sometimes, I think that all I can do is feel sorry for myself, and how I ended up in this life.

I changed my clothes quickly, everything I do tonight has to be fast, and without a second thought, it does me no good to be slow and questioning. I walked back into my room to see my mother standing in the doorway, glaring at us all. She never bothered me much, but I know she never left my sisters alone.

"I expect you all to be perfectly behaved tonight. Your father's siblings have come from all over the country to finally meet you brats. Don't you dare disgrace your father's name tonight by behaving like imbeciles. Am I understood?" She asked, her voice sounding like nails on a chalkboard.

"Yes Ma'am," All four of us said in unison. She didn't bother to say anything else to us, she turned her head to the door, motioning us all to follow her out of the room.

I could feel my siblings watching me, waiting for me to act first. I had to do what she wanted, it's too much of a risk to disobey anything she says. I can't take any risks knowing my siblings are going to follow whatever I do. I didn't want to do whatever she wanted, but I had to. I've never had a choice in my life, and my freedom certainly isn't going to begin tonight.

By the time we reached the bottom of the stairs, there were two more men and another woman standing with our father, and I could only assume these people were the rest of his siblings. They certainly all looked like they could be related.

"This is ridiculous," I heard Anastasia mutter under her breath. Not that I disagreed with her, but she had to understand that speaking out isn't a good choice.

"Stop talking," I muttered back. She's too outspoken for her own good. It's an admirable quality, but in this house, it's the most dangerous thing she can possess.

"Children, this is Leonard, Edward, and Michelle, my other siblings," My father said, first motioning to a tall man with brown hair and light brown eyes that glimmered with kindness. Then, a more average-height man with light blonde hair and blue eyes. He almost looked like Alastair, except for the eyes. And finally, a short woman with blonde hair and brown eyes, she looked like what I envision Anastasia will look like when she's older. It's almost eerie how similar we look to our father's siblings. You can tell we're all related.

Does he hate us because we remind him of them? Does he hate me because I remind him of himself?

"And these are my children, Atticus, Alastair, both seventeen, Anastasia, sixteen, and Annabelle, fourteen," My father said, pointing to each one of us.

"You would have thought by now we'd know what our nieces and nephews look like," Aunt Michelle said sarcastically. I watched Uncle William turn to her with a sympathetic look, and she quickly looked away from him. Based on the thirty seconds I've known her, she's exactly like Anastasia.

Does he hate all of us because we remind him of his siblings and his childhood? What happened to him when he was younger that made him so spiteful to anyone who bears the slightest resemblance to the people he grew up around?

"Yes, well, there's never been a good opportunity for you to come and meet them, Michelle," My father said back, his tone slightly snappy.

Why is he like this?

"How about when they were born?" Uncle Edward said, his eyebrow raised, almost like he wanted to say more than he did. I feel like I'm getting closer and closer to understanding why my father is the way that he is, but I feel like the closer I get, the more complicated everything becomes.

"What's done is done," My father said. It's clear for anyone to see that none of his siblings enjoy his company. Why are they even here? Do they feel some kind of obligation to show up because they've never met their nieces and nephews before?

"Michelle, doesn't Anastasia look exactly like you did at her age?" Uncle William asked, clearly trying to defuse the tension.

"Yes, I suppose she does," Aunt Michelle said, examining Anastasia. She almost looked pained to see my sister, like she was looking in a mirror that only brought suffering and agony, like seeing Anastasia in real life hurt her entire being.

"Our other guests should be arriving soon. Our waiters will begin coming around shortly to fetch you whatever you desire. Please excuse me," My father said, moving toward the gigantic kitchen. Not that he ever cooked, he only told the chefs on duty what to do and what not to do.

"Which one of you boys is the oldest?" Uncle Leonard asked Alastair and I, eyeing us up and down.

"I am, Sir," I responded quickly with a smile. Just like my father told me to. It was such a habit to always act exactly how he wanted in front of guests, without even thinking about what I was doing.

"Please, never call me Sir again," He laughed, almost sounding disgusted.

"William, is your husband coming tonight?" Aunt Mary asked, abruptly changing the subject. I think the bluntness reminded me of Alastair. I wonder if my siblings and I are all some kind of mix of Sebastian's siblings. Maybe that's why he hates us.

"Oh God no, you know how Sebastian is. He doesn't even know I'm gay," Uncle William laughed. I wonder if I should talk to Uncle William about Gabriel. At least I know he'd understand what it's like to be so different when you're surrounded by someone who'd kill you for trying to live your own life.

Before I even had a chance to pull him off to the side, the doorbell rang, signifying that the first guests had already arrived. I suppose I could always talk to him later, as long as he plans on sticking around for at least tonight.

I quickly dashed to the door, ready to greet our guests. I should have known that with my luck, I'd come face to face with Gabriel and his mother on the other side. I don't know why he seemed so surprised to see me answering the door, I did live here after all, no matter how much I hated it.

"Atticus," He began.

"Welcome in, Mr. and Ms. Lumone," I said, ushering them inside.

"Mr. Lumone?" He asked, shocked I'd address him so formally.

"Just a formality for my father," I whispered to him as he walked in the door behind his mother.

"Where is he?" He whispered back.

"Why?" I asked. I knew why, I only wondered if he'd admit it.

"Just curious," He lied, exactly what I expected.

"I can't let you go confront my father, Gabe. We'll talk later," I said, dropping the subject. It's not that I didn't admire his willingness to defend me, but I simply couldn't allow him to take that kind of risk.

Ms. Lumone went around the room, introducing herself and Gabriel to all of my father's siblings, clearly forgetting their names moments after hearing them. She tried her best, but she could never seem to remember much about anyone.

I knew my chance was now or never. I quickly walked right beside Uncle William, leaning in toward his ear.

"Do you think I could talk to you for a few minutes?" I whispered, feeling my heart pound in my chest. I don't know why I felt so afraid, it's not like I had to be nervous in front of the only person in this family who would understand what I was going through.

"Of course, is everything all right?" He whispered back. I believe that part of him deep down knows something isn't right here. Maybe he thought I'd be brave enough to ask him for his help to get us away from our father.

"Yes, I just want your opinion on something," I said, motioning him up the stairs. He nodded, quietly following me to my bedroom, sitting down on the bed as I closed the door.

"What is it you want to talk about?" He asked.

"You're the only person in this family I think I can talk to about this, so I'm trusting you to keep this between us,"

"Are you alright?" He asked. Something within him has to know something isn't right. Every word he says points to a realization he knows he can't say out loud.

"I am, I'm just gay and don't know what to do because I didn't know my boyfriend was coming tonight," I blurted out. I didn't even think about what I was saying, I just sort of said it. I guess that was the easiest way to handle that sort of thing.

"That boy was your boyfriend?" He asked. He didn't seem surprised that I blurted my biggest secret to him, he just went along with it.

"Yes, and I didn't mean to say it the way I did, but Gabe's the only one who knows, and I don't know how to tell anyone else,"

"It's alright, Atticus," Uncle William laughed, cutting off my rambling.

"I don't know what to do. I mean, I love Gabriel, and I want to be able to tell everyone that for so many reasons. But I can't, and it's destroying me to have to keep him a secret from so many people. My brother doesn't even know," I said. I don't think I had to explain myself to him, I think he just knew. At least, I hope he knew.

"It's a hard thing to keep hidden. Do you think your brother would tell your father?" He asked. I think Uncle William might be the first adult in my life to genuinely care about me. Maybe he sees a little bit of himself in me.

"I don't know. I know that I'm scared to tell him. I don't think he'd tell my father, but at the same time, anything can happen, you know?" I shrugged. Of course, I wanted to believe the best of Alastair, but I don't know if that's a risk that I can take.

"Believe me, son, I know. It's a terrifying thing to tell anyone, even if you know how they're going to react. But I've just met you, and even I can see that your brother loves you, and nothing you can tell him is going to change that," He said with a smile.

"You think so?" I asked, looking for his reassurance.

"I do. And if there's anything else you want to talk to me about, and I do mean anything, don't hesitate to come and steal me away from this incredibly boring and pretentious party," He said, again focusing his attention to my eye.

I think he knows about the sinister things his brother does. He's known Sebastian his whole life, and it's not like there's a switch that flips in someone's head to turn them into an abusive piece of shit. Something tells me that Uncle William has his own experiences with Sebastian, and doesn't know how to start that conversation with me. Or maybe he never will. In any case, he knows something that I don't.

We knew we had to head back down to the party, more and more guests had been arriving with every single moment we were away, and if we had been gone for too much longer, that would only make my father even more suspicious.

Immediately after coming down the stairs, Alastair was urging me off to the side, almost like he was waiting for me to come and rejoin the event.

"What were you two talking about?" My brother asked, almost as if he was suspicious of me. At this point, I think he knows about me and Gabriel, and I believe he's only waiting for me to confirm his suspicions.

"Wouldn't you like to know?" I laughed, moving away from my brother, and toward Anastasia. I feel as though I never talk to her, she's always so closed off that trying to communicate with her is like trying to talk to a slab of concrete.

"I know how much you hate these things, trust me, I hate them as much as you, but please, I am begging you, don't say anything stupid," I whispered to her.

"And what exactly qualifies as stupid in your mind?" She whispered back, a sense of sophistication in her voice.

"Anything that would get you in trouble with father,"

"So I can't even breathe?" She said, louder than she should have. I understand her anger, better than anyone does. But I also understand better than anyone how dangerous it can be to voice that anger.

"Listen to me, we can bitch about these parties and Sebastian all you want after this is over, but it's not safe for you to say things like that right now, you know that," I urged her. She's not stupid, she knows she shouldn't even bother speaking at these parties unless someone speaks to her first.

"This whole house isn't safe," She scoffed.

"Anastasia, I know you're not dumb. Stop fucking talking like that. Not here, not now. I swear to you that you can say whatever you want about anything after this is over, you can call me a stupid bitch after this for all I care, but right now, I am begging you to shut up," I pleaded. She looked me up and down, looking at my bruised eye, staring deep into my soul. She'd never admit it out loud, but she knew she should listen to me. She knows I've been through more with Sebastian than I'll ever tell anyone, and that I know how to survive these irritating parties.

"Fine, but don't expect me to be his perfect daughter,"

"I want you to be safe. Don't do anything stupid," I said. She didn't bother to respond to me, she simply walked away.

I don't know why she refuses to talk to me, I just want to be there for her. I wish she'd give me the chance to be someone she can depend on, but it feels like every time I take a step closer to her, she takes two steps away from me.

"You don't seem to be enjoying yourself," Aunt Mary laughed, coming closer to me. From what I could tell, she seemed like a kind young woman. Then again, it's very easy to present yourself one way in a crowd full of people.

"Sorry, I feel a little dazed today," I said, instantly trying to explain myself. I knew I couldn't say the truth, not even to someone who probably understood better than I did exactly who my father was.

"Trust me, Atticus, none of us are enjoying ourselves either," She said, smiling.

"Do you mind if I ask you something?" I began. I needed to start getting answers about things, even if it wasn't a good idea.

"Ask away,"

"Why did you all come here tonight? You've never come to these events before. Why did you all decide to come for the first time tonight?" I asked. She seemed surprised that this is what I chose to ask her. I think she presumed I had other questions I wanted answered, potentially even questions about my father.

"It was now or never," She said, filling me with even more questions than answers. Typical response of a DuVonet.

"I don't understand,"

"I don't expect you to. Not yet at least. But you will soon enough," She smiled, walking away from me. It was like she was speaking in some foreign language that only she could understand.

She vanished like smoke into the swelling crowd of people, disappearing from my sight. This entire family is so strange in so many ways. Things have been going on deep within this insanely fucked up bloodline for much longer than I would have first thought.

Every single one of my father's siblings seems to know more than they're letting on, and I can't figure out why they won't come right out and say what they know. Do they think they're protecting us from the truth?

"Atticus, I'd like to speak with you, dear boy," Uncle William said, coming up behind me, and slapping his hand onto my shoulder.

I could feel my father staring at me from across the room. I noticed him pull a waiter to the side as he stared me down, whispering something to the man.

"Earth to Atticus," Uncle William laughed, directing my attention to him.

"Yes, sorry. I got distracted for a moment," I said with a smile.

"We need to have a conversation. There's a lot of things that you don't know, that you need to be aware of," He began, instantly transforming from a happy and smiling man, to a serious slab of stone.

"Such as?" I asked, curious as to what he could be trying to tell me.

"Your father is a sick and sinister man," He began. As if I didn't already know that. Before he continued his sentence, the very same waiter my father had been speaking to came up to my uncle, handing him a glass of champagne.

"For Mr. DuVonet's toast," The waiter said regarding my uncle's confused expression. Uncle William nodded, and the waiter quickly moved on.

"We don't have much time then, so I'll make this fast. I know what your father does to you and your siblings, he did the same things to us when we were growing up. Your mother is not really your mother. Your real mother is," The clinking of glass cut off Uncle William from finishing.

I felt sick to my stomach. I felt like I was going to throw up, or pass out, or both. I couldn't see straight, everything around me was fuzzy. I couldn't believe I was even still standing.

"I'd like to thank you all for joining me tonight, it truly means the world to me that so many of you came," My father began. I couldn't even hear him, his words were ringing in my ears. It wasn't long before the room

began to holler their cheers and begin to take their drinks.

My heart was pounding in my chest, I turned to face Uncle William,

watching him take a large sip of his champagne, seemingly struggling to get

it down. Maybe he wasn't much of a drinker.

"Your mother is," He began. He couldn't even finish his sentence. He

began coughing violently, and I could see the blood escaping his mouth as

his legs gave out on him, causing his body to slowly lower to the ground.

"Uncle William?" I said, trying to bring him to the ground safely. He

couldn't speak, he kept coughing as more and more blood spewed out of his

body.

"Someone call an ambulance!" I screamed in the bustling room.

Everything in the room was so loud, that I don't think a single soul heard my

desperate pleas for help. I couldn't stop myself from crying. It didn't matter

that I'd only known him for an evening, he understood me in a way no one

else did.

"*Mary,*" He managed to cough out, the life leaving his body while his

corpse remained in my arms. I couldn't move. I tried to scream, but no sound

existed in me. I didn't know what to do, no one even noticed the fucking

corpse in the corner laying on my body.

"Uncle William, please," I said, begging for something I knew wasn't possible.

Through my blurry vision, I noticed Alastair coming toward me. Sometimes, he makes me wonder if twins truly are telepathically connected.

"What the fuck?" He asked, crouching down the moment he noticed the blood on our uncle's face.

"He's fucking dead," I pushed out.

"What happened?"

"I don't know, he drank the champagne and now he's dead," I said, my voice shaking as Alastair helped pull William's corpse off of my body. I tried to look away, I tried looking into our backyard to watch the water ripple in the pool that no one ever used, but something else in the water caught my eye.

"Alastair," I began.

"What?"

"Is that a fucking body floating in the pool?" I asked, unable to look away.

"Holy shit," He said, confirming my sightings.

"What are we supposed to do?" I asked. I doubt he knew either, but I couldn't even process the world around me right now. How has no one else noticed the two dead bodies at this house?

"I think we need to see who it is," He said, staring at me.

"Stay here and try to get someone's attention, and have them call the police or something, I'll look outside," I said, moving to the door.

"Atticus,"

"It's okay," I cut him off, moving closer to the door.

I walked outside without thinking about it, trying to get a closer look at the body floating in the shallow water, close to the edge of the concrete. I didn't have to get much closer to recognize the brown hair that was identical to my sister's.

"Mary," I choked out, rushing back to the house, noticing heads turn toward me as Sebastian quickly sped over to me.

"Who is that in the pool?" He quietly asked, clearly trying to keep the attention off of the fact that this party had a rising body count.

"Mary, Sir," I whispered.

"William is dead as well?" My father whispered as I noticed the faint smell of chlorine on his hands and his slightly damp sleeves.

No.

As awful as he is, there's no way he did this.

He couldn't have.

He's not capable of murdering his own siblings, is he?

"Yes, Sir. Both of them," I answered, not letting him know of my suspicions.

"Start getting people to leave," He ordered. I didn't know how to get people to leave, it's not like I could tell them that I believed my father just murdered two people.

Would he risk his image at this party, just to keep his children from finding out the truth about him, and everything he's done? I didn't even get a chance to ask Mary if she truly was my mother. I don't think William would have lied to me, especially not about that, but now I don't think I'll ever know for sure.

I motioned for Alastair to help me start urging people out of the house, but it's not like either of us knew what to do. He didn't even know the truth, and he still didn't know how to react. I didn't pay any attention to who I started ushering out, I just did what my father told me.

"Is everything okay?" Gabriel asked me, I didn't even realize I was anywhere near him until he spoke to me.

"Far from it," I whispered to him.

"What happened?"

"A lot of insanely fucked up things and I promise I will tell you everything tomorrow, but right now I need you to leave," I whispered. He didn't bother to question me, he knew if I was urging him out of the house like this, things were beyond fucked up.

It felt like it took forever to get everyone out of the house, and no emergency services had even arrived. My father knew he couldn't start his screaming yet, not when the police could arrive at any second.

"What happened?" Anastasia quietly asked me. I didn't even know she was standing right beside me. I couldn't bring myself to answer, I only stared at the ground, noticing Uncle William's blood on my shoes. Everything around me seemed to fade out of existence, except for my uncle's blood and the ringing of his last words to me.

"Atticus?" I heard Annabelle's muffled voice ask. I didn't bother to even attempt to look at her, I couldn't.

"Atticus, talk to us," Alastair begged. They've never seen me like this. I wonder if my silence scared them. Maybe it told them that something was very wrong. Maybe they simply didn't understand.

I mean, how exactly am I supposed to tell any of them that my mother isn't actually my mother, and our father is even worse than we thought?

"Atticus, what happened tonight?" My father asked. I couldn't even look at him. How could I ever look at him again, knowing that he was a murderer? How could I look at him, knowing what William told me?

"I don't know," I said, my eyes never unfocusing from my bloody shoes.

"You do know," He pushed. I think he really only wanted to know what the brother he murdered told me with his dying breath.

"William drank the champagne and started coughing up blood, and then he died in my arms. I looked outside and saw Mary floating in the pool, Sir," I responded, fighting against the tears in my eyes. I finally removed my gaze from my feet to look at my brother. He looked like he was in pain, I don't think I can handle making that pain worse.

"What did he say to you?" My father asked.

"That I reminded him a lot of himself when he was my age," I lied. For the first time in my life, I confidently lied to my father's face. He nodded, I assumed he believed my lie and accepted it as a good enough answer.

There was a knock on the door, I assumed it had to be the police. I still couldn't move, I didn't care enough to move. Instead, I let my father answer the door.

"Are you okay?" Alastair whispered.

"No, I'm not fucking okay," I whispered harshly. I didn't want to give him an attitude, but if he asks dumb questions, what else does he expect?

It felt like hours that I was forced to answer dozens of questions the police had for me. I couldn't tell them the whole truth, I knew I could only say bits and pieces for my own safety.

Before they left the house, I noticed my father talking to the officer who seemed to be in charge, and I saw my father hand the man a check.

Of course.

He's paying off the fucking police to cover up what he did tonight.

I felt the numbness fade away, slowly being replaced by pure seething rage. I can't trust myself to behave if he says one more fucking word to me. He has to pay for what he's done, and I don't care if he kills me for getting justice for his brother, and my real mother. He's pushed people around his entire life, and it's about damn time someone starts pushing him back.

"Children!" He screamed once the officer left the house. He didn't have to say it, we all knew he was demanding for us to form a line at the stairs for him. The four of us slowly walked to stand before the absolute monsters we were forced to call parents.

"We're both incredibly disappointed in you all after tonight's events," Elizabeth said.

"How could you let this happen?!" Sebastian screamed. I don't know how much longer I can keep myself from doing something I'll probably regret.

"Do you have any idea what this is going to do to our reputation?" Elizabeth scolded.

"Don't you know that we have an image to uphold? That we're the most perfect family?!" My father shouted, getting in my face, like he was trying to intimidate me or something, thinking I was afraid of him.

Nope.

I'm fucking done.

"You sick fucking liar!" I screamed in his face.

Chapter Six

"What the fuck did you say to me?" Sebastian asked, shoving me.

"You fucking heard me!" I shouted, shoving him right back. I wouldn't listen to his bullshit anymore. I could see Alastair's face out of the corner of my eye, like he was afraid both of me, and for me.

I knew what my father was planning to do, it was like a sixth sense. I saw his fist bunching up, ready to swing at my face. I didn't even let him get the chance, I took my shot at him first, knocking him clean across the face with my fist, something I've wanted to do my entire life.

I could feel everyone in the room staring at me. I might have majorly fucked up, but it was definitely worth it to for once give my father what he deserved.

"You stupid child!" He yelled, holding the spot on his face my fist collided with, a red mark forming on the skin.

"You sick bastard!" I shouted, his open palm striking my face. I didn't let myself focus on the stinging feeling building underneath the surface of my skin, it didn't matter. I knew the truth, I knew what he did.

My father grabbed my shirt collar, his grip tight, and yanked me toward him, forcing me close to his face. And for once in my life, I wasn't afraid of him.

"You have no idea what you're talking about," He growled.

"I know exactly what I'm talking about. I know what you did," I pushed back. He needed to realize that he couldn't scare me anymore, he's not the one in control any longer. I think that would terrify him more than anything.

I guess while I wasn't paying attention to my sisters, Elizabeth had taken them up the stairs, and the sounds of their screams were the only thing that reminded me that they were still in the house.

"What the fuck is she doing to them?!" I shouted in his face, pushing him off of me.

"Nothing that concerns you!" Sebastian yelled, slapping me across the face once again. It didn't even hurt me anymore. The stinging only served as a reminder that I was stronger than him. He can't hurt me anymore, not really, not in a way that matters.

I tried to move past him to get to my sisters, but he kept pushing me away, preventing me from getting up the stairs.

"Alastair, go to your room right this instant. Do not deter from the path to your room, or there will be hell to pay, do you understand me, boy?" He said to Alastair, the only other person remaining on the same level as us. He hesitated for a moment, like he was questioning if he should listen to our father, or risk his life to help me.

"Yes, Sir," Alastair obediently said, rushing up the stairs, away from this entire situation, no matter how much he didn't want to leave me alone down here. I don't blame him for running, there's no need for both of us to risk our lives tonight.

I watched my father reach into his pocket, slowly pulling something out of it.

"I didn't want things to have to come to this, but you've pushed me too far, dear boy," He began, his breathing heavy.

Is that a fucking knife?

He slowly opened up the object, clearly enjoying himself, and what he was doing.

Holy shit, it is a knife.

"But, you've forced my hand, Atticus," He continued. I didn't even think about it, I just bolted for the door, practically ripping it off of its hinges, running for my life out of the house.

"Atticus!" He screamed, chasing me to the door. I didn't look behind me, I couldn't, I had to keep running and hope for the best. He wouldn't chase me through the streets, if anyone saw him chasing his son with a knife, that would tell the world everything they needed to know, and the image he desperately tried to cling onto would be gone in an instant.

I ran to the only safe place I could think to go, arriving there in record time, thanks to pure adrenaline and fear guiding me the entire sprint. I pounded on the door, begging anyone on the other side to let me in, and keep me away from my father.

"Atticus?" Gabriel began as he opened the door and I pushed my way inside.

"Close the door,"

"What's going on?"

"Close the fucking door, Gabe!" I shouted, cutting him off. I didn't want to yell at him, but I didn't know if my father followed me, or sent someone else after me. Gabriel seemed to immediately notice my fear and quickly shut the door, locking it behind him.

"What the fuck?" He asked, clearly confused as I fell to my knees trying to catch my breath.

"Is it okay if I stay here tonight?" I asked as the oxygen slowly returned to my lungs that felt like they were on fire.

"Yeah, of course. Is everything okay?"

"Everything is so far from okay," I laughed as the pain in my face finally registered, the stinging heat rushing through my entire body.

"What happened?"

"I'm going to need you to be a bit more specific," I laughed. Am I in shock? I feel like I'm going insane. Nothing about this is funny, yet I can't seem to stop myself from laughing. Is this what it's like to lose your mind?

"Start from what happened once you left my house earlier," He said, kneeling on the ground with me.

"I got home and there was this guy standing right by the entrance of the house with my father. Turns out, this mystery guy is my uncle, and the rest of my uncles and aunts were going to show up at the party. I never knew I had any aunts or uncles so you can imagine my surprise," I started.

"Your father has siblings?"

"Apparently so, quite a few of them at that," I answered.

"Alright, so you just learned they exist, and they're on their way to your house for this party. Then what?" He asked, prompting me to continue.

"Well, fast forward to when they all showed up, I found out that the mystery guy, named William, is gay, so naturally, I want to talk to him and get his advice. After you showed up, we went upstairs and talked. I told him about you, and after a little bit, we came back downstairs and some other stuff started happening, not that important," I quickly explained.

I could see that Gabriel was in his own state of panic, trying to piece together everything all at once, while also ensuring I didn't completely lose my mind while recounting the events of this night.

"The important part comes right before my father's toast. William starts to tell me some *things* about my father, including the fact that he was an abusive piece of shit to his siblings too. Then, he begins to tell me that my mother isn't actually my mother. Then, the toast happens, he drinks the champagne, starts fucking dying, and with his dying breath tells me who my mother really is. Then, he died in my arms, and no one heard me screaming for help. Fast forward a little bit, and I find my Aunt Mary drowned in the pool. Everyone starts leaving, and I confront my father about what William told me. I punched him in the fucking face, and then he pulled a knife on, me so I ran, and now I'm here," I finished, breathlessly. Gabriel looked beyond horrified, to say the least.

"What the fuck, Atticus?" He said, looking completely traumatized at the fact that I said all of this so casually and so easily. I guess I forgot that what seems like normal family behavior to me is beyond horrific to him.

"So that was my evening. Oh, and I'm convinced my father killed William and Mary. Him trying to kill me only further solidified that in my mind,"

"Hold on, back up a bit. Who is your real mother?" He asked. I'm surprised that was the first area he decided to focus on.

"Mary," I said, almost gagging on the word.

"As in your father's sister, Mary?" He asked, horrified.

"Yeah, apparently, Alastair and I are a product of fucking incest, so I feel absolutely fantastic right now," I said, finally realizing exactly how disgusting my existence feels.

"Did you tell Alastair?"

"No, I don't exactly know how to tell my brother that our now-dead aunt is actually our mother. It's not exactly a very casual thing that you can bring up in passing," I said, feeling my attitude flare.

"Are you okay? Like, mentally?" He asked. He obviously didn't know how to respond, he probably couldn't even read how I was feeling. I don't think I even knew how I felt.

"Not even a little bit,"

"Let's move on, okay? You confronted your father, and then he pulled a knife on you?" He asked, redirecting my story.

"Oh, I did more than confront him, Gabe. I punched him in the face. I called him a sick liar, and told him I knew what he did. And then, he sent Alastair to his room, and decided to try to fucking stab me, so I ran here as fast as I could. This was the only safe place I could think to go to," I said.

"And why do you think he killed William and Mary?" He asked. Of course everything seemed obvious to me, but Gabriel didn't see any of these things happen. He didn't really know who my father was.

"He could see I was bonding with William, and he knew William knew the truth about him, and what he's done. So he tried to keep him from telling me anything. I saw my father talking to a waiter, and not long after the same waiter came over and gave William a glass of champagne. After William drank the champagne, he started coughing up blood and then, he died. I assume he killed Mary to keep me from asking her for the truth. Right after I found her body, my father asked me who it was, but I noticed that his hands smelled like chlorine and his sleeves were wet," I explained.

I felt like a goddamn detective. Although, I suppose it wouldn't be too difficult to figure out my father's sinister truth if you know who he truly is behind the mask he wears. But Gabriel didn't say a single word, and I think that terrified me more than anything my father could do to me.

"Please say something," I said, breaking the long silence.

"I don't know what to say. This is insane, and I don't know what to do," He finally explained. I understand that it's not like any of this is an easy situation to respond to. There's not a single area he can focus a response to, every single thing that's happened tonight has been beyond insane.

"Yeah, I know. I came here because I didn't know where else to go. I obviously couldn't stay there,"

"No, it's fine. I'm glad you came here, but this is a lot to process at once. How are you feeling?" He asked. I don't think Gabriel even knew what to think or feel.

"Numb? Everything? Nothing? I don't know. It's not every day that you find out that your aunt is your mother, and your father murders the one adult in your life that could understand you, and your mother," I explained.

I think I'm still trying to process this entire situation, and not a single thing makes sense to me. None of this is something that can be rationalized, it's just an insane circumstance that you have to deal with, and try to wrap your head around, hoping you'll still have your sanity by the end of the night.

"Do you want to try to talk about it?"

"I don't know. I think I might need to bang my head against the wall for an hour," I said, looking down at my shoes, again noticing the blood splattered on the front of my shoes.

"I don't really think that's going to help your sanity," Gabriel said, examining my face. I couldn't help but smile at his stupid comment. Even if it felt like my entire life was falling apart right before my eyes, at least I still had Gabriel at my side.

"I don't think anything in my life is going to help my sanity," I said laughing, leaning my head onto his shoulder.

"I think I should take offense to that," He said, wrapping his arms around my shoulders.

"I think you should too," I added.

We sat together in silence for a while, I don't think either of us actually knew what to say, I don't even think there was anything to say.

"Your life is really fucked up," He finally said, laughing.

"You think so?" I asked in a very dramatic tone.

"Maybe a little,"

"What if my father was waiting outside the door with his little pocket knife he was going to murder me with?" I burst out laughing.

"Atticus, why the fuck would you even say that?" Gabriel asked, smacking my arm. He clearly wasn't a fan of all of my jokes.

"Because it's funny," I said, feeling myself grow more and more exhausted with each passing moment. I felt like I could fall asleep right there on the ground, it's not like it'd be an unfamiliar feeling to me.

And I suppose I did fall asleep right there, because before I knew it, I was being shaken awake for school. It felt so strange to me that I was still expected to go to school like everything was completely fine, despite the events of last night. But no one could know about any of the things I had just experienced. Life had to proceed as normal.

"I seriously have to go today?" I asked as Gabriel tossed me some of his clothes to wear today instead of my suit from last night.

"Yeah, you do,"

"Can't I be excused for having my fucking uncle's corpse drop on my body?"

"Unless your father's going to call the school and excuse you from classes for today, no," He said, extending his hand to pull me off the ground.

"That's bullshit," I quietly said, walking to the bathroom to change my clothes. I stared at myself in the mirror for a long time. I wonder if my childhood self could see me now what he'd think of me. What he'd think of the fact that I've gone toe to toe with my father, and escaped with my life. I wonder if he'd think that he became brave, stupid, or suicidal.

"Does Alastair know you came here last night?" Gabriel called from the other room, snapping me out of my head.

"No, he doesn't even know I was chased out with a knife," I said, walking back into the room. I didn't have any of my school things with me here, I had to hope that one of my siblings would bring them for me. It was a quick walk to the school, and it was a walk filled with silence. We still didn't know how to address any of the events of last night.

The schoolyard was full, and I felt dozens of eyes on me as I walked closer to the building. I could only assume people found out about the body count at my father's party last night.

"Why are so many people staring?" Gabriel whispered to me.

"They probably heard that two people died in my house last night," I whispered back, as I found Alastair standing in the yard. He seemed to notice me at the same time, and he instantly started walking toward me, carrying two backpacks.

"What happened last night?" He asked, handing me my bag.

"I had to get out of the house," I calmly explained. I didn't want to cause a panic for him so early in the morning, or in such a public place. All I could do was pretend to be calm.

"What?"

"There were some things that happened after you got sent upstairs, and I went to Gabriel's and stayed there for the night," I shrugged.

"No, don't fucking shrug at me, what the hell happened last night?" He asked, demanding clear answers.

"Alastair, right here and right now is really not the place for this kind of conversation," I explained. I can't tell him everything about last night in the middle of the schoolyard.

"Why not?"

"Because it's insanely fucked up. How are the girls?" I asked, changing the subject. I cared more about how they were, than having to tell Alastair about why I left last night.

"Not good. Everything really screwed with them," He began, I noticed him eyeing Gabriel up and down.

"He knows," I said, knowing the question that he had in mind. I know I made Gabriel promise not to tell Alastair he knew, but the events of last night changed things. Alastair deserved to at least know about that.

"You told him?"

"Yesterday before the party," I said. I couldn't tell how he felt about my decision. Maybe he was angry, but maybe he understood.

"Well, the girls have burn marks all over their arms now, courtesy of our mother. And they're a little scared of you," He said quietly.

"What?" I felt my heart shatter. Did I truly scare them that badly? Did they see pieces of Sebastian in my explosive anger?

"They've never seen you like that. Atticus, that shit was terrifying. You're not a violent person, you never have been, and they saw you punch our father in the face. You physically fought back against him. You wouldn't even take a swing at me when I hit you first. I've never seen you so angry. What the fuck caused that?" He said, almost trying to justify my siblings being afraid of me.

"I found out a lot of things last night, and there was a lot going through my head. I'm sorry I scared you guys, but if you knew what I know, you'd understand," I said, feeling arms wrap around the back of my stomach. I turned around to see who the arms belonged to, surprised to see Annabelle holding on to me.

"Where did you go?" She asked, looking as if she was about to cry.

"I had to leave last night, I couldn't stay home," I stuttered out. I didn't want to lie to her, but she's too young to know the truth. I had no choice but to lie.

"Why?"

"Because I made a mistake. I did something really stupid and the only way to keep myself safe was to leave for the night," I said gently. I couldn't tell her the truth, it would wreck her. She doesn't need to know about what happened to me while she was being tormented by Elizabeth.

"When are you coming back?" She asked, finally letting go of me. I didn't have an answer for her, I didn't know when I was going back, if I was even going back. I felt obligated to go back, if only to be there for everyone else.

"Soon," I said. There was nothing else I could say, but I couldn't destroy her by telling her the truth. Alastair is the only one who needs to know the entire truth about the events of last night. He deserves to know about who we truly are.

"You should get to your class," Alastair said to Annabelle, gently urging her away. I don't blame him for wanting his answers as soon as possible, but I can't give them to him here, it's not right. This isn't something you can say out in the open, like it's not a big deal.

"You should get to class too," I said, copying exactly what he did.

"Don't think this conversation is over,"

"Far from it," I said as he walked away.

"How are you going to tell him?" Gabriel asked as we started walking to our first class.

"I have no idea. It's not exactly like this is a light conversation topic, this is going to turn our entire lives upside down," I said. And it was true. My entire world feels like it's been tilted sideways, and I can only imagine how Alastair is going to take the news.

"We could always skip our classes today," Gabriel said. He's not the kind of person to ever want to skip class. He only wants to help me process everything wrong with my life.

"You don't want to skip,"

"No, but if it's going to help you, then I don't mind,"

"The school would call my father and make everything worse. I'll survive," I reassured him. I knew he cared, of course, but I also knew how to survive my father.

"Are you sure? Because we could turn around and leave right now," He said as we walked into our first classroom.

"It's a little late for that, don't you think?" I laughed as we took our seats in the back of the classroom, trying to stay hidden from anyone else who might know of some of the events of last night.

"Atticus, I can't believe you're here today!" Some girl I've never even seen before said, taking the seat right next to me. She had long red hair and dark brown eyes, and clearly, she knew me, but I had no idea who she was. Although, I suppose most people know who I am, especially after the events of last night.

"Well, I am," I said, trying to be dismissive of her. I don't like talking to people I don't know. I always try to get them to leave me alone, but of course, they never leave.

"How are you feeling?" She asked, putting her hand on my arm. Is she trying to flirt with me? Or is she one of those weird overly-friendly people? I didn't even have to look at him to know that Gabriel was staring at her.

"Sorry, who are you?" I asked. She seemed shocked I didn't know who she was. Why would I have known her? I've never seen her before. We might be in the same class, but I've never seen her face before now.

"It's me! Isabelle!" She laughed.

"Isabelle?" I asked. How long would it take for her to realize that I don't know her? Was she delusionally convinced we had some kind of history together?

"Isabelle Soline!" She said, beaming.

"I have no idea who you are," I said. Did she think we were friends or something?

"Seriously?"

"Sorry," I awkwardly said.

"I can't believe Alastair never told you who I am!" She said, shocked.

So she's friends with Alastair? What does that have to do with me? Just because we're brothers doesn't mean we have to share the same friends. I couldn't tell you the names of any of his friends, and I think he likes it that way.

"No, he hasn't. Why are you so surprised I'm here?" I asked, deciding to borrow my brother's bluntness.

"Well, after what happened last night," She whispered.

"What do you know about what happened?" Gabriel interrupted. I always forget how defensive he can get.

"Alastair told me some of your family passed away last night, and that you and your father got into some kind of *argument*," She whispered.

What the fuck is Alastair doing? I don't even know who this girl is, and he's telling her my business? He has no right to tell anyone what I did last night, especially not someone I've never met.

"I don't know what you *think* you know, but I suggest you forget he told you anything," I said, turning away from her. She finally took the hint, and left me alone, not bothering to pester me any further.

"What the hell is wrong with her?" Gabriel asked.

"I don't know. I don't even know who she is. I'll have to talk to Alastair about her when I see him,"

"Why would Alastair tell some random girl you don't know about what happened with you and your father last night?" He whispered.

"I don't know what exactly he told her, and I don't know why. I didn't even want to tell you anything, I wasn't ever going to. The only reason I did was because you figured out I was lying to you," I explained, feeling my emotions start building up, trying to understand my brother's idiotic actions.

"Why weren't you going to tell me?"

"It's not something I want to admit. And in my mind, if one person found out, it would only be a matter of time before more people found out, and then everyone would know," I never expected Gabriel to understand, and I'm glad that he doesn't, but I can't always explain my rationality to him. He either understands it or he doesn't.

"But if more people know, they can try to get you guys help," He's too naive for his own good.

"Not when my father pays off the police,"

"What?" He asked. I realize now that I forgot to tell him about what else my father had done last night.

"When the police showed up and started asking questions, he gave whoever was in charge a check before they left last night. And then, he left the house. He didn't ask any other questions, he grabbed his stuff and left," I explained.

"Atticus, you can't go back there," He said.

"I don't have a choice. I have to go back, I can't leave them there,"

"Atticus,"

"You saw Annabelle this morning. I won't leave them there," I said firmly. I understand that he wants me to be free of my father, but he should also understand that there is nothing in the world that will convince me to leave my siblings there with him.

"I'm not going to be able to change your mind, am I?" He asked, finally realizing that trying to argue with me about this was going to get him nowhere.

"Now you're getting it," I smiled.

The day seemed to move slower, and slower as I waited for my chance to see my brother, and figure out exactly what the hell he was doing telling random strangers my personal business. I knew it wouldn't be smart to cause an argument with him, but at this point, I don't think it can really be avoided.

My chance finally arrived, and I still didn't even know what I was going to say to him. I didn't want to be too aggressive, that's only going to make things a million times worse. I didn't even get a chance to talk to him until the last few minutes of our only class together.

"Alastair, did you tell someone about what happened last night?"

"What are you talking about?" He asked. He was trying to act stupid, which only pissed me off further, but I couldn't let him see my anger.

"Did you tell some girl named Isabelle about last night?" I asked, this time, almost more like I was telling him, rather than asking for confirmation.

"You know Isabelle?" He asked, dodging the question. It was like he was trying to get me to crack, and completely lose sight of what I asked him.

"I didn't before my first class, but I do now because she decided to come up to me, and Gabriel, and ask me why I was here today, considering last night's events, and my *argument* with our father," I said. He couldn't play stupid now. I don't know why he even bothered trying to cover up his conversation with her, isn't it obvious to him that I already know?

"I told her some things. Believe it or not, I do have friends other than you," He snapped back. He's obviously mad at me for not telling him about the things I learned last night.

Fine.

If he wants to know what I'm burdened to know so badly, then I'll tell him, right here, right now, and he'll just have to stay calm.

"Fine, you really want to be like this? Elizabeth isn't our mother, our mother is Mary, and our father murdered her and William last night," I whispered harshly.

"What?" He loudly asked.

"Remember, Alastair, you have to keep quiet about this, and stay calm. You know, for the girls' sake. We can't let them be afraid of both of their brothers," I said, grabbing my things and leaving the classroom.

I still didn't know if I was going home after classes ended that day. I have to apologize to my sisters, but I doubt they even want to see me, they're probably still afraid of me.

Do they think I'm exactly like our father?

Why did I do that?

Was it really worth it?

Was attacking Sebastian worth it to have my sisters be afraid of me?

Obviously, he deserved it, but does that mean it was right for me to do it in front of my siblings?

Are they going to be afraid of me forever?

Did I really ruin everything with them?

"Atticus?" Gabriel asked, lightly shoving me, pulling me out of my mind. What was he doing in here? He's not in my eighth hour.

"Why are you here?" I asked, almost sounding kind of rude. It's not that I didn't want to see him, but I didn't feel like talking to anyone right now.

"They have to combine our classes today, were you not listening to your teacher?" He softly asked.

"No, honestly, I wasn't," I said, leaning back in my chair, silently wishing I could disappear. I didn't want to think about my own existence right now, and how disgusting it was. I wanted to vanish into a dark hole, never to be seen again.

"Are you okay?" He asked, noticing that some part of me was off somewhere else that no one could find.

"I told Alastair what I learned last night,"

"You mean, while you two were in class together?" He asked, shocked that I would do such a thing.

"Yeah,"

"Why the hell did you do that?"

"He was being an asshole about me not telling him what I knew. So I told him, and reminded him that he had to be completely calm about it, and couldn't say anything to anyone. He can't let his emotions get the best of him, we can't let our sisters be terrified of both of their brothers," I said in a cocky manner.

I don't know what's happening to me. I feel like I'm losing sight of who I am, and I don't like the way I'm behaving, and who I'm becoming. I'm changing into someone who isn't me, someone I don't want to be. I feel like I'm becoming more and more like Sebastian every single day.

I can't help but feel like my fate is to become exactly like him, continuing on a horrible cycle that I don't know how to escape, if there even is a way to escape who you are, and what you're destined to become. I don't want to be anything like him.

But I don't think I have the strength to stop myself.

"They're not really scared of you, I think they're just surprised that you stood up to him," He said, trying to change my mind.

"You didn't see their faces last night. I saw the way Alastair looked at me. Whether he admits it or not, he's afraid of me. I've never seen him look so terrified before, not even of our father, but last night? He looked at me with pure fear, like I was a monster," I said. I didn't want my siblings to be scared of me, I'm their brother.

Maybe this means I am exactly like my father. His siblings have spent their entire lives afraid of him, two of them were even murdered by him. The other four vanished after their siblings turned up dead, probably trying to save themselves from the same fate.

Am I the Sebastian DuVonet of our generation?

I'd never hurt my siblings, I'd sooner die than hurt them, but that doesn't remove the fear from occupying their minds. They've seen me behave in a way that they never thought was possible. They don't know what I'm capable of, and honestly, I don't know either.

I think the potential to change who you always thought you'd be stems from many different places, and I don't think that change is always positive. I think more often than not, that change is the most terrifying thing a person can undergo. It doesn't matter who they want to become, they end up shoved into a mold of what their situation has forced them to transform into, for better or for worse.

"You're going back home, aren't you?" Gabriel finally asked, again forcing me to suddenly remember where I was.

"Maybe not with them right after classes, but I have to," I answered. I could tell he didn't like my answer, but he understood. He knew this was something that I had to do.

The end of our class quickly approached, and for the time being, I went home with Gabriel, I had nowhere else to go that I knew would be safe.

"How much longer are you going to hide out here?" He asked as we sat at the table in his home library.

"Until the sun sets," I said, looking out the window to watch the sun slowly dip below the horizon. It's not like I was avoiding talking to my siblings, it's that I was avoiding having to deal with my father, I can't trust him to not try to kill me again.

It wasn't much longer before there was no light from the sun remaining in the sky, and I knew my time was running out. The longer I stayed away, the more strained my relationships with my siblings became. I had to go fix the mess I made, and I had to do it tonight.

I slowly left Gabriel's house, making my way through the night toward the house I didn't really belong to, trying to figure out a way to get to my siblings, without risking running into my father.

I walked around the side of the house, remembering the tree that could be climbed to lead right into Alastair's bedroom. It wouldn't be the most conventional way into the house, but it would work. I made my way up the tree as quietly as I could, quickly reaching my brother's window, noticing it was open, and sliding in as silently as possible.

Chapter Seven

"Dude, what the fuck?" Alastair quietly asked after I entered the room. I couldn't help but notice the girl sitting on my brother's bed, I think I even recognized her.

"Why is there a girl on your bed?" I asked, blinking at him.

"Why did you crawl in through my fucking window?" He snapped back.

"Hi, Atticus," She said. I turned to look at her, finally giving myself a chance to determine who she was.

"Hi, Isabelle," I said, acknowledging her, and turning back to my brother. "Why is Isabelle on your bed?"

"What are you doing in here?"

"Honestly, I think I could ask you the same thing. There's a girl on your bed, Alastair," I said, feeling like I was utilizing the bluntness I see so often from him.

"Brilliant observation. What do you want?" He asked, clearly annoyed with my presence. Not that I really cared.

"Well I did come to talk to you, but if you're busy, I suppose I could come back another time," I laughed, trying to be as quiet as possible.

"I'm going to go," Isabelle began, making her way back to the window.

"Isabelle," Alastair began.

"It's fine, I'll see you tomorrow," She said, waving goodbye, and exiting the window as I tried to contain my laughter as best as I could.

"Are you happy with yourself?" He asked.

"I kind of am now," I said, smiling.

"Yeah, yeah, yeah. Laugh it up, you caught me with my girlfriend in my room," He scoffed.

"I will laugh, this is absolutely hilarious," I said, trying to keep my laughs silent.

"At least I have a girlfriend," He huffed. Is he stupid? I thought he knew about me and Gabriel. Or was he trying to make a jab at the fact that I'm not into girls?

Either way, that's not what I came here to deal with.

"About earlier,"

"I don't really want to hear about that," He said, cutting me off. I can't say that I blame him, but that doesn't mean we didn't need to talk about it.

"Not acknowledging it doesn't make it any less true," I said, trying to force a conversation that I knew neither one of us wanted to have.

"I'd like to stay in denial about being the product of incest for a little while longer, if that's alright with you," He said. Of course, I wanted to be in denial too, but the truth is, we don't have the privilege of pretending this isn't our reality. William died telling me this, I can't pretend it isn't real.

"You were the one who wanted to know what I found out so badly. Did you ever stop to think that I didn't tell you for a reason? Did you ever even think that I didn't want you to know how fucked up our existence is? I didn't try to keep this from you for no reason. I did it because this isn't something that anyone wants to know. William knowing this, and telling me got him killed," I explained, trying to justify my actions. I probably could have said all of this a little bit better, but this was the most honest truth.

"What makes you so certain that our father killed William? And what makes you think that's the reason?" He asked. Did he not believe me?

"I saw him pull a waiter to the side and the next thing I know, that same waiter gives William his glass of champagne, and moments after drinking it, he dies. That's not a coincidence," I explained. I don't understand how this wouldn't be obvious to anyone who knows what kind of man my father really is.

"Our father already told us that William had some kind of weird allergic reaction to something that was in the champagne," Alastair said, turning away from me.

"And you seriously believe him over me?" I asked, louder than I should have.

"Yeah, because what he told us makes sense. I know our father is terrible, but he's not a murderer," He said. There's no fucking way he actually believes our father would tell him the truth about anything.

Why was he defending him? This isn't like my brother at all. Is this his way of trying to get back at me for how I reacted to him earlier? Why would he believe Sebastian over me?

"You seriously don't believe me?" I asked, feeling defeated.

"No, I don't. What you're saying doesn't make any sense. You're obviously lying for fucking attention or something stupid," He shot.

"Attention? You seriously think I'd lie about something like this for attention, of all fucking things?" I asked, no longer hurt by my brother's words, but beyond pissed off instead.

"It seems like you'd do a lot of fucked up things for a lot of reasons, Atticus," He hissed, his words landing like knives.

"What are you even talking about?" I asked, trying to mask my building rage. I knew I couldn't lash out at him, that would only make things worse.

What is he doing?

Is this some kind of game to him?

Why does he suddenly think that I'm his enemy, when all I've ever done in my life is try to help him in any way that I could?

"You think you're so much better than all of us, like you're above all of this. You think you can run out on all of us when you fuck up, and leave the rest of us to deal with your mess, because you don't know how to grow the fuck up, and deal with your mistakes," He said, almost looking like he was planning on trying to fight me. Again.

"You honestly think I ran out for no good reason last night?" I asked. He has absolutely no idea what he's talking about, and he's focusing all his anger on me, because he doesn't know the half of what happened.

"Yeah, I do, because you abandoned all of us without any warning. You just left," He huffed. He couldn't have been more wrong about everything.

"Before you start accusing me of being some kind of monster, maybe you should make sure you have all your information straight. Because I didn't just leave last night," I pushed back.

"Bullshit," He laughed.

"Really?"

"Really,"

"You seriously have no idea what you're talking about," I said, feeling my blood begin to boil underneath my skin, like a fire was lit inside my body.

"I think I know exactly what I'm talking about," He said, taking a step closer to me.

"Oh, so you know our father chased me out of the house with a knife last night?" I said, stepping closer to him, getting right in his face.

"What?" He asked, stepping back.

"So you didn't know that?" I asked in a snarky tone. I didn't feel bad about making Alastair look like an asshole, he deserved it.

"That's why you left?" He quietly asked.

"Yeah, because if I didn't, he would have killed me. Do you still think he's not a murderer?" I asked. I don't understand why my brother even considered believing what our father told him, it's not like he ever tells anyone the truth about anything.

"I didn't know,"

"No, you didn't. You didn't know shit, you decided to jump down my throat because you thought I just left. Just like you didn't know that Gabriel was begging me to not come back here, but I refused to listen to him. Because I knew I could never leave you three here, no matter what. Even if Sebastian fucking kills me for coming back here," I said, cutting him off from even getting the chance to explain himself.

I didn't want to hear his excuse for instantly trying to blame me for a situation so far out of my control, without even bothering to hear my side of the events of last night. The fact that my brother even considered for a second that I would leave them all here cut me deeper than any knife or icepick could. I've passed up more opportunities to get out of here than I can count, all so I wouldn't leave them alone.

No promise of freedom is good enough to even make me contemplate leaving my siblings behind to receive the pain that belongs to me. I can deal with it long enough for us all to find a way out, I refuse to pass anything along to them in place of me.

"Why didn't you tell me earlier?" He asked. Not that he even gave me a chance to explain myself earlier, even if I wanted to.

"When are you going to learn that everything I do is to protect you and our sisters? You didn't need to know. You don't have to suffer with the knowledge that I do, and neither do the girls," I explained, letting myself begin to calm down.

"What are you going to do now for answers? Considering the fact that the main people who could tell you anything are dead?" He asked after a few moments of silence.

"I'm going to find at least one of his other siblings before they leave town, and see if they can give me any other information. And before you even ask, no, you can't come with me," I said, not even giving him a chance to ask to tag along.

"How do you know any of them are even still in town?" He asked.

"I don't. But I have to at least try to find one of them,"

"Leonard might still be here," He said, having some sort of realization.

"Why?"

"He mentioned something about having a hard time traveling because of whatever illness he has, he said he'd probably be here for another week or so," Alastair said, his expression looking like he'd just won the lottery.

"Any idea where he would be?" I asked, he remained silent for a few moments, clearly trying to think.

"He said he likes poetry slams, maybe check a cafe that hosts them, or something like that," He said, like a lightbulb started shining brightly above his head.

"That's perfect," I said, rushing to climb back out of the window.

"You better come back and tell me what you find out," He rushed. I was surprised he actually listened to me, and didn't rush himself out of the window right behind me.

"No promises," I said, moving to scale the house as quickly as I could.

I sprinted out of the yard, running back to Gabriel's house. If anyone knew where there'd be some sort of poetry slam, it'd be Ms. Lumone. I knew she never left the house much, but I'll be damned if that woman didn't love poetry.

I rushed into the Lumone home, first spotting Gabriel sitting in an armchair by the door, reading. He slowly looked up at me as I tried to start catching my breath.

"Glad to see you're still in one piece," He said, shutting the book.

"Where's your mother?"

"What?"

"Where is she? I need to ask her something," I said, breathlessly, barely keeping myself standing.

"She's at some poetry slam. Did you run here?" He asked, slightly changing the subject, noticing my breathlessness.

"Where exactly is she?"

"The cafe that's about four blocks from here, why?" He asked, clearly growing more and more confused with each passing moment.

"I need to find my uncle,"

"What does my mother have to do with your uncle?"

"He's at the poetry slam," I said, rushing back out the door, starting to sprint toward the cafe, soon hearing Gabriel's footsteps following behind me. It was nice to know that he would willingly follow me blind on whatever strange mission I found myself on.

"Why are we running?" He asked, catching up with me.

"I don't know how much longer he's going to be here," I answered, picking up my pace, trying to get to the cafe as fast as I possibly could. I felt like if I didn't run fast enough, the entire world would fall apart beneath my feet. And maybe it would.

It didn't take long for me to arrive at the cafe, with Gabriel right behind me, and I spotted my uncle in the crowd almost instantly. I think he discovered me at the exact moment I found him, as I noticed him rising from his seat carefully and walking toward me.

"Atticus?" He asked, almost like he was surprised to see me. I think Gabriel understood that he couldn't be a part of this conversation, and he instead went to his mother. I think he just didn't want me to go alone.

"I was hoping I could talk to you about a few things," I said, out of breath from pushing my lungs to their absolute limit.

"I think I can imagine what those things are," He said, giving me a small smile, placing his hand on my shoulder.

"Can you really?" I asked. Does he actually know the answers to my questions? Or is he only pretending to know?

"I can. But of course, we can't talk about that here. Is there somewhere else we could go?" He asked.

"Not really," I answered.

"You and I will take a walk then," He smiled, leading me outside. The cool air felt nice, now that I could finally enjoy it without racing to an end goal.

"What can you tell me about my father when he was growing up?" I asked, jumping right into my most burning question.

"He was just as bad then as he is now," He answered. He didn't look at me as he spoke, and I couldn't help but wonder if he believed that looking at me would bring back memories of his own adolescence, and the horrific things that must have happened to him.

"Did you ever tell anyone?"

"One person, the love of my life. And your father killed him when I was fifteen," He said, clearly saddened by the memory of the man he used to love. I couldn't help but fear that this would become Gabriel's fate. Had I made a mistake in telling him the truth about my father?

How many people has my father murdered in cold blood?

"Him?" I asked, hoping he would understand what I was trying to say to him.

"Yes, him. You're less alone than you think, Atticus. Just because your siblings don't understand you, doesn't mean that no one does," He said, turning to me. I thought for a while before I asked anything else.

"If it's not too much to ask, why did my father kill him?" I asked, not wanting to pull too much from my uncle, but still hoping to get answers.

"Your father is a bitter man. He can't handle the fact that other people can be happy, and he can't. He's not a man that's ever faced true joy in his life. His only pleasure derives from causing pain to other people. I've never understood why he was so awful to us when we were growing up, and I don't think I ever will. I'll never understand why your father killed him, and I don't believe there is a true reason behind it. Some people are simply terrible monsters, and that's all they'll ever be," He explained.

"Do you know why he is the way he is?" I asked. I didn't think this was a question that had an easy answer, but it was something I had to ask.

"I don't think that's something that has a simple explanation. Your father is seven years older than I am, I always remember him being the way that he is. William was probably the only one who could answer a question like that," He said sadly. I wonder if he knew why his brother was murdered. I didn't know if I should tell him what I knew about William's death. But I knew that if I was him, I'd want to know.

"I think I know why my father killed William," I said quietly.

"What?" He asked, stopping dead in his tracks, and turning to face me. He didn't know what his brother had done?

"Sebastian poisoned William," I slowly began to explain something that, again, I thought was incredibly obvious.

"You're certain of this?" He asked, grabbing my shoulders. I think he and William were close, maybe that's part of why he's still in town. I didn't want to ask him, it didn't feel right to try to pry any more information out of a man clearly grieving the loss of two of his siblings.

"I can't prove it, if that's what you're asking, but I know what I saw. I can't prove he murdered Mary either, but I'd be willing to bet anything that he's behind both of their deaths," I said. I didn't want to give him a false idea of what happened to them, but he deserved to know what I knew.

"What makes you so sure that Sebastian did this?" He asked. I think he believed me without even having to hear my evidence. He's known my father his entire life, by now, he has to know what Sebastian is capable of better than me.

"I saw him talking to the waiter who gave William his champagne right beforehand. After he took a drink, he started dying. And moments after, I found Mary in the pool. When Sebastian came up to me, his hands smelled like chlorine and his sleeves were wet," I explained.

Obviously, there's no solid way for me to prove what my father's done, but he did this. There's not a single doubt in my mind that he's behind his siblings' deaths, and maybe even more deaths. My father has a body count larger than what I know, and I can only imagine how much it's going to continue to grow.

"I really wish you were wrong about this, Atticus," He said, his head bowing.

"Leonard, how many people has my father killed?" I asked, feeling my nerves skyrocket. I was afraid to know, but I need to know exactly what kind of monster I was living with, and who I had to protect my siblings from.

"I don't have an exact number, son, but I know that it's high. I've never been able to prove anything, but I've always known that my brother was behind many murders. I don't know how he's always gotten away with it, but I know what he's done. Why would he kill William?" He asked, shaking his head.

"William told me the truth about my mother," I began.

"Elizabeth?" He asked, interrupting me. Leonard didn't know? Were William and Mary the only ones that knew the truth?

"Elizabeth isn't my mother,"

"Your mother is Michelle then, yes?" He asked casually.

What?

"No, Mary is my mother," I corrected him.

"Who is Michelle the mother of then?" He asked himself, as I felt myself grow sicker and sicker.

"Wait, you mean to tell me Elizabeth *isn't* actually my sister's mother either?" I asked, feeling my stomach drop.

"No, I remember now, Elizabeth was never pregnant, but I remember Mary being pregnant twice, Michelle being pregnant once, and then I never even saw their children. They never told any of us when their children were born. It took me a while to put two and two together, and realize that you four were the children, but it all clicked together once I found out that Sebastian somehow had four children, although his wife was never pregnant, and then I knew exactly what he'd done," He explained. I was disgusted, to say the least, all four of us were part of something so sick and sinister.

I wanted to throw up.

I wanted to scream, and run away, but I had to know everything.

"Annabelle looks exactly like Mary, and Anastasia looks like Michelle. So does that mean that me, my brother, and Annabelle are Mary's children, and Anastasia is Michelle's child?" I asked, my voice shaking with disgust.

"I can't imagine how you must be feeling right now, but you deserve to know the truth," He said as my balance faltered. I couldn't stand straight.

I felt myself fall over, Leonard catching me before I had a chance to hit the ground. I felt everything and nothing all at once. I didn't know what to do, I couldn't breathe, I felt myself gagging at the thought of what my father had done. Everything was so much worse than what I first thought it was, and I can imagine everything is only going to get worse from here.

"How could he do this?" I asked, unable to prevent myself from throwing up on the sidewalk any longer.

I felt like I was a kind of dirty that you could never wash clean. My existence itself was some kind of sick and twisted joke. This couldn't be true, this has to be some kind of fucked up prank, this can't be real.

"Sebastian is a sick man. And sick men do sick things, trying to justify their disturbing existence in any way that they can. But this isn't something you can justify. I know you didn't want to know any of this, but you need to know the truth about him. If you know who he really is, you have power over him, you have the strength to destroy the foundation he's built himself on," He explained.

"I can't do this," I said, coughing.

"You can. And you need to," He said.

Why does all the responsibility always have to fall on me? I'm seventeen. I can't be the soldier that everyone needs me to be. I can't be the one to destroy my father. I'm not the strong, defensive line everyone wants me to be. I'm not brave enough to stop him, I'm not powerful enough to help anyone. I can't do this. I'm not the weapon everyone can depend on to fight their battles.

I'm just a kid.

"Why do I have to be the one to fight back against him? Why am I the one who has to give up everything to protect everyone except myself?" I asked, feeling tears forming in my eyes.

"Because you're the only one selfless enough to stand up against him. Everyone else makes selfish decisions that are only in their best interest. You care about everyone before yourself," He said, like that was supposed to comfort me, and make me want to continue to throw myself on the front lines of the war with my father.

"And look where it's gotten me! My entire body is covered in bruises! I have to hide everything I am! I have to lie to everyone, about everything! I got chased out of the house with a knife for trying to stand up to him! I have to be the picture-perfect son and the brave older brother! I can't keep doing this, it's tearing me apart!" I screamed. Everything about me was breaking down and crumbling into pieces, and I didn't care to try to stop it anymore. I was falling apart, and nothing could hold me together anymore.

"Then stop lying. Tell everyone the truth. Let people know what you're going through. The next time someone tries to give you an attitude about being a part of the perfect family, tell them the truth. Blow up on them, scream in their face, but don't bother to lie anymore," He advised. This sounded like an easy way to get myself killed.

"No one is going to believe me!" I shouted.

"You don't know that, Atticus. Does that boy that ran after you believe you?" He asked, referring to Gabriel.

"Yes, but,"

"There. Someone believes you," He said.

"It's not that easy,"

"It's easier than you think it is," He said, interrupting me.

"If it's so easy, why did you never tell more people?" I asked. Doesn't he realize that trying to tell someone about what I go through on a daily basis is one of the hardest things I can do? I never even wanted to tell Gabriel. I never wanted to have to tell anyone, but I was left without a choice, typical of my life.

"I couldn't risk losing anyone else, Atticus," He said, almost sounding ashamed of himself.

"So you want me to risk Gabriel? You want me to risk everything I have, all because you could never be brave enough again? You're expecting me to get myself and everyone I love killed, because none of the fucking adults can grow a spine and stand up for literal fucking children? No. I'm not your soldier, I'm not some pawn that you can force to be everyone's protector all because *you're* weak," I shot back. There are a lot of things I'm willing to do, but risking Gabriel's life isn't one of them. I'd rather die than put him in any kind of danger.

"I understand you're tired of all of this, but,"

"No, I don't want to hear whatever bullshit reason you're going to come up with. I'm done. I'm done fighting everyone's battles for them. Haven't I been through enough already?" I asked, not even bothering to try to hide the millions of emotions I felt pushing up to the surface.

"You've been through a lot in your life, I know that, and I understand. But you can't turn your back on the people who need you to be their voice," He said. Why is he so adamant about me being some kind of warrior for everyone in this family who's been damaged by my father?

"I'm not turning my back on anyone. For once in my life, I'm trying to take care of myself. I've given up so many chances to get out of here because I couldn't bear the thought of leaving my siblings behind. But now, they hate me, they're afraid of me. I'm done getting my ass beat for even breathing to protect everyone else," I said. I didn't feel like I owed him an explanation, but I couldn't stop the words from escaping. No matter what I say or do, I always feel like I have to justify every little thing I do.

"Atticus, you don't mean that, that's not who you are," He began.

"You don't know shit about who I am!" I screamed, cutting him off. He's known me for one day, and he suddenly thinks he knows everything about me? I don't even know everything about myself. I don't even know who I am half the time. I can't even recognize myself in the mirror, but a man I've known for twenty-four hours knows every little detail about me?

"I know that whether you admit it or not, you want to protect as many people as possible. You could have skipped town years ago, you're smart enough to make it on your own, but you've stayed here. You've stayed here because you couldn't handle the thought of leaving your siblings here alone," He said. I knew within me that he was right, but that didn't matter. I'm sick of having to be there for everyone all the time, it's destroying me. Obviously, I want to keep my siblings safe, but I don't think I can do it anymore.

I don't know why everyone believes I'm some sort of invincible force that can handle protecting everyone, and take on my father. I can't make him stop. I can't do anything but sit there and accept what he does.

I couldn't stop myself from crying, and I couldn't tell if I was crying for myself, or for the damage everyone else would have to begin taking if I stopped being their barrier. I felt guilty, but more than anything, I felt hurt. And I'm so tired of hurting all the time.

"If you can't confront your father, then I will," Leonard eventually said, starting to walk back toward my house.

"What?" I asked, following right behind him.

"I'm already dying, it's not like I have anything to lose. It doesn't matter if he kills me, I've already got one foot in the grave," He said, laughing.

"You can't be serious?" I asked.

"I am. If I have to die, it's going to be doing something right for once in my life, not because my body is ripping itself apart from the inside out," He explained. I suppose I understood his reasoning. He was afraid, that much was obvious, but maybe he felt like he had to redeem himself after what happened when he was younger. Maybe he felt like he owed it to everyone my father's hurt to at least try to protect as many people as he could.

The rest of the walk back to the house was filled with a painfully loud silence. Was he really about to risk his life for people he barely knew?

The house looked as menacing as always. It didn't have even an ounce of personality, it looked like a miserable prison that crushed your soul the moment you stepped through the door. Leonard didn't even take a moment to collect himself, he barged right inside, with me right behind him, following him along like a lost dog.

"Sebastian!" He hollered the moment he entered the house. My father instantly came down the stairs, noticing me hiding behind his brother.

"What the hell are you two doing here?" He demanded. He was clearly still angry about what I did yesterday, his face still looking red and swollen where I had attacked him. I didn't feel bad in the slightest, in fact, I wanted to laugh at him, knowing he finally got what he deserved, and knowing that I was the one to give it to him.

"What the hell is your problem?! That you're awful enough to treat your own children like punching bags?! Horrible enough to rape your own sisters?! Cruel enough to murder your own brother and sister in cold blood for threatening to expose who you truly are?!" Leonard shouted, moving closer and closer to my father with every single word. If Leonard was afraid, he was strong enough to hide it from Sebastian.

I wondered if anyone else in the house could hear what my uncle was saying, and if they could, I wondered why they chose to remain silent and hidden away.

"I have no idea what you're talking about! You've gone mad, Leonard!" Sebastian spat back.

"Bullshit!"

"And you!" He began, pointing to me, "What makes you believe you're welcome back in this home after what you've done?!" He shouted at me.

"Leave the boy alone!" Leonard said, pushing me further behind him. Is this what it felt like to be protected? To have someone care about me enough to defend me from my father by putting themselves in his line of fire?

"You have no idea what you're doing, dear brother," Sebastian said. It was like my eyes were trained to notice even the smallest adjustment of my father's hands.

Everything seemed to stop, it was like time had ceased to progress, and everything was frozen in place. I tried to warn him, I tried to say anything, but the words refused to fly off my tongue.

I couldn't warn him, he didn't even have a fighting chance. Leonard walked into this house tonight, knowing he was going to die at his brother's hand. He had accepted his fate long before Sebastian plunged the knife into his abdomen. He accepted his fate before he even stepped through the door.

I should have prevented this. I should have done what Leonard told me and stood up to my father myself. I shouldn't have made him stand up for me, all because I was sick of being the one that people depended on. I could have saved him.

But I was too selfish to keep him alive. We both knew what was going to happen to him, and I let it happen anyway, all because I guilted him into giving up his life for me. I made him give up everything for me, just because I was afraid.

His body slowly started to drop to the floor, and I knew I had to catch him. I couldn't let him fall alone, not after he had sacrificed his life for me. I helped him lower to the ground slowly and peacefully, trying to treat him with as much respect as I could.

"I don't regret what I did," He whispered to me with his final breath.

His last words were a lie, they had to be. His defense of me got him killed. I think he just doesn't want me to feel guilty about his fate, but I'm the one to blame for what happened to him. No words would ever change that.

It's my fault he's dead. It didn't matter if he would have blamed me or not, the whole truth is that it's entirely my fault that he's dead. It didn't matter that my father was the one who stabbed him, I was the one who killed him.

Chapter Eight

"Atticus!" My father screamed, yanking me off of the ground, away from Leonard's body, pulling me away from the corpse of my uncle.

I didn't want to think about what was happening to me. Maybe if I didn't let my mind register what was going on, it wasn't real. I didn't have the strength to fight against my father. Or maybe I didn't care enough to try to stop him.

I felt my face growing hotter, and hotter with each stinging strike. My body grew weaker, and weaker. I felt myself make contact with the ground, where I saw my uncle's body right beside me, slowly being dragged away.

I don't know who was taking the corpse away, I didn't care to know. I didn't want to think about who had to drag Leonard's dead body away from the spot where he was murdered. I didn't want to imagine who was so unlucky that they had to dispose of my father's latest victim. I guess they don't feel unlucky, knowing that they've survived another day.

With each passing moment, I felt myself begging for death more and more. How many more people have to die because of me? How many people are going to risk their lives trying to help me? How many people are going to make the ultimate sacrifice to try to stop my father? Can he even be stopped? Is this the way things will always have to be? Am I just another one of my father's nameless victims, who will never truly get away from his abuse?

The pain slowly started to melt into pure numbness, like I was outside of my body, floating away into outer space, unable to come back down to earth, destined to float into the vastness of the galaxy.

I felt my eyes wander to the staircase, I could almost feel the energy shift in the room, like I was no longer alone with my father. The moment I looked at the stairs, I noticed Annabelle, standing there, staring in horror at what was happening to me, tears running down her face.

I couldn't speak to her, I couldn't risk my father realizing that she was standing right there, who knows what he'd do to her?

I tried to silently plead with her to get her to leave. She didn't need to see this, no one did, especially not her. She's just a kid. Annabelle looks at me as her number one defense against our father. She thinks I'm some kind of impossibly strong superhero, she shouldn't have to see me as anything less than what she needs me to be. She doesn't deserve to be forced to witness me at the lowest I've ever been.

She deserves to still believe that her older brother can protect her from anything. She deserves to believe that her brother has no weaknesses. She deserves to believe that I'm capable of keeping her safe, even when things seem impossible.

It was like she was frozen on the stairs, she made no effort to move. I couldn't say a single word to try to comfort her, I had to silently beg her to walk away, and act like she didn't see a single thing.

It's not like I was asking an easy thing of her, but I hope she understands that it's necessary for her safety. I know she'll want to talk about this later, and I'll gladly listen to every word she has to say, but she has to know that right now, she has to go anywhere but here.

Annabelle isn't stupid by any definition of the word. She's a scared kid who needs something to cling to in order to ever feel even remotely okay in this house, and that something happens to be me. I wish she could read my thoughts and understand that she needs to turn around, and walk away, forgetting she ever saw anything.

It's not an easy thing to forget, it's truly impossible to forget. But to survive in this house, she doesn't have a choice. She has to pretend that nothing is happening, and everything is perfectly fine. She needs to believe that *nothing* is happening to me, and walk away.

She finally began to slowly retreat up the stairs, her eyes still never leaving me. She was probably beyond horrified. She's been through so many things in this house, and she's seen so many awful things, but I don't think she's ever seen anything this terrible.

I had to lay there on the ground, feeling my father cut me up with a knife. It didn't hurt, I only felt the cold metal separating my skin, feeling my blood start to slowly pour out of the open wounds that covered my body.

It was like my father wanted to test how many times he could cut me open before it would kill me. It was like he was enjoying slicing me to bits, dragging his knife along my face, my arms, my abdomen, anywhere he could reach. Maybe he wanted me to see the scars that would form, and understand that no matter what I do, I'll never be able to forget him. He will forever be a part of me, leaving his anger all over my body.

I wanted to cry. I wanted to scream for help. I wanted someone to burst in and save me from my life, and the things I've been doomed to suffer through. But I knew deep within me that things would always be like this. There would be no happy ending, no fairy tale life. This is how my life began, and this is how my life would end.

There's no one coming to my rescue, no one is going to save me from my father. I can't keep wishing for an impossible savior, trying to live in the hope that eventually, one day, everything will be okay. Nothing will ever be okay, none of this is ever going to end. Everyone who's ever tried to take a stand against my father is dead. And I can only imagine that one of these days, I'm going to be the next person to fall victim to my father's cruelty, and thirst for blood, and drag everyone I love down into the grave with me.

The only thing I could really do was wonder when it would finally be my turn to die at the hands of the man who was supposed to protect me, the man who was supposed to raise me and help me become a good man.

But I suppose an awful man can't truly raise a good son. Awful men don't know how to raise another person, especially not a good person. It's his fault that I don't think I actually have the capability to be a good man.

I don't know how long my father spent torturing me, I only know the moment it ceased. I could feel the blood rushing through my entire body, almost as if it was trying to heal the dozens of wounds that now covered my skin, trying to form scars as a reminder of what I've survived.

But I don't want to remember. I want to forget everything. I don't think any of this is making me stronger, it's making me weaker. It's ripping my mind apart, it makes me feel like I can't trust anyone, even if they truly do have good intentions.

I don't think I can trust anyone other than myself, I can't count on anyone to truly have my best interests at heart. Not when my own father has lied to me my entire life, and has tried to destroy me in every single way possible, tearing my life away from me, removing my freedom to choose anything in my own life.

"Atticus?" I heard Alastair's voice ask, his voice being the only thing that pulled me out of my thoughts, reminding me where I was.

"Yes, dear brother of mine?" I asked, trying to laugh. I couldn't look over at him, I didn't know if he was alone. I heard his footsteps coming close to me, right beside my head.

"Annabelle saw everything," He whispered, crouching down close to my face, extending his hand close to mine.

"Not everything," I groaned, grabbing my brother's hand to sit myself up, feeling lighter as more blood gushed out of every area of my body.

"You're bleeding," He noticed, standing up.

"Yes, thank you for pointing out the obvious," I said, still using his hand to stand up, my balance faltering. This time, I was the one who failed to account for how blood loss would affect me. I guess we really are a lot alike.

"Like, a lot," He said, grabbing my left side to keep me standing the moment he noticed I couldn't stand on my own.

"Wow, I didn't notice that,"

"Don't get smart with me, jackass," He said, leading me toward the stairs, where Annabelle grabbed onto my right arm, draping it over her shoulders.

Shit.

I didn't know she came back down here with him.

"Are you okay?" She whispered.

"I'm fine, just a little tired," I lied. She didn't need to know the truth, that's not her burden to carry. She didn't need to know that I thought I was going to die on these stairs, the loss of blood finally getting to me, causing my battle to finally end.

They brought me to my bedroom, leading me into the bathroom, Alastair forcing me to get into the bathtub so he could play nurse. I guess it should be alarming that we've had to do this for each other in less than a week's time.

"Annabelle, go to your room, I'll take care of him," Alastair said, urging her away.

"But,"

"It's okay, Alastair's got this," I smiled at her, letting her know that I would be alright. She nodded, and silently left my room, returning to her own.

"How much pain are you in?" Alastair asked, first starting to clean the cuts on my face, the stinging liquid causing my eyes to water.

"Not as much as you would expect," I explained, removing Gabriel's now bloody sweatshirt to allow my brother access to the other wounds that covered my body, also allowing him to see the countless other scars I've given myself. He knew about them, but that didn't mean the sight of them shocked him any less.

"Why did you come back?" He asked, refusing to look at my face, his sights trained on the cuts on my arms.

"I didn't come back alone," I responded, trying not to move.

"What are you talking about?"

"I came back with Leonard. Alastair, our father killed Leonard right in front of me. And it's all my fault," I whispered. I think I believed that if I admitted it quietly enough, that would erase my guilt. Alastair didn't say anything. He just sat there, cleaning cut after cut after cut.

"It's not your fault," He finally said.

"Yes, it is. I made him come back here, I made him confront our father, all because I was too selfish to do it myself. Sebastian killed him, and it's entirely my fault," I pushed back.

There was nothing he could say to convince me otherwise, I was as guilty as my father. Alastair clearly didn't want me to blame myself, but there was no one else to blame. If I didn't make him come back with me and do what I wasn't brave enough to do, he'd still be alive. If I didn't make him confront my father for me, he would still have a beating heart.

Nothing my brother could say would change the fact that I'm the reason people are dead. Just because I didn't deliver the fatal blow, doesn't mean I'm not responsible for their deaths. It's the exact same as if I had plunged the knife into their chests myself.

I'm a murderer. Whether my brother admits it or not, I'm as bad as our father. I'm a killer, and it's my fault so many people are dead. I couldn't save William. I couldn't save Mary. And I couldn't save Leonard.

"You couldn't have known," He tried to reassure me.

"I did know. We both knew that whoever spoke against him was going to die, and I let him sacrifice himself for me," I explained as my brother finished cleaning and wrapping the wounds on my left arm.

"Then it sounds like it was his choice. If you both knew what was going to happen, and he still decided to try to protect you, then it sounds like he made the choice to risk his life for you. You didn't force him to do anything, he made that decision on his own. Just because the outcome was bad, doesn't mean it was your fault. Leonard knew what he was risking, and he still decided to go through with it. That doesn't make it your fault, that made him someone who cared enough about you to sacrifice his life to try to keep you safe," He said. I really hate when he makes sense about these kinds of things.

I didn't say anything to him, I didn't have anything to say. Part of me knew he was right, whether I wanted to acknowledge it or not, Alastair was right.

But I still can't help but feel responsible for Leonard's death. I feel like somehow, I could have prevented it, if I had done even one thing differently. If even the smallest change had been made to my actions, maybe he'd still be alive, and maybe his brutal murder would have never happened.

But I can't control fate, I can't control time, I can't control anything but my own actions. And the sooner I accept that, the better off I'll be.

It didn't take long for Alastair to finish cleaning and wrapping all of my injuries. Over time, he's become quite fast and efficient at taking care of my countless wounds, always having to be the one to take care of me when I can't even find the strength to stand.

"You should talk to Annabelle," He said, helping to lift me out of the bathtub, and grabbing the bloody sweatshirt off the floor.

"I know. But I also need to figure out what to tell Gabriel about his sweatshirt," I said, trying to lift my brother's spirits even the smallest amount.

"I'm sure he won't care that much, he'll just be glad you're alive. But you still need to talk to Annabelle," He restated.

"I know, I'm going. But I don't know what to say to her," I said, walking toward the door, almost afraid to reach it.

"Then don't talk, just listen to her. Think about it, Atticus. She watched you get your ass beat horrifically. She knows it happens, but she's never actually seen it before. She's probably traumatized, and she doesn't know how to deal with that. She looks at you like her knight in shining armor, she's never seen you like that, she doesn't know what to do," He said. I seriously hate it when he's right.

"I know,"

"So just be there for her, listen to whatever she has to say. You're the only one she'll talk to about this stuff. She won't talk to me, and I don't think she's ever even held an actual conversation with Anastasia," He said.

And he was right. I knew I had to talk to her, and maybe try to explain something to her, but that didn't make doing it easy. The truth is, I was terrified to face her after what she just witnessed. I don't know what she thinks of me, and I'm afraid to find out. She's seen me for who I really am, a weak kid who can't even really stand up to his own father.

I moved into the hallway, making my way to her bedroom, hoping she was ready to talk to me. I knew I couldn't force her to say anything to me, or even convince her to want to see me, but I had to at least try.

Chapter Nine

"Annabelle?" I asked, knocking on her door, and waiting for her to let me in. At least, I hoped she was going to let me in. I wouldn't blame her if she didn't want to. But, I wasn't waiting for a long time, the door slowly opening, revealing my sister on the other side after only a few short moments.

"Atticus," She said, stepping aside to invite me into the depressing room. It's hard to really know, and understand who she is based on the blank walls in her bedroom. It's sad thinking that none of us can express anything about ourselves in our rooms. They're only places we stay in, not live in.

"Do you want to talk about what you saw?" I asked, walking in and closing the door behind me.

"Why did he do that to you?" She asked. I wish I had an answer for her.

"Some people aren't good people. They do bad things, and there's really no reason behind it. They're bad people who want to hurt other people, because they think that hurting someone else is going to take away their pain. And it won't, it never will," I tried to explain in the best way I could. I guess there really isn't a way to explain why some fathers hate their children so much as to make their lives a living hell. Maybe it's something fundamentally wrong with them that can't be explained.

"Why did you hit him yesterday?" Was her next question. I couldn't tell her the truth, not about something like that.

"He's been lying to us about a lot of things our whole lives. I guess last night was my breaking point, and I couldn't handle his lies anymore. I'm sorry if I scared you," I apologized, while trying to avoid the entire truth.

I didn't want to lie to her, but the truth would destroy her entire world, it'd rip her apart. She's too young to know any of this, she's too young to know the truth about our parents.

"What has he been lying about?" She asked.

Shit. Of course, she had to ask something I couldn't give her an answer to. It's not that she doesn't deserve to know, it's that she *shouldn't* know about these kinds of things. No one should. But she's just a kid. I don't want to destroy her entire perception of herself so young.

"Annabelle, I think it's for the best that you don't know about that stuff,"

"Why not?" She interrupted. She was rightfully sick of being treated like a child. But it was my job to protect her, no matter what, even if she didn't like my methods. I'm not going to let him destroy her like he destroyed me.

"It's a lot of bad stuff, and you don't need to be thinking about those kinds of things. Listen, when you're older, I promise I'll tell you everything, but,"

"But I'm just a kid? So I don't get to know anything because I'm too young? That's bullshit, Atticus, and you know it," She snapped back. I understand that she's upset, and that's fine, I don't blame her at all. I only need her to understand that I'm only hiding things from her to keep her safe.

"I promise you, I'm only keeping this from you because it's what's best for you," I tried to explain, but I don't think she was going to believe me. She's a young teenager. She's going to think there isn't a single person in the world, other than her, that knows what's best for her.

"You don't get to make that decision for me," She said, obviously growing more and more upset by the moment.

"Can you please try to understand why I'm doing this? I only want to protect you, and I can promise you that knowing shit like this is only going to hurt you. Annabelle, what I know is why I did what I did last night. You know that's not who I am. Do you really think I attacked Sebastian for no reason?" I asked. She wanted to be treated like an adult, and I understand that. But she needs to realize that sometimes people do things they don't want to, all to protect the people they love.

"Well no,"

"Then understand that I'm trying to do what's best for you. I wouldn't keep secrets from you if it wasn't for the best," I explained, interrupting her.

"I can handle it," She tried to object.

"No, you can't. I can't handle it. Alastair can't handle it. And neither can you," I said. I wonder how long it's going to take her to realize that she's not going to change my mind.

"Why do they hate us?" She asked, sitting down on her bed.

What's with her asking questions that don't have answers?

"I don't know. It's nothing that any of us did. They're bad people who don't know what it means to love someone. There's *nothing* that we can do to change that. That's just how it is. They're bad people who are so miserable in their own lives that they take it out on us," I explained, sitting down next to her.

"Most of the time, I can't help but think there's something wrong with me. If I was just the daughter they wanted me to be, they wouldn't be like this. I think about what my life would be like if they loved me. But I do *everything* they say, and I do everything they want, and it's still not enough. They still don't love me. And I think there has to be something wrong with me, something that I can't change," She said, leaning her head on my shoulder.

"There's nothing wrong with you. And as much as it sucks, there's nothing that you can do to change them. They're bad people, Annabelle, they always have been, and they always will be. And there's nothing you can do about it. The only thing you can do is pretend it doesn't bother you, no matter how much it might hurt. If you let them see that they're hurting you, that's how you let them win. People like our parents only want to cause other people pain. That's what makes them happy. But if you show them that they can't hurt you, you're taking away their power. That's what I did, I pretended that nothing they could do actually hurt me, and eventually, it became true. They can't hurt me anymore, because I don't let it hurt me. I push the pain away, and I tell myself it doesn't exist. And that makes it go away," I explained.

I didn't know if she understood what I was trying to tell her, I didn't even know if my words made any sense.

"So you told yourself it didn't hurt, and eventually, it actually stopped hurting?" She asked, as I noticed the water welling in her eyes that she was trying her best to fight off.

"That's exactly it. If you take control of your pain, nothing can hurt you. Their actions and their words only have power if you give them power. The moment you take that power away from them, they can't do anything to hurt you anymore,"

"How do you take control of your pain?" She asked, confusion written all over her face. I guess it's not really something that makes a lot of sense, but it's what works. It's what makes life in this house bearable.

"Let your mind wander somewhere else. I like to look into my future, and think about what my life will be like in ten years. And that brings me some kind of peace. You have to find that place for you, the place that brings you the most amount of happiness, the most amount of peace. Once you find that, things can only hurt you if you let them," I said.

I didn't feel like my words were making any sense, but Annabelle seemed to understand them, nodding along to every word I said. She was trying to think of her own safe place, I could see the concentration etched across her features.

"How do I know if I'm controlling my pain?" She asked. I didn't know a good way to explain it. It's the sort of thing that you don't realize you're doing until you really think about it. But that explanation wouldn't make any sense.

"You'll just know. It's not exactly something you can describe, but something you'll sort of do without thinking. It'll become second nature once you start thinking about it," I explained.

I hope she understood what I was trying to tell her. I'm not exactly the best at trying to explain living in your own mind when you can't deal with the life you have to live, or the world around you. It's not something that's easily explained or understood.

"How did you realize you could control your pain?" She asked. I don't know if I ever had a moment of realization, or if things suddenly stopped hurting me.

"When no matter what was happening to my body, I didn't feel anything. Things stopped hurting," I shrugged. I don't know if she really understood what I was saying, or if she only pretended to understand because she didn't know what else to do.

"Do you think things are always going to be like this?"

"I don't know. I hope not. But I do know that once you get out of here, they can't hurt you anymore. They won't be able to get to you, and you'll be somewhere far away from here. Somewhere they'll never be able to find you, somewhere that no one will ever hurt you again. I know it seems impossible right now, but you *will* get away one of these days, and you'll never have to feel trapped again. You'll finally be in control of your own life, and you'll be free to do whatever you want, whatever makes you happy," I said, smiling at her.

I didn't have the heart to tell her that I didn't think I would make it out of here. But I knew I had to tell her what I wish someone would have told me so many years ago. Maybe then, things would have turned out differently for me, and maybe I'd actually believe that a life existed for me beyond this house.

"What about you?" She asked, seemingly confused that I didn't make any mention of my own freedom from this hell.

"What do you mean?"

"Where are you going to go after all of this?" She asked. I guess I never really picked a specific place to go, I don't think I ever actually survived that long in my head to form an actual plan for life outside of this place.

"I don't really know. Maybe somewhere in the mountains,"

"Mountains?" She laughed.

"They have a nice view," I laughed back, nudging her shoulder. Her laughter slowly died out, filling the room with nothing but silence.

"Are we going to be okay?" She finally asked, turning to look at me.

I had to think about it for a few moments. I honestly didn't know if we would ever really be okay. I think we would simply learn how to live with what we've survived. I don't know if there is a way to truly be okay with something as horrific as the things we've been through, but I do think we can eventually learn to accept that this wasn't our fault, and there was nothing we could have done to change our situation.

"I think so. Maybe not right now, but I think we will be soon. I think peace is finally on its way to us, and things are going to change soon enough. You just have to hold on a little bit longer," I said. I had to give her something to cling onto, even if I didn't fully believe it myself. She deserved to believe that life would get better one day, even if I wouldn't be around to see it.

I hope I didn't destroy all of the hope she had left in her. I know she probably didn't want to hear everything I told her, and as much as I didn't want her to know the whole truth, she still deserved most of my honesty.

I heard my father's footsteps slowly thundering up the stairs, approaching Annabelle's door. I instinctively stood up, standing directly in front of her, acting as a barrier between the door and my sister. Anyone who wanted to come in here would have to go through me first. I don't care how weak I felt, I'd do whatever I could to protect her.

I stood silently, listening for where my father's feet moved, trying to pick up on even the slightest movement, or the faintest creak in the floorboards. It wasn't long before I heard five other sets of feet coming up the stairs, coming closer to my sister's room. I turned around to face Annabelle, leaning close to whisper in her ear.

"If that door opens, I need you to run and lock yourself in your bathroom. Don't worry about me, and don't look back. Just lock the door, and stay quiet, do you understand me?" I asked her, keeping my voice low so that no one other than my sister could hear me. She nodded in acknowledgment of my statement.

I felt sick to my stomach, if that door opened, I could only imagine what would happen to my sister. No one was expecting me to be in the room with her, they expected her to be alone, defenseless against a hoard of men much older than her, with no one in there to try to protect her. I knew there was probably only one thing they were there for.

It was silent on the other side of the door, the footsteps never went away, they remained on the opposite side of the door, almost as if they were waiting for their perfect moment to strike.

If they wanted to play the waiting game, I had no problem staying in here until the sun rose on the horizon. I'd wait in here as long as I had to, if it meant keeping whoever was waiting for my sister away from her.

The door quickly sprang open, and Sebastian rushed into the room with five men much larger than him following him. I could try, but there was no way I'd be able to fight off all six of them. I wasn't strong enough to do something like that, and I don't think I ever would be. I could give it my everything, but I knew I'd never win that kind of fight.

Annabelle didn't move, she stayed frozen behind me. I knew she didn't have much time, she had to go, and she had to go now.

But she didn't.

The men began to form a circle around the entire room, entrapping Annabelle and I where we were. I grabbed her hand, making her stand, hoping she realized that if any of the men moved to attack me, she had only a few seconds to run out of the room, and get as far away from here as she possibly could.

Not a single person moved. We all stood in our places, like actors on a stage waiting for the show to begin, not daring to even breathe. It was a question of who would be the first to move, and I didn't plan on it being me.

"Atticus, move," My father demanded, getting right in my face, like he was trying to scare me. That seems to be his only scare tactic, and he actually seems to believe it's effective. I will admit that it used to work, but not anymore.

"Go fuck yourself," I pushed back, getting in his face, making sure to keep Annabelle close behind me, not letting her get more than an inch out of my reach.

"Do you truly believe you scare me, dear boy?" He asked, tilting his head down at me, as if that was going to help him.

"I could ask you the same thing, dear father," I snapped back, looking directly into his eyes.

I might be fast, but sometimes, Sebastian's faster than I am.

I didn't even have a moment to react. I never even saw his hand move. But before I knew it, his hands were at my throat, dragging me away from Annabelle, as it felt like my vocal cords were being crushed in his grip. I tried to fight against his hands, hearing Annabelle scream as I saw two of the men racing toward her, grabbing at her as she tried to fight against them.

It was no use, they were too strong. It didn't take them long to drag her out of the room, and I could still hear her screams echoing through the hallways, my adrenaline building enough to allow me to break out of my father's grip.

I didn't even make it to the door, one of the men still left in the room beat me there, pointing a knife at my throat, and the other two men grabbed me from behind. I couldn't try to fight against them, I'd only end up getting my throat sliced open. I could hear my father laughing, coming closer to the door, standing next to the man holding the knife.

"When are you going to learn, Atticus? You can't stop me. You can't protect any of them, you can't even protect yourself. Nothing you can do here matters. You're fighting a losing battle. The sooner you realize that, the easier things will be for you. Give up now, before you get yourself trapped somewhere you can't get out of," He said with a wicked laugh.

"I swear to you, I will fucking kill you," I said, never breaking eye contact with him. I wasn't scared of him, not anymore. And I want more than anything to be the one to put him six feet under.

"I'll be looking forward to it," He laughed, turning to the man with the knife, "Take him to the backyard, and have your fun with him," He said, exiting the room, walking in the direction of Annabelle's screams for help that still haven't stopped.

I knew those screams.

I knew what they were doing to her.

I wanted to die, hearing her suffer through that. No one deserves to be violated in such a horrific way, their freedom of choice stripped away from them. No matter how many times she begged for them to stop, they wouldn't. Because people like my father, and his shitty friends don't care about the choices other people make. They just assume that they have the freedom to make those decisions for them.

They don't care that she's trying her hardest to fight against them. They don't care that she's a fucking child. They don't care that she's saying no.

The three men dragged me out to the backyard, keeping the knife pressed to my neck the entire time. It was useless trying to fight. I couldn't help Annabelle. It didn't matter what happened to me. They could kill me for all I cared.

She has to suffer through what they're doing to her, she has to live with that for the rest of her life. And I'll never forgive myself for not preventing it. It's my fault that I couldn't stop them.

I could feel their fists colliding with every area of my body, I didn't bother to try to control my pain. I wanted to feel it. I deserved to feel it. I let every single blow hit me as hard as they possibly could. I didn't deserve to try to hide from the gut-wrenching pain that I felt soaring through my entire body. I had to just let it happen, because *I deserved it.*

If I couldn't protect Annabelle from this, how could I be expected to keep her safe from anything? I couldn't keep those men away from her, and now she has to suffer the consequences of my weakness. I didn't know where she was, but I could still hear the sounds of her desperate cries for help ringing in my ears, and the sound of her pain hurt me more than any punch ever could.

I can't even offer emotional support for her after this, she's not going to want to talk to me. She's not going to want to talk to anyone. She's going to force herself to deal with this on her own, and it's my fault. My sister is suffering, and there's nothing I can do about it.

I could taste my blood filling up my mouth, the sour taste a familiar and bitter feeling that I can never seem to escape. It's one of those things that seem to follow me everywhere I go, always right by my side.

I almost felt numb, like all my senses were slowly fading out of my body, and I didn't care enough to try to stop it. I wanted to let myself suffer, and lose the ability to feel anything at the same time.

I didn't want to think about what was happening to my sister, but it was also the only thing on my mind. Even if she doesn't blame me, it's all my fault, and there's nothing I can do to change that.

Maybe my father was right. Maybe I can't help anyone. Maybe I'm supposed to be a silent figure, who only accepts the things that are happening to him, because he knows he doesn't have the power to do anything to stop it.

It was at least an hour before Annabelle's screams stopped, and the men stopped attacking me. I wanted to go find my sister, more than anything. But I didn't have anything left in me. Not strength, not energy, not even the willpower to force myself off the ground, which seems to be my fate most nights. The pain had me paralyzed, and left me feeling like I was already half dead.

I don't know how long I stayed there by myself, staring at the stars, making wishes on anything I saw moving in the night sky. It didn't matter what it was, I just hoped it had the potential to end my misery.

"Atticus?" I heard Alastair's voice ask.

I wonder how many times he's going to be forced to have to lift me off the ground, and drag me to my room when I can't move.

"I need your help," I groaned.

"Of course you do," He said to himself, grabbing my left arm, and hoisting me off the ground, letting my arm fall on his shoulder as he dragged me back inside the house. I did my best to try to walk alongside him, my feet shuffling along the ground.

At this point, I think he was tired of gently setting me down, and he instead practically threw me onto my bed, the fast movement adding even more pain and discomfort to my aching body.

"Ow," I whispered.

"Sorry. I guess I didn't think that was going to hurt," He shrugged, looking under my bed for my hidden ice packs that were practically our saviors in this house.

"Why would that not hurt?" I asked, turning to look at my brother. I really did question his intelligence sometimes. Alastair is a very complex person that I don't believe I'll ever really understand.

"I don't know, I just think you don't feel pain most of the time," He said defensively, handing me the ice packs. He wasn't wrong, but that didn't mean he had to test his theory.

"So you decided to throw me?" I asked, feeling my tone rise.

"I did not throw you!" He quietly defended.

"Bullshit!"

"Atticus, you know damn well I did not throw you! What did Annabelle have to say?" He asked, changing the subject. I didn't know how to discuss the events of the past three hours with him, I didn't even know if he could hear her screaming for help.

"Did you not hear her?"

"When?"

"Like an hour ago,"

"No, I didn't hear anything. I was with Anastasia in her room. I mean, we heard Sebastian come up here and start trying to argue with you, and we heard Annabelle scream a few times, but that was it. I heard her get taken down the stairs, and after that, it was like radio silence," He explained. So he seriously didn't know what had just happened to her?

"After that, you heard nothing?" I asked, confused. How could he not hear her screaming for help?

"No, nothing," He answered, clearly clueless as he sat down next to me.

Of all the sounds he's been practically trained to listen for and notice, how could he not hear Annabelle?

"You didn't hear her screaming at any other time?" I asked, looking for clarification.

"Nothing. Why?" He asked, not knowing a thing about the horrors our sister just had to endure for the past hour.

I didn't know if I should tell him about what happened, it didn't feel like it was my place to tell him anything. That's something for Annabelle to talk to him about, if she ever feels comfortable enough to even mention what happened to her.

"No reason," I said, shaking my head. I didn't like keeping things from my brother, but it's not like I actually had a choice in the matter. I feel like he could tell that I wasn't being honest with him, but he didn't bother to question me any further, he simply sat silently with me. I think if nothing else, he was finally beginning to understand why I withheld things from him when I did.

It's still hard to talk to him about things, despite everything we've survived together. Trying to talk about what we've experienced is something that I believe is always going to be difficult, no matter what.

We know we can depend on each other for anything, but that still doesn't mean we know how to communicate. I think our screwy upbringing has completely damaged any, and all ability we may have once had in terms of communication. It was never going to be something that we were good at. We've been told our whole lives that our voices didn't matter, and that they shouldn't be heard. Why would we ever think to use them with each other?

I could feel the exhaustion pushing itself through my body, all of my systems feeling like they were shutting down. I needed to rest, to take time to let my body try to heal itself before it was pushed beyond the point of recovery.

Chapter Ten

I woke up to the sound of my father hollering for us all to come downstairs. I couldn't imagine what he wanted, and I honestly didn't care that much. But I didn't have a choice, I had to comply with his demands. I was still in an unbearable amount of pain, but I had to pretend that it didn't exist as I slowly made my way down the stairs, following right behind Alastair.

I stood in a line at the bottom of the stairs with Alastair and Anastasia to my left, facing my father while still struggling to keep myself standing. I had to hold onto Alastair for some kind of support, I knew I couldn't stand long on my own.

Where's Annabelle?

"You three should know how disappointed we are with your younger sister, Annabelle. She's brought so much shame and disgrace to our family name," My father began. I felt my heart beating out of my chest, I felt like I couldn't breathe.

"Where is she?" I asked, feeling the air escape my body.

"The disappointment killed herself last night," Sebastian growled, giving me an evil glare.

No.

She couldn't have.

She didn't.

He's lying, he has to be lying.

He's hiding her somewhere, she's fine.

My body felt like it was shutting down on me, like everything within me was crumbling to pieces, shattering my soul and everything that I am. This can't be true, this all has to be some sort of sick joke.

"Her selfish actions have tarnished our good name," Elizabeth spat.

Did they even care?

"You're lying," I whispered, trying to hold the tears still in my eyes, not allowing them to fall. I knew I couldn't let him see me cry.

"I don't lie," My father said, moving closer to me. I couldn't believe him, how could he have the audacity to call Annabelle selfish for doing the only thing she could think to do to escape him? How can they say that she ruined the family name by trying to save herself?

It's his fault she's dead.

But it's also my fault.

I couldn't help her last night, I couldn't stop what I knew was happening to her, I couldn't do anything to save her.

If I had fought a little harder to keep everyone away from her, she'd still be here. She'd still be alive, she'd be okay, and I'd still be able to hold her, and tell her everything was going to be okay, even if I didn't fully believe it.

She's dead, and it's my fault.

"You three need to get going, you still have classes today," Sebastian said, acting like we didn't care that our sister was dead.

"You're seriously going to make us go?" Anastasia said, stepping toward our father, Alastair quickly grabbing her and holding her back.

"Go," Elizabeth barked, forcing the three of us back up the stairs silently. We didn't have a choice. Because we never have, and we never will.

We had to get ready to go to school like we weren't just told our sister was dead. Like our entire world didn't just fall apart right in front of us. I had to walk out of the house, plastering a fake smile on my face, acting like I wasn't the reason my sister was dead.

The three of us walked silently, everything seemed so bare without Annabelle. I looked at Alastair and Anastasia, their hands shaking, the same as mine, as we got closer and closer to the schoolyard. We didn't even bother to say anything to each other, the three of us went our separate ways, Anastasia to her friends, Alastair to his, and I scanned the yard for Gabriel.

After a moment, I saw him waving me down, and I quickly made my way over to him, hearing nothing but the sound of my heart thundering in my chest.

"Where did you go last night?" He asked as I got closer to him. I didn't bother to answer him. I let myself fall into his arms, clinging to him like he was the only real thing left in the world. I didn't care if anyone saw me, I needed him right now.

"Are you okay?" He asked, trying to process the situation as he wrapped his arms around me.

"Annabelle's dead, and it's all my fault," I sobbed into his shoulder.

"What?" He asked softly, keeping his tone quiet, almost as if he was quiet enough, she might still be alive.

"I couldn't protect her last night, and she fucking killed herself because I couldn't do anything to stop them from," I stopped. It was like I couldn't even say it.

"When did you find out?" He asked.

"Maybe twenty minutes ago," I explained, pulling away from him and wiping my eyes. I knew I had to try to keep myself together, no matter how badly I wanted to sink into the ground, never to return.

"Why are you even here right now? And what happened to your face?" He asked, studying my face, clearly noticing the cuts that weren't there previously.

"My father said we had to go, despite Annabelle's disgraceful and shameful actions," I explained. I couldn't believe those were the words he used to describe his own child.

His fourteen year old child.

"He seriously said that?" Gabriel asked, his anger building. He knew there was nothing he could do with his anger, and I think that hurt him more than anything.

"I don't know what to do. People keep dying because of me, I can't help anyone, I just end up killing everyone. I can't stop my father, I only get everyone I care about killed," I said, letting myself cry.

"None of this is your fault,"

"All of this is my fault. It's my fault William died, it's my fault Mary died, it's my fault that Leonard died, and it's my fault Annabelle killed herself," I rushed, interrupting him.

I felt like I was going insane. I keep getting everyone killed, and I don't know how to stop it. I can't save anyone, I can only make people suffer. Everyone I try to help ends up dead, and it's all because of me. I've led too many people to their deaths, it doesn't matter if I felt their life leaving their bodies. I led them to my father. I killed them.

"Atticus, you didn't kill any of them. You didn't poison William. You didn't drown Mary. You didn't kill Leonard. You didn't do anything to

Annabelle. Their deaths are not your fault, and the only person who has any responsibility for what happened to them is your father. You didn't do any of this. None of this is your fault," He explained, grabbing onto my shoulders, like he was trying to keep me from floating away.

No matter how many times he tried to say that I was innocent, I knew I would never believe him. He's lying to me to keep me from losing my mind from the guilt.

"I don't know what to do," I whispered as I began walking toward our first class. I didn't even think about it, it was like it was a force of habit to pretend that everything was okay, no matter what was actually going on.

"You need to realize that it's not your fault, for one," Gabriel said, following me. I think he was too afraid to let me out of his sight. I don't think I blame him. I think if I'm left alone, I'll have to kill myself to keep anyone else from dying.

"It is my fault,"

"It's not. You couldn't have known, there was nothing you could have done. You did everything you could to help Annabelle, there was nothing else you could have done," He explained, trying to comfort me.

"I could have,"

"Atticus, there was *nothing* else you could have done. And the sooner you stop blaming yourself for everything, the better off you'll be," He interrupted as we walked into our classroom.

I don't know where my mind was, it certainly wasn't this classroom, or this lecture. I didn't care to pay attention to anything that was going on, I didn't care about any of this. Nothing really mattered to me.

My sister is dead, and I have to act like I don't care. I have to act like she's not even dead, like she didn't even exist. Like she's only real in my mind. Like I'm the only person who even knew who she was. Like she's a faded page in a book of stories that no one believes in. I'm supposed to let her disappear to time, like she was never even real in the first place.

I don't know where the rest of the day went. I don't even remember moving from the first seat I was in. I didn't speak all morning, I gave up on trying to find words, there was nothing to say.

"Atticus," I heard Alastair say as he sat down next to me.

"Alastair," I quietly responded.

"What are we going to do?" He whispered, as if I had an answer for him. It almost terrified me to think that despite everything, Alastair and Anastasia would still look to me for guidance, but I had none to give.

"I have no idea. She's gone, and there's nothing we can do," I whispered back. He didn't know it was my fault, he didn't know about anything that happened to her last night. And now, he never will.

"How does he expect us to pretend that nothing is wrong?" He asked, his voice wavering. I could tell he was trying to fight crying, but he shouldn't feel like he has to fight his emotions, not when it comes to something like this, not ever. He didn't know what to do, that much was clear. But I don't think any of us really knew what to do either.

I certainly didn't.

I felt nothing but anger building up inside of me. That seemed to be my most common emotion lately. I never used to be an angry person, but now, it seems like anger is all I ever feel. I'm always angry about everything, there's always something getting under my skin, and I don't think I can control my own emotions anymore. Or maybe, I don't care enough to hide how I really feel anymore.

I'm going to end up getting myself killed one of these days if I keep letting my father know how I truly feel, but I don't think I care if I die anymore. Maybe if I die, the people around me will stop dropping like flies, and might actually have a fighting chance in their lives. Maybe it'll be like their curses have been lifted, and they can go about their lives without being constantly afraid that my father will kill them for simply associating with me.

"Because he thinks we're all heartless monsters like him that don't care when someone dies. He doesn't realize that we actually love people and can't pretend that they didn't exist when he removes them from our lives. He doesn't recognize the fact that not everyone is a monster who lacks empathy, and doesn't care that someone has tragically died," I said.

I'd love nothing more than the ability to completely rip my father apart in front of the entire world, exposing him for who he really is, and not some persona he puts on in front of everyone to disguise the monster he truly is.

"Have you told anyone what happened to her?" He asked.

"Only Gabriel," I responded.

"Why does it seem like you tell him every single detail about everything?" Alastair asked, almost as if he was judging me for having someone I trusted that wasn't him.

"Why does it matter?"

"Because haven't you ever thought that maybe telling him *everything* isn't a good idea?"

"He's the only person I've told anything,"

"But still,"

"He's my best friend, Alastair. I trust him with my life," I explained. That wasn't far from the truth, he is my best friend. He might be my only friend, but he's still one of the most important people in my life. I wonder if Alastair was offended that I called Gabe my best friend. But Alastair is my friend by default. I think if we didn't grow up together or have the same face, he and I would have never spoken to each other.

I think he could tell there was something more that I wasn't telling him. And maybe he already knew what I kept hidden from him, but if he did, he didn't say anything about it. Whatever he knew, or didn't know, he kept it to himself.

The rest of my day was filled with a painful silence. The only sounds I could even hear were the sound of my breathing, and my heart trying to escape my chest.

I met Alastair and Anastasia in the schoolyard after our final classes ended. None of us wanted to return home without Annabelle, but we didn't have a choice. We knew we'd only make things worse if we didn't go back.

The walk was still silent, there was nothing to say. There were no words that could encapsulate our grief. We hadn't even begun to process the loss of our sister, we had to put on a happy face the entire day, acting like we weren't told the most heart-shattering news early in the morning.

We walked through the door, instantly seeing Sebastian and Elizabeth blocking the stairs, preventing us from going up the stairs to cry to ourselves in our bedrooms.

"Shut the door," Elizabeth demanded, and Anastasia complied, being the last one in the house.

"Atticus, who is Gabriel Lumone to you?" Sebastian asked as I felt my heart plummet in my chest. The world around me felt like it was shrinking, and like everything was going to disappear, leaving nothing behind but me, standing there, afraid for my life. Afraid for what was going to happen to me. Afraid that I was about to be killed for something I couldn't control about myself.

"He's a friend of mine, Sir," I responded, feeling myself begin to shake.

"Don't lie to your father!" Elizabeth shrieked, slapping me across the face.

He knows.

I don't know how he knows, but somehow, he knows. He knows everything that I've spent my entire life trying to hide from him.

I couldn't breathe, I felt my heart racing, like it was trying to run out of my body, leaving me to die facing my father.

"Tell me the truth, boy. Whatever you think you're hiding, I already know," He demanded, stepping closer to me, and grabbing me by the collar of my shirt.

"He's my boyfriend, Sir," I whispered, refusing to look him in the eyes. I couldn't look at him, I couldn't look at anyone. I had to stand there, feeling like I had confessed to a heinous crime, when my only crime was loving another man. Which to my father, was an act worse than murder. Not that murder really meant much to him anyway, being something that he can do so casually, and without remorse or guilt.

I could feel Alastair and Anastasia staring at me. I never intended for them to find out, especially not like this.

"You disgust me," He said, throwing me to the ground. I didn't know what to do, I couldn't run out, I couldn't go anywhere. He'd catch me before I could even reach the door.

"Did you two know about your brother's shameful behavior?" Elizabeth asked, turning to Alastair and Anastasia.

"They didn't know," I answered, my voice shaking as I turned to look at my surviving brother and sister.

"No one asked you!" My father shouted, kicking me in the stomach, knocking the air out of my lungs.

"No, Sir," Alastair answered quietly, staring into my eyes. I couldn't tell how he felt. Maybe he felt betrayed. Maybe he was shocked. Or maybe, he knew this entire time, and understood why I never told him directly. I don't know, and I don't have any intentions of ever asking him. I don't intend to ever mention this to him ever again.

I truly don't believe he knew, I believe he had his suspicions, but I don't think he actually knew anything. At least, I hope he didn't.

"You sick bastard," Sebastian said, kicking me again, acting like his violence was going to change who I am.

"I'm the sick one?" I asked, coughing.

"You are!" He responded, stepping on my chest, pressing all of his weight on my upper rib cage, like he was trying to snap every bone in my body, and puncture my organs.

"Then what does that make you?" I said, trying to lift his foot off of me.

"Disappointed, ashamed, embarrassed," He said, pressing even harder with each word, causing me to scream out in pain.

"No, that makes you a fucking monster," I breathed heavily, trying to fight back against him.

"You don't know what you're talking about,"

"I might be sick, but at least I didn't rape my sisters, and murder anyone who tried to tell the truth," I spat, feeling the pressure on my chest grow heavier, and heavier, making breathing even harder.

I could feel every set of eyes locked on me, never looking away for even a moment. No one knew what to say, I believe everyone was in a shared state of shock at the fact that I had confronted my father in such a way.

"You've let them fill your head with lies, haven't you?" He asked, almost as if he truly believed he could convince me that what I'd learned was all fiction.

"It's all true, and you know it is. You killed William. You killed Mary. You killed Leonard. And it's your fault Annabelle is dead," I pushed, his foot pressing down harder on my chest, invoking another scream of agonizing pain.

"It's *your* fault, Atticus. You couldn't help her, you couldn't help anyone! If there's anyone to blame, it's you. You're the reason they're all dead, and you know it. You're the last person who should be pointing fingers at anyone other than yourself. You're the one who should be carrying the guilt, not me," He said, his weight feeling heavier, and heavier.

Somehow, hearing those words from him instead of myself changed my thinking. If he believed it was truly my fault, then it wasn't, it couldn't have been. He always uses me as a scapegoat for the things he's done, and if he's blaming me, he knows he's guilty. He knows he's a murderer.

"I didn't poison William. I didn't drown Mary. I didn't plunge the knife into Leonard. And I didn't send those men after Annabelle. You think you can blame me for everything, because you're not capable of admitting what you've done. You think that somehow, everything is my fault, when you're the only one to blame for the terrible things you've done. I know who you really are, and I know what exactly you've done to the people around you your entire life. You can't convince me I'm responsible for any of the things you've done," I said, feeling his weight release off of my chest for a moment, just long enough for me to push him off of me, quickly, breathlessly, standing up.

"You can't honestly believe that anyone told you the truth,"

"I know that I believe them over you. They had no reason to lie to me, you've had every reason to make things up, and lie to me my entire life. You've never told me the truth about anything, and you know you haven't. All you've done is *lie* to us all, because you thought you could get away with it for the rest of your life," I said, feeling like I had all the power in this situation. I don't think I really did, but I felt like I had enough to finally make a difference in my life.

He didn't know what to say, I don't think there was anything he could say. He never knew how to communicate, especially not now. All he knew how to do was use his fists to solve his problems.

And so he did.

He knocked me straight on the jaw, blood slowly pouring onto my teeth. Again. All I could do was look at him, and smile, blood covering my entire mouth.

I knew he wasn't going to give up, he was going to keep swinging at me until I stopped trying to defy him. It almost made me laugh that he was so intimidated by a seventeen-year-old kid with a loud mouth, who didn't know when to give up, and would test what exactly he could do before he got pulverized.

"You know, I almost feel bad for you. You obviously don't know how to talk to people, and your solution to everything is to hit the people you don't agree with, because that's so much easier than admitting the truth. You can try to hide from what you've done for as long as you want, but the truth is that you can't hide, not really. I know what you did, and there's not a single thing stopping me from telling everyone exactly what kind of monster you are," I said. I wasn't afraid of him, at least I don't think I was.

"No one will believe you,"

"They will. You can't keep me silent forever, I'm not afraid of you anymore," I said, finally trying to take control of my life instead of letting my father control everything about me.

I hope he was afraid of the thought that I was going to tell everyone the truth about him, and I hope he knew that I didn't plan to give up until the whole world knew exactly who he truly was. A disgusting monster that has the ability to silence anyone who dares to go against him.

I knew I was risking my life by threatening to expose him to the world, but I didn't care. I wouldn't let him control me any longer. I'm stronger than he is, and he can't scare me into obedience any longer.

"You're going to regret this, Atticus," He said, waving his hand, signaling to someone.

Before I had a chance to react, two of the men from last night came down the stairs, and stood directly behind my father. I didn't get a chance to move, I didn't even have a moment to think, or process what was going on.

The men grabbed onto both of my arms, forcing me to stand in front of my father, unable to break away from them, or go anywhere.

"You're not going to do anything unless I allow you to," Sebastian said, taking out his knife once more.

You've got to be fucking kidding me.

He's not seriously going to kill me in front of so many people, is he?

My father took the knife, slashing me across the stomach with it. He knew the injury wouldn't kill me, but it would keep me from being able to fight against him, and prevent me from trying to escape.

I wouldn't let him know that the slash hurt me in any way, I almost let him believe that I enjoyed the pain. I could feel Alastair and Anastasia watching me, looking for any kind of sign that I was in pain, but I provided none.

"You know what to do with the sick bastard," My father said, walking away up the stairs.

The men started dragging me away, toward the kitchen as I tried to kick myself free. I knew exactly where this was going.

I knew it wasn't a good idea, but I couldn't stop myself from trying to fight against them, feeling the blood pour out of my wound the more I struggled, stinging and aching with every single small movement. This was going to kill me if I didn't stop, and I knew that, but somehow, I didn't care enough to stop fighting.

I couldn't go back in there, I can't do it again. The garage is the only punishment that can still break me, chopping me down like a tree, and leaving nothing but a stump as a reminder of what used to be. And this time, I have a feeling it's going to last a lot longer than just one night. I worried I would never leave this garage ever again.

My father knows that this is the only thing that can still hurt me, and he's going to use that to his advantage to scare me back into submission, thinking I'll be at his mercy the moment he lets me back out of the pitch black, freezing garage.

But these men didn't care. They didn't care about what they were doing, they only did whatever my father told them to do, no matter the moral price, and no matter how awful.

Because that's what my father surrounds himself with. People who are as bad as him, all so he can feel as if he has some moral high ground over everyone else. It's the only thing that makes him feel good about himself, finding people exactly like him.

And unfortunately for the DuVonet children, the world was never in short supply of horrific people exactly like our father. They're everywhere you look, and no matter how fast you may run, or how you may try to hide, you'll never be able to escape from them. They will always be right around the corner, watching you, waiting for you.

Chapter Eleven

They threw me into the garage without a second thought, sealing me away in the darkness, and ignoring my pleas for freedom. It didn't matter what I said, or how much I begged. No one would listen to me, no one would set me free. I didn't even care to look for my ice pick, I just sat against the wall, holding myself.

I didn't bother to hold in the countless emotions I felt building up in myself. I screamed as loud as my lungs would allow until my voice gave out on me, and the faucet turned on in my eyes, creating an unstoppable flow of water, a flow that I didn't want to stop. I wonder if they could hear me on the other side of the door.

I felt strange letting myself express every single bottled-up emotion I've hidden from everyone my entire life.

When I get locked in the cold emptiness of this space, I can't help but think about everything in my life, there's nothing else to do in here. I feel forced to think about everything about who I am, and how I got so unlucky in life. I don't know why my life has turned out the way it has, I don't know if I did something to deserve all of this. Maybe in some other life, I pissed off some ancient God, and this is my punishment.

I can't help but feel that because of what I've faced, I'm going to turn out exactly like my father. And that terrifies me more than anything, thinking that I may become the very thing I've fought against for so long.

But I don't know how to be anything different. That's the kind of man I've grown up around, I've never had an example of a good man in my life. I don't think I'd know the first thing about being a good man, a good father even.

I don't want to be like my father, I want to be the exact opposite of him, but I don't know how to be anything different. I know how to be a shitty man and a horrible father, thanks to him, but I don't know how to teach myself to be better than him.

I don't know if there is a way for me to learn how to be a better man. Maybe I'm stuck becoming what I was raised by, and it's not possible for me to be anything different. Maybe I was doomed from the day I was born.

I think the lives we're born into are a trap, and it shows you your only options in life, no matter how awful they might seem. But it's not like we can choose our circumstances, or how we're raised. Maybe we don't even get to choose what we do with what we learned as children. Maybe it just sort of happens, and there's only the illusion of free choice in our everyday lives.

Maybe we're forced to be part of a vicious cycle that will never truly end, all because we don't have the strength, or the courage, or the power to end the evil chain. We simply have to exist as a part of something we never had a choice in.

Fate is a weird thing, and I'm not even sure I believe in it. I don't know what I believe anymore. Maybe life is some shitty game you have to play in the hopes of finding something better waiting for you in the afterlife. Maybe there is no afterlife, maybe there's nothing beyond this. Maybe there is.

But I know that I don't believe in a God. Not anymore. What kind of sick and twisted God would allow these kinds of things to happen? Children becoming victims of heinous crimes, thanks to their father? Children feeling like they have to walk on eggshells around their own parents, because even the smallest mistake will set off a chain reaction that ruins their entire lives? Children afraid to tell anyone the truth about their parents, because they're afraid that no one will believe them?

I wouldn't let myself put any faith into a monster that could stand aside, and let things like this happen, it's sick and sadistic. No loving power would allow these things to happen. So either God hates everyone, or he doesn't exist. And in either case, I want nothing to do with him, whether he's real or not, I don't want him in my life.

Maybe I'm overthinking everything, and I'm just trying to make sense of things that don't have an explanation, because I feel like I have to understand everything, or nothing will have any meaning in my life, and I'll always be trapped in this garage, and I'll never *really* get out of it.

Maybe I'm only driving myself insane, because that's all I can do in here. All I can really do is lose my sanity in the hopes of understanding things that will never really make sense. But I don't think anything makes sense anymore. I don't even know how long I've been in here. It might have only been twenty minutes, but it could have been an hour.

Two days.

A week.

A year.

I don't have a concept of time in here, there's no way to keep track, I'm surrounded by darkness.

I don't care to keep track of the time though, every single moment of every single day feels the same in here anyway, it's not like the amount of time that has passed really matters.

No one ever opened the door to the house either, so not an ounce of light ever poured into the abyss, I simply sat silently in the dark, my voice didn't even work anymore.

I knew I was going to be locked in here for days, with no end in sight. I wondered what Gabriel would say. I knew he'd ask questions about where I was, I just didn't know what my brother would tell him. I didn't know if Alastair would tell him the truth, or if he'd make up some lie about why I wasn't in classes, and why he couldn't talk to me.

I don't know if I wanted Gabriel to know the truth. Obviously, I didn't want to lie to him, but I didn't want him to know about what was happening to me either. I didn't want him to blame himself for this, it's not his fault.

I still don't know how my father found out about him, I don't think I wanted to know. All that mattered to me was making sure that Gabriel didn't find out that Sebastian knew, he'd never forgive himself. It didn't matter that it wasn't his fault, but he'd place all the blame on himself. I guess we're a lot alike in that regard.

I couldn't stop myself from thinking about him while I was locked in here, wondering how he'd react to my situation, and what he'd do, because I know he'd refuse to sit back silently and pretend as if this never happened. I thought about a lot of things every single time I was stuck here.

Who I am.

Who I'm going to become.

My life.

My siblings.

Who I wish I would become.

I've never had this much time in here, so I've never had this long to think. Oddly enough, this is the only place where my thoughts are totally safe. They never exit this room, and no one but me will ever know about the things I've thought about, and discovered in here.

I felt my body growing weaker and weaker, I don't even know when the last time I ate anything was. I don't know how long I've been locked in here, forced to share the silence with my screaming mind, unable to tune out the dark thoughts I felt creeping into my head. I never know what to do with these thoughts, or how to make them go away. It feels like they're a part of me, a part that I can't get rid of, something that will always be with me, no matter where I go. I don't want these thoughts to be a defining piece of who I am, but I don't think that's something I have the power to change anymore.

I think it's something I'm cursed to live with, and it's not something that can vanish, or be thrown away, it's a piece of me. It's a piece that I hate, a piece that I wish I could banish, as if it was never something I've been forced to live with.

I wanted to cry, but I didn't have anything left in me. I think it's been several days that I've been alone with myself, but I can't be sure. All I know is that I haven't slept at all, feeling cursed to stay awake and suffer, unable to rest, and unable to forget anything about who I am and what I'm forced to suffer through.

I don't know how much more of this my body can take, it's already been through so much, and I don't know if it can handle anything more. I want all of this to end, and I don't care if it kills me anymore. It's getting harder and harder to find reasons to carry on, allowing myself to suffer every single day that I still have a pulse.

I don't know if I could run away, and *really* be able to get away.

How do I know that my father won't find me?

That he won't kill me?

That I'll actually be safe?

I don't even know where I would go. I'd have to leave everything here behind, go to another state, another country even, and I wouldn't be able to tell anyone where I was going. I'd have to disappear into the night like a cloud of smoke, leaving without a single trace or hint of where I could be.

Was that something that I actually wanted to do?

Or was it something I felt like I *had* to do?

Something that I felt I didn't have a real choice in?

Was that just a survival tactic?

Will I ever actually be safe?

Or will I only keep trying to trick myself into believing that everything is going to be okay eventually?

The door slowly pushed open, but I didn't bother to get up. I knew this wasn't my signal of freedom, it was more of a test to see if I was still alive, or if I killed myself yet.

I wonder if my father locked me in the garage with the intention of driving me insane, or if he locked me in here because he knew he wouldn't have to see or hear me, and he wouldn't have to acknowledge his disgusting, shameful son.

Whoever was on the other side of the door pushed a small bottle of water and some scraps on a small tray into the garage, leaving it right by the door, quickly closing it, and leaving me in the dark once again.

I knew this was just to keep me alive, this was the bare minimum for survival, but I didn't care to fight for my survival. I was ready to let go, and finally have peace for once in my life.

But I couldn't.

Something within me wouldn't let me give up on myself.

And so I didn't.

I sat in the cold garage, on the bitter and unforgiving floor, trying to understand myself, trying to understand anything that I could possibly rationalize, it's not like there was anything else to do in here.

I like to think I'm a good person, but I don't know if there's a way for me to determine that. Just because I try to help people, doesn't mean I'm a good person. I don't seem to be very good at helping people, everyone I've ever tried to help, or save has only ended up dead either way, like nothing I did even mattered.

Maybe I try too hard to change the things that can't be changed, and I let myself believe I have more control over the world than I actually do. Maybe I'm trying to convince myself that I'm a good person, I just try too hard to help people, and end up ruining their lives in the process.

I don't know.

I don't understand myself, and I don't understand morality. I don't know what makes someone a good or bad person, and I don't know where I fall on that spectrum. Maybe I can't even be defined as a person at all.

I don't know who I am. I don't recognize the skin I wear, and I don't know the face I see in the mirror. I don't ever know what to do. I always feel like I'm floating, and I can't come back down, like I have to stay up in the sky, and I'll never be able to come down.

Maybe I'm dead. Maybe I died a long time ago, and I have no way of knowing if I'm still alive. If I have a life still worth fighting for, or if I'm simply a ghost, forced to haunt the halls of the house that destroyed me, crushing me in the rumble as it crumbled to the ground, killing anything that stood in its way as it crashed down, far beyond saving.

Am I going insane?

Is there a way to know if you've completely lost your shit?

Or are you supposed to assume that you still have your sanity, and you can carry on in life as normal, as you've always done, no matter what was actually happening?

Is life simply always pretending to be okay, despite the nightmare fuel you have to survive every single day?

Are we all going through the same thing, pretending to be fine when we really feel like we're dying on the inside?

Or are there people out there who actually manage to be happy every single day?

Are they just lying?

Are we all suffering?

Is that all there is to life? Pain and suffering? Unable to heal, or move on from the things that have been destroying us our entire lives, forced to put on a happy face to please the world around us?

Can we ever tell the truth about how we feel, or are we expected to tell lies to everyone our whole lives?

Is there anyone we can trust with the truth, or can we only ever trust ourselves? Are we forced to keep our deepest and darkest secrets buried under six feet of dirt, along with our dreams, and eventually our own bodies?

I never know what to do anymore. I feel like every single decision I make is wrong, and I'll never be able to make the right choices. I'll always be a fuck up, ruining everything I touch, damaging anything and everything I come into contact with, no matter what my intentions are.

For once in my life, I want to feel like I'm making the right decisions, instead of tearing everything apart. I want to make a real difference. I want to be able to help someone without hurting them, but I only seem to be capable of getting people more hurt than when they began.

Maybe I'm making everything a bigger deal than it is, I don't know anymore. I don't know why I always get like this, why I always feel like it's my responsibility to take care of everyone, like *I'm* the one that has to be everyone's savior.

I think I wish I had someone to save me, and I've taken it upon myself to be that person for everyone else, because I know that no one is coming to rescue me, and I'm all on my own.

I really wish I wouldn't analyze myself like this sometimes. I always end up hurting myself more than I thought was possible.

I want everything to stop. I want to be okay. But I don't even believe that's possible anymore. I feel like I'm a person that's doomed to suffer their entire lives, and never know peace.

Who am I really?

Who is Atticus DuVonet?

Does he even still exist?

Or did he die with his spirit many, many years ago?

Is he just a memory that you might be able to stumble upon in a dusty old photo book one day?

Was he ever even real?

Does anyone remember who he is?

Is there anyone who cares to know who he is?

Does his existence really matter to anyone, or does he let himself believe that he's important to someone to keep him from killing himself?

Would anyone even give a fuck if another victim dropped into a grave with his name plastered on it?

Does his name mean anything to anyone at all?

Is his grave just a forced marker in the name of remembrance of a soul that will never truly be missed by anyone who knew him?

Or should he let himself fade away, leaving not a single trace of the fact that he was ever even alive, letting himself remain a mystery to anyone who might stumble upon his name by accident?

I feel myself falling into a place I don't know if I'll be able to get out of. But I don't think I care enough to stop myself, or to fight it. I think I want to let myself disappear one night, without another word, letting myself be known as a ghost, or some urban legend that no one can confirm. Just a rumor that circulates every so often, leaving more questions than answers. I think that's what I want to leave behind.

But I feel like I have an obligation to stick around. Like too many people need me to be here, so I have no choice but to continue to suffer through life, trudging along, acting like I feel strong enough to survive this life. I feel like I have to be the one to bear the burden of being a DuVonet, and deal with my father. Because no one else knows how to stop him.

Maybe he can't be stopped, maybe he's meant to be this all-powerful monster that no knight can slay, a beast who will always torment the people around him, making their lives eternally miserable, making them wish they were dead. But maybe that's what he wants. If we have no will to live and survive him, he can get away with anything, because we don't care enough to fight for ourselves, accepting anything that he throws at us.

I hope he never gets what he wants, but this stupid fucking garage is depriving me of the capability to care about anything anymore.

I wish I would just fucking die.

I don't know how I'll die, I don't think that's something I've thought about that much. I like to think it'll be peaceful, but given the way my entire life has gone, I don't think that's an option for me. Maybe I'm simply a person that's meant to suffer, no matter what I do. I'll always be in pain, and no one can do anything to change that.

I think the only reason I'm still fighting for my life is that I still have love to give. Somehow, despite everything I've had to survive, I still feel overwhelmed with love. And I'm going to continue to give it, even if my father kills me for it.

I don't have a plan for telling Gabriel about what happened when I finally get out of here. Part of me doesn't want to tell him, but part of me feels like he deserves to know. I've been away for a long time, at least a week, maybe longer, I don't even know. I don't think I can leave him with no explanation, but I don't want him to blame himself.

I still don't even know how my father found out about Gabriel. The entire time we've been so incredibly careful, we did everything we could to avoid anyone seeing us. Did my father have someone following me?

Someone always watching me? If someone was tailing me this entire time, why did my father wait until now to do something about it?

I don't understand, and I don't think I ever will. I don't think I'll ever really understand anything about my life, or my father. I still don't know why he is the way that he is. All I know is that he's always been like this, but that doesn't mean I understand it.

Maybe some people are simply born monsters, and no matter what they do, they can never escape what they are. They'll always be horrible people who don't care about anyone but themselves. It doesn't have to make sense, and it probably never will, but that's reality.

I couldn't stop myself from wondering what Gabriel was thinking. Where did he think I was? Did Alastair tell him what happened? Was he looking for me? Did he know exactly where I was? If Alastair told him everything, how was he reacting to it?

I almost find it strange that any time something major happens to me, he's always the first thing on my mind. Nothing else occurs to me first, it's always him. There could be a million things happening all at once, but he's always the first thought in my mind. He's the first thing I think about when I wake up in the morning, and the last thing on my mind before I fall asleep at night, when I can actually sleep. No matter where I am, or what's happening to me, he's always on my mind. And I can't help but wonder if he experiences the same thing for me.

I like to think that he does, but I don't know if I'll ever really know. It's not like I can peer into his mind, and understand every single thought that races through his head. I don't think I'd want to be able to do that, it feels like a violation.

The door opened again, another small bottle of water and food scraps being pushed into the void, the door closing as fast as it opened. I don't know who on the other side was trying so hard to keep me alive, but I can't imagine that it's my father. Maybe it's Alastair. Or maybe it's Anastasia.

I wish I could understand Anastasia. I hope she knows that even if she doesn't talk to me, I still love her with everything that I am. Maybe I only serve as a reminder of the things she has to deal with. I feel like I don't even know her. She's my sister, and I live with her, but she feels like a complete stranger to me. I don't know who she is, I barely even know anything about her. I don't know why she doesn't like talking to me, maybe she doesn't even like me, but I wish she'd open up to me at least a little bit.

Maybe one day she'll be okay with talking to me. I wonder if she believes that if she doesn't talk about the things she has to deal with, they'll go away. Maybe she's more like me than I thought. Maybe we're complete opposites. Maybe I'll never know. But maybe one day, I will.

What I do know is that the longer I'm locked in here, the more I can feel myself slipping away. I don't know if I'll still have my sanity after this, I'm not even sure if I'll still know who I am. I don't even think I know who I am now.

I know that sometimes, I'm not convinced anything in my life is real, and it's all some sort of delusion I've created in my mind. A sad attempt to rationalize the world around me, even if I know it will never make sense.

I think the world is too messy to actually understand. I think everyone only pretends to know themselves, and what they want. I don't think anyone knows anything at all, and we're all pretending to be put together for the sake of reputation.

People pretend to be okay with themselves and their lives because they prioritize being known for being happy, and successful over their own well-being. I think that's why so many people don't survive in this society that values material possessions over true happiness.

Maybe I'm out of my mind, and I don't know anything. Maybe I only talk about complicated subjects and issues to make myself sound smart. I have no idea what I'm talking about, I'm just trying to make sense of things that have no explanation, because I don't know what else to do with my life.

There's nothing else I can do with my life.

I have to put on a happy, perfect face, and pretend to understand everything that gets thrown at me, because that's what people are supposed to do. They're supposed to cope with the life they're given, and accept the fact that they can't do anything to escape who they are. It's a vicious system that doesn't care about the casualties it causes, or the lives it destroys, claiming to be building society for the better. I wonder who people would become if they actually had a choice in their situation, and the environment they're enclosed in.

I wonder who I would be if I had a real choice, and what my life would be. I don't even know what I would choose, I don't know how to make things better for me. I think I've accepted this is how my life has to be, and there's nothing I can do about it.

I don't know how much longer I'm going to be trapped in here, but I do know that I can't keep dealing with this for long. Being stuck in here, in the dark, alone with my thoughts is driving me insane. There's nothing to do in here but think about everything that's wrong with me, and how I ruin everything. I don't like who I become when I'm left alone with myself for too long. It's like I become the worst possible version of myself, so wrapped up in my own mind that I don't even know what's going on around me. It's like I get lost in a world I don't understand, and I can't escape it. I simply have to deal with it, and hope I snap back to reality soon.

It doesn't help that the only sound in here is my own breathing. It almost makes me wonder if my senses are vanishing, or if they're enhancing.

I just want to get out of here. I can't take it in here, always feeling like I'm on the brink of insanity, never knowing if there's going to be a moment that I finally snap.

Is any of this even real?

Is it all in my head?

Is there a way for me to know for sure if any of this is actually happening, or am I supposed to blindly assume that everything around me is real?

This is insanity.

I need to get out of here, and I need to get out now. I can't take this anymore, I don't even know if anything in my life is real at this point. Is Gabriel someone I made up in my head? Is he someone I know, but not someone who cares about me?

I don't know why I care so much about getting out of here, it's not like anything is going to be any different when I emerge on the other side of the door. Sebastian is still going to make my life a living hell, and I'm still going to wish I was dead.

The door slowly opened, a blinding, bright light pouring into the otherwise pitch-black room. The light was so bright that I couldn't see anything, my eyes were too adjusted to the vastness of the dark.

"Atticus?" Anastasia said, her voice ringing in my ears. I couldn't see her, I could only make out her figure being reflected in the brightness that shone around her, almost making her look like an angel looking down on me.

I didn't want to speak, I don't even think I could if I wanted to.

"It's been a month. Sebastian is finally letting you out," She said, walking toward me.

A month?

Have I really been locked in this hellhole for a full month?

"Atticus, say something," She said, her worry clearly beginning to grow. I wonder if she thought I'd lost my mind.

Maybe I have.

I didn't have anything to say. No words could describe how I felt. There wasn't a single thing I could say that would make any of this any better.

I lost a *month* of my life, because of something I have no control over.

I lost a month of my life, all because I'm in love with a man.

There are plenty of things I'll never forgive my father for, and this is definitely one of them. I don't think this is something that I'll ever be able to move on from.

It doesn't matter what I say, or what I do. Everything I do is wrong, and everything I do is going to get me thrown back in here for another month, time chipping off of my life that I'll never get back.

"Are you okay?" Anastasia asked, grabbing my hands to help me off the ground. I wanted to answer her, but something in me just couldn't. No words can describe what I went through while I was locked away like an animal. Nothing is ever going to make any of this okay.

Chapter Twelve

I left my sister's question unanswered as I slowly walked back into the house, and moved upstairs to my bedroom. I didn't want to talk to anyone, I don't even think my mouth remembered how to form words, it felt like some forgotten practice to me. I could tell she was worried about me, but I don't think I really cared. Nothing would make any of this better.

I wasn't expecting Anastasia to follow me to my room, but I think she was afraid of leaving me alone in this state, considering what happened to Annabelle.

"Can you please say something? Even if it's telling me to go fuck myself and leave you alone?" She asked, almost as if she was trying to make me laugh. Normally, it would have worked.

But I still didn't say anything. I just shook my head as a response.

"Weren't you the same one always lecturing me about talking about these kinds of things? Don't you think you should take your own advice?" She asked.

I looked at the clock that sat on a nightstand next to my bed. It was early in the morning, and I knew it had to be a school day. She wouldn't have been bothering me otherwise.

"Shouldn't you be getting ready for school?" I croaked out, my voice barely existing anymore. It hurt to speak, it felt like I was being stabbed in the throat with each word.

"Only if you do," She said, nudging me. I don't think I really had much of a choice. My options were to go to school and pretend that nothing happened, or stay here and deal with my father.

Pretending that nothing happened was clearly the better option.

I don't know what explanation I was supposed to give people for my absence for an entire month.

"He told the school you were really sick and nearly hospitalized," Anastasia said, finally walking out of my room, as if she was reading my mind.

I didn't have much time to get ready, so I rushed through making myself presentable after a month of living in the shadows. I never really cared much about how I looked, but this time, I had to care.

It wasn't long before I was on my way to the school, walking alongside Alastair and Anastasia. Neither of them tried to talk to me, I think they understood that I wasn't willing to say a single word.

A part of me didn't want to look for Gabriel as I entered the schoolyard, I knew he'd be asking for answers I couldn't provide, filled with questions I didn't know how to respond to. It's like I was afraid to see him.

He was all I thought about in that garage, but I was terrified of being reunited with him.

But I didn't have to look for him, because he spotted me the moment I set foot in the yard. He practically sprinted over to me, grabbing onto me as if he let me go, I'd fade away. I guess it didn't really matter if we tried to hide our relationship anymore. My father already knew, and that was the worst possible situation.

I held onto him, letting myself believe that there was nothing else around me. I wonder if he knew the truth about where I've been for the past month.

"Where have you been?" He asked, as I felt my shoulder becoming wet.

So he didn't know.

I wasn't surprised he was crying, he probably assumed I was dead. It's simply in his nature to always assume the worst when he doesn't hear from me. Especially over long periods of time. Not that I blame him, and if I had been left in there any longer, I probably would have been dead.

"Locked in the garage," My voice cracked. I didn't even sound like myself. I didn't recognize my own voice, it was so faded away from not speaking for so long.

"What?" He asked, slowly pulling away from me, examining me with his tear-stained face.

"Sebastian locked me in the garage for a month," I said, my throat feeling like it was bleeding.

"Why?" He asked, his tone slowly growing more and more rageful.

I didn't want to tell him the truth, but I owed him an explanation. He's the only person that deserves to know exactly what happened to me.

"I don't know how, but he found out," I began, my throat scratching, feeling like it was closing up on me.

"Found out about what?" He asked. I could see the color draining from his face. I don't think I even needed to tell him, I think he just knew.

"Us. Everything," I quietly explained, grabbing my vocal cords.

"How?" He asked, looking like he was experiencing every single emotion all at once. And I couldn't blame him for it. I had processed this all a month ago, with the exact same reaction.

"I don't know, I don't care to know. But he knows everything. I don't know what to do about it, because now Alastair and Anastasia know too. I lost the ability to choose when to tell them, and the ability to even tell them at all," I said, feeling more defeated than anything. It hurt knowing that my father ripped away the chance for me to tell my siblings, more than anything he had ever done to me.

Gabriel was pissed, that much was clear to see. I didn't blame him for being angry, I understood why. I could tell he wanted to do something about it, but there was nothing for him to do. There was nothing anyone could really do about it. What's done is done, and I can't do anything to change what my father knows, no one can. I have to accept whatever my fate is going to become.

"You can't go back there, Atticus, you know that, right?" He asked. But I think he knew that I *had* to go back. He hated admitting it, but he knew I couldn't leave, no matter how badly I wanted to.

I was too afraid of what might happen to me if I allowed myself to let go of what I'd been stuck in my entire life. I don't know if I would know how to function outside of the bubble that the house put around me. I didn't have the strength to defy my father by staying away, he'd find me no matter where I went. I'd always be looking over my shoulder, afraid that he might appear behind me, dragging me back to everything I tried so hard to escape.

He locked me in the garage to keep me under his control, and it worked every single time. He knew it was the only thing that still terrified me, the only thing that would convince me to shut up, and deal with everything he forced me to survive. I don't know why it always worked, but it did. Just when I thought I might actually be able to make a difference in my life, and get the hell out of here, he finds a way to keep me tucked underneath his thumb, only doing things that he's permitted me to do.

I wonder if my life is one that's still worth fighting for, or if I should save myself the trouble, and give up. I should make my peace with whatever happens to me, because I'm not powerful enough to change anything. I have to accept that I can't stop anything. There's nothing I can do to prevent the cards that fate has laid out for me. And it's time I made my peace with that.

"I have to go back, Gabe. I can't walk away. I don't expect you to understand, but I do need you to support me. I can't explain it, but this isn't something that I think I'm ever going to get away from," I said. I had to stop talking, every single word felt like a knife digging itself into my vocal cords. I don't think I've ever felt so helpless in my entire life. Nothing is ever going to get any better. There's no end to any of this in sight.

I don't know how much more of this I can take before I completely lose who I am, if I even still know who I am. I feel lost, like I'm floating above this body that I don't even understand, forced to watch every cruel thing happening to this body, unable to do anything to stop it.

I don't even see a point in still trying to exist in a life where every little thing I do is wrong, and I can't do a single thing right. What's the point in trying to communicate with someone when every word I can say is wrong?

Is there a point to anything? Or is my life cursed to be meaningless and filled with nothing but pain and suffering?

I don't want to think about my life. I don't want to think about anything. I don't understand anything. I don't even know who I am. Do I even have a personality? Or am I simply a mess of flesh and blood that wanders around without a purpose, or any understanding of anything around me?

I don't remember ever moving out of the schoolyard, I didn't even know that time still continued to move forward, pushing the day along while I felt frozen in time, watching everything around me fade away, disappearing before my eyes.

"Atticus," I heard Alastair ask, placing his hand on my shoulder. I don't know how I got here, I can't remember a single thing happening after my conversation with Gabriel.

Is this what it's like to lose your mind? To be melted down into a brainless zombie that can't even think for themself? A creature that accepts anything that happens to them without ever bothering to question if there's a God, and if there is, why he hates you?

"Atticus, please, say something," Alastair pleaded, keeping his hand firmly on my shoulder.

I could tell he was getting worried about me, but I didn't care. Nothing mattered to me anyway. Everything is going to vanish one day, including me, and there is *nothing* I can do to stop it.

"We don't have to talk about what happened, but please, say something," He continued. I turned to look at him, a blank expression on my face.

I didn't care enough to call him out for his ridiculous audacity to make any sort of mention of the complete hell I faced for the past month, when he never cared enough to try to check on me.

Everyone left me alone to die in that garage, either by suicide or starvation. I don't know who gave me the bare minimum to survive, and I probably never will, but I don't believe it was my brother. I do believe it was Anastasia, but I don't think I'll ever know for sure.

"Atticus, you're really starting to worry me, and a lot of other people. Can't you say one word?" He asked. He was becoming desperate, that much was clear to see. But it didn't matter to me.

I already felt like I was dead, why would I not start acting like it too?

If people were so concerned about me, why did no one ever bother to try to save me from the life I was trapped in? If people cared so much about me, why did no one help me? Why did everyone leave me to die on a sinking ship? Because they cared more about saving themselves than ever trying to protect me.

It's bullshit. That's all it is.

No one is concerned enough to actually do something to help me, like no one else cared enough to help Annabelle. She could have been saved, I could have saved her. And maybe somebody could have saved me.

But I'm too far gone to be saved at this point. I've lost too much of who I am. I've been burned down to the ground too many times to ever be salvaged. The only thing left of me is piles of ash that litter the ground, slowly being carried away by the wind, until nothing remains of the person I used to be but stories and memories.

"Say anything at all, please. I'm begging you," Alastair said. I couldn't help but wonder how long it would take him to realize that I've given up speaking, it never seems to get me anywhere but a cold garage.

And besides, I don't know who's listening to every word I speak. I don't know if my father has sent someone to follow me around, and report every word I say back to him, which is only going to make everything in my life that much worse.

It's not safe for me to speak, I don't think it ever has been. It's best if I stay silent, that way, I can never say the wrong thing, because I simply won't speak at all. I can't make a mistake, or be wrong if I don't speak.

But I'm sure my father would still find a way to blame me for every little problem he has to face in his life. Because somehow or another, everything is my fault, and I'm always the one to blame for every problem, no matter how small.

I'm the root of all horrible things, and I hold the blame for every single minor inconvenience anyone has to face. Every little thing is always my fault, and never anyone else's. It all falls on me.

"Atticus, I'm worried about you. A lot of people are. Please, say something," Alastair said, continuing his meaningless pleading. Sometimes, he's too stubborn for his own good, and he doesn't know when to give up.

I think that's my brother's problem. He never knows when to give up, or when he's fighting a losing battle. He doesn't know when to jump off the sinking ship, and take his chances in the water. At least in the water he can try to swim to the shore, but if he stays on a failing ship, he's only going to drown.

"Listen, I'm sorry about what I did, okay? I know it wasn't right, but please, talk to me," He said.

What was he talking about?

What did he do?

And why did he feel the need to apologize for it?

Maybe if I stayed silent for long enough, he'd tell me what he did.

"I'm sorry I told Sebastian about Gabriel, I'm a shitty brother, okay? But I'm sorry. I don't expect you to forgive me, but please, talk to me," He said.

He fucking told Sebastian?

He's the reason I was locked away like a caged animal for an entire fucking month?

He's the one who betrayed me?

"You did fucking what?" I finally said, not caring about the pain that burned through my throat as I turned to face my brother, seeing nothing but red.

"I'm sorry, but please, let me explain," He began as we were dismissed from our class.

I didn't want to hear whatever bullshit excuse he was going to give me, nothing he could say was going to make this any better. I can't trust him anymore, not with anything, and there's nothing he can do to fix that.

He might be my brother, but I have no idea who he is anymore.

I don't even feel like it's right to call him my brother anymore. He's just a stranger who looks like me.

"Stay the fuck away from me, and stay away from Gabriel," I said, quickly standing up and rushing out of the classroom, rage being my only guide. I didn't even give him a chance to explain himself.

Whoever he is, he's not my brother anymore.

I couldn't believe him, I never thought he would be the one to stab me in the back like this. I never would have imagined my own brother would hurt me like this.

I didn't bother to go to any of my other classes, I just sat in the bathroom the entire rest of the day. Not many other people came in there, and the ones that did, didn't bother to try to speak to me. They simply let me be alone with my thoughts.

"Atticus?" I heard Gabriel ask me during the last class of the day, as he moved to sit down next to me. I don't know how he always manages to find me, but it's like his own little superpower.

"How do you always find me?" I asked with a hoarse voice. Gabriel handed me a water bottle, nudging me. He always knows exactly what I need.

"You're like six feet tall, you're pretty hard to miss," He said with a small laugh that I didn't return. I didn't know if I should tell him about why I no longer have a brother.

"I found out how my father knew about us," I whispered, feeling my voice slowly return. I knew I should tell him, but I didn't even really know where to begin.

"Wait, what? Seriously?" He asked, turning his full attention to me.

"It's why I only have a sister now," I began explaining.

"What are you talking about?"

"I don't have a brother anymore. Alastair is the one who told my father about you. I don't know why he did it, and I really don't care to hear his bullshit excuses. I'm never going to forgive him for that. He fucking destroyed me, and I'll never be able to forgive him," I said. I was pissed, and I wasn't going to make any attempts to hide it.

Alastair ruined my life. He took away the freedom I had to tell people who I am. He's the reason I'm never going to be safe at that house ever again. Not that I was ever safe, but now I have to worry about even more people enlisted by my father trying to kill me.

And Gabriel.

I don't care what kind of justification he tries to give, it doesn't matter to me. There's no excuse for what he did, and I'm never going to be able to forgive him. After everything I did to try to protect him, he still betrayed me like this.

"Are you sure he told your father?" Gabriel asked, almost like he didn't believe Alastair was capable of such a thing. I guess I wouldn't have believed it either if he didn't flat-out tell me himself.

"He admitted it to my face. He *told* me that he was the one that did it. I don't know what to do. I don't ever want to speak to him again, I have nothing left to say to him," I said.

I don't believe I was thinking logically, but I didn't really care.

I knew what I was feeling, and I knew that I couldn't trust Alastair, not anymore. Maybe I never really could, and I only let myself believe I could blindly trust him with anything, all because he was my brother. I never bothered to consider the fact that the person closest to me would be the one to hurt me the most.

I was beyond hurt, I didn't even know how to describe the level of pain I was feeling. I've never felt so betrayed, so damaged in my entire life, despite everything I've been through in the seventeen years I've been on this Earth. Nothing has ever damaged me so much, no knife has ever cut me so deeply, and no wound has ever bled this much.

And I don't believe anything else will ever hurt this much, nothing else will scar me so intensely, leaving me broken and damaged to die, wondering why I've been betrayed in such a brutal way.

"Maybe he had a valid reason,"

"Why are you defending him? Do you even realize I almost fucking died in there?" I interrupted. It angered me that Gabriel would even bother to try to defend what Alastair did, what got me locked away and left to die in the garage for a month.

What if I did die in there?

Would he still defend Alastair?

Would Alastair feel guilty?

Would anyone even care?

"Atticus, I'm not defending him. I just want you to consider that maybe he had a reason before you act like he's not your brother," He said. Whatever reason Alastair claimed to have would never justify nearly getting me killed.

"He's not my brother. Because my brother wouldn't do something like that, no matter what. My brother would never betray me like that. So I don't have a brother anymore. I only have Anastasia," I said.

I didn't want to sound like I was erasing Annabelle's existence, that couldn't be further from the truth. But the truth is that she's gone, and she's never coming back. No matter how much I may scream, and cry, and beg for her to come back, she never will. I don't have her anymore. I only have one sibling left, and I barely even knew her. But she was the only one who remained, and she was the only one I could still trust.

"You can't act like he doesn't exist, Atticus. He's still your brother,"

"He's not," I spat, standing up and exiting the bathroom.

I couldn't believe that Gabriel was actually trying to defend Alastair, or trying to get me to change my mind, knowing what I went through this past month because of him.

I don't think I've ever felt more alone in my entire life. I've never felt so abandoned, so unheard. It was like no one was actually listening to any of the words I said, and they only pretended to acknowledge the countless thoughts I felt bubbling in my head. Thoughts I couldn't silence, thoughts that I couldn't push away. I had to deal with them, trying to keep them from taking control of my entire life, running me off the road like a mad driver on the highway.

No one understood the pain I was experiencing, and I don't believe they really cared either. Not a single person bothered to even *attempt* to understand what I was feeling, which only made me feel even more isolated than when I was locked in the garage.

It made me feel like I never actually got out of there, almost like I did die in there, and my ghost is out wandering the world, trying to act like everything is going to be okay one day, and I'll eventually be able to move on.

But I don't think I can move on.

I think I'm always going to be stuck in this rut, and I'll never be able to get out. Always feeling like there's nothing beyond this pain and betrayal, never escaping what I've been cursed to live in. All I want is to have happiness in my life, happiness that I'm not afraid is going to fade away at a moment's notice. That's all I've ever wanted, that's the only thing that I've ever tried to find in life.

But I guess that's something that isn't meant for me.

I'm supposed to live an unhappy life, a life where I'm constantly ignored, where no one actually listens to a single word I say. A world that makes me question if life is even worth living. A world that makes me question if I should simply give up on myself now, before I'm forced to deal with even more pain that I don't know how to cope with.

I felt like no one was on my side, like it was me against everything in my life. And I had to deal with all of it on my own, because no one else cared enough to try to help me bear the burden of my life, it was just a war that I was the only soldier in.

But I'm so tired of fighting.

I'm so tired of always having to be strong, no matter what.

I'm tired of never being understood, and being expected to be endlessly strong, never losing strength for even a moment.

The last class was finally dismissed, and I was unintentionally right outside Anastasia's classroom. She was the last person left in the room, and I could see her talking to the teacher, so I stood at the door, waiting for her.

I don't know why she was talking to him for so long, it's not like Anastasia's a bad student, she's exceeding in all of her classes. I recognized her teacher, Mr. Wilis, I had him last year for chemistry. He still had the same flat brown hair and dead brown eyes.

He was a man that made me somewhat uneasy. I never really understood why, he was significantly shorter than me, and I towered over him. But to me, something about him always seemed off.

Anastasia's best subject is chemistry, why is she taking so long to talk to her teacher?

I felt my stomach doing flips, something about this felt strange to me. This isn't like my sister, this shouldn't be taking her so long.

I looked closer into the classroom, trying to see what was going on, immediately noticing Mr. Wilis standing way too close to my sister. I remember him always standing really close to the female students. Everyone in my class always thought it was weird, but no one ever did anything about it, there was nothing anyone could do.

I kept my eyes on him, never looking away. I didn't care if he saw me staring at him, I wasn't going to take my sight off of him for a second. I couldn't tell what they were talking about, or why it took so long.

Anastasia clearly seemed like she was trying to get away from him, like she was uncomfortable being in the same space as him, like the thought of him made her physically sick.

And then I felt like throwing up.

The fucking teacher kissed my sixteen-year-old sister.

The disgusting forty-something teacher kissed my teenage sister.

I didn't even think twice, I barged into the room, walking up to my sister.

"Get your fucking hands off of her!" I said, pushing him away from her, and putting my sister behind me.

"Atticus DuVonet! Listen, I don't know what you think you saw," He began, trying to defend himself as he took a step back.

"I saw you kiss a fucking teenager!" I said, pushing him away again.

"Atticus, can we please go," Anastasia whispered to me, grabbing my arm.

"This isn't over, you sick pervert," I said.

"Atticus," Anastasia pleaded, as she dragged me out of the classroom, leading me into the hallway.

"Are you okay?" I asked the moment we were out of his line of sight.

"Can we please not talk about this," She said, starting to walk away from me.

"Ana, you have to tell someone about this," I said, grabbing her arm. I wouldn't let my sister be a silent victim, not when it comes to something like this.

"No, Atticus. Can we pretend this didn't happen?" She said, releasing her arm.

I don't understand why she's refusing to acknowledge what that creep did to her. I saw it happen, it's not like anyone wouldn't believe her if she has a witness.

"Anastasia,"

"No!" She shouted, cutting me off before I could even begin my sentence, storming away from me, toward the schoolyard, beginning the walk home by herself, not even bothering to wait for Alastair.

Now I really don't understand her.

Maybe I never will.

I don't know.

Maybe she'll keep everything to herself, because she doesn't know what else to do.

I can only hope that one of these days, she'll finally realize that she can talk to me, and that she's not alone, no matter how empty this cruel world might seem. She'll always have me at her side, whether she believes that or not.

I wish I knew how to communicate with her, but I don't think she even knows how to communicate with anyone. I don't even know if she ever talked to Annabelle. Maybe she did, but maybe she didn't. It feels impossible trying to understand Anastasia when she's so closed off about everything.

Chapter Thirteen

I didn't bother to look for Alastair, I just walked home silently, by myself. I didn't see a point in trying to talk, all I did was piss everyone off every single time I tried to speak. It's not like I tried to constantly irritate everyone by simply existing, it just seems to happen. I didn't even want to see Alastair. He *betrayed* me, I didn't want to speak to him, I didn't even want to acknowledge his existence.

"Atticus, please, talk to me," Alastair begged, running at me from behind. The harder he tried, the more he pissed me off. I have nothing to say to him, and I'm not willing to listen to a single word he has to say.

"Fuck off, Alastair," I said, walking faster to get away from him, but I knew he wouldn't give up so easily.

"Can we please talk about this?" He asked, following right behind me.

"I have nothing to say to you," I said, trying everything I could to get away from him.

He quickly ran ahead to get in front of me, forcing me to stop walking and look at him. Everything in me wanted to ignore his presence, and act like he wasn't there. Like he was a ghost I could look right through, as if he was never real.

The other part of me wanted to knock his teeth down his throat.

"Then let me explain!" He shouted.

"I don't want to hear your bullshit," I scoffed, pushing him aside so I could walk past him, tossing him away like a child tosses an old toy. Maybe I didn't really care about him anymore.

I've trusted Alastair my entire life. I've always defended him, feeling like I could depend on him for everything, never once believing it would be possible for him to betray me.

And now, I can't even trust him enough to walk next to him. How can I be certain that he isn't holding a knife in his hand, waiting to stab me in the back the moment I take my eyes off of him?

"You know what? Fuck you, Atticus," He said, pushing me from behind.

"Really?"

"Really," He said, like he was trying to act tough. Now, I was beyond pissed at him. He's trying to act like I'm suddenly the villain here, as if he didn't ruin my entire life. As if he didn't get me locked in the fucking garage for a *month*. As if he didn't bring me the closest I've ever been to genuinely killing myself.

I felt my anger reaching an uncontrollable level, almost as if I wasn't in control of myself. I didn't even try to stop myself. I punched him straight in the jaw, exactly as he did to me not that long ago. I didn't even think about it, I just did it. And I don't think I regretted it or even felt bad about it. He deserved it.

"Asshole!" He shouted, grabbing his face.

"You fucking ruined my life!" I screamed. I didn't care if someone heard me, everyone deserves to know the truth about the perfect Alastair DuVonet. The perfect Alastair DuVonet that only cares about himself, and making his life better. The perfect Alastair DuVonet who doesn't care if he has to destroy his own brother to protect himself.

"You won't even listen to me!"

"I don't care about your shitty explanation! You ruined my entire life, I don't want to hear a single fucking word from you! You're not even my brother anymore!" I said. I don't care if that seemed too far, it was the truth, and he needed to hear it.

"Don't say that," He said, his tone dropping to a low level.

"Go fuck yourself," I said, starting to walk away once again.

"You're still dating Gabriel, aren't you?! Your life isn't ruined!" He shouted. I didn't want to respond to him, but he seemed to be unable to realize exactly how much damage he's done.

"But now, I have to be afraid for his life! I have to be terrified that our father is going to fucking kill him! Every single moment he spends with me, he's in danger, and it's entirely your fault!" I said. I could see him speaking, but I don't know what he said. I couldn't hear anything clearly except for the ringing in my ears, and the pounding of my heart.

I hope Alastair felt bad about what he did, he should. And if he had any empathy at all, he would. I don't want to understand why he hurt me like this, I don't think it's possible for me to ever actually understand. I can't trust that any explanation he'll give me is the truth, I can't blindly believe that he isn't lying to me to save his own ass.

I don't care to listen to anything he has to say. And to me, no reason is valid enough to completely betray your own brother, the same person who's always done *everything* he possibly could to keep you safe, the same person who's done nothing but try to keep you out of harm's way. The same person who was willing to sacrifice his own life to try to protect you.

I subjected myself to so much hell for Alastair, losing so many pieces of myself that I'm never going to be able to get back. I was willing to give up anything to try to protect him from the wrath of our father, and this is how he repays me. By destroying my life, ruining any chances I had at ever being truly happy. Instead, now I always have to be looking over my shoulder, everywhere I go, never knowing who's watching, never knowing who's going to try to kill me for something that I spent so many years wishing I could change about myself.

I couldn't help but wonder if I should skip town. I could do it, too. At least, Leonard believed I could do it. Maybe running away is how I can protect Gabriel, he wouldn't know where I went. No one would be able to track me down, and no one would ever be able to hurt me ever again. I don't know what I'm waiting for, if I'm even waiting for anything, or if I just don't know how to do something like that.

I don't even think I know where I'd go, I think I'd simply start running and hope for the best. Not bothering to stop for anything, not even giving myself a chance to catch my breath, just continuing to run, never looking back.

I don't think it would be difficult. I think running away is something that requires a level of courage I don't have, or is something that you don't even consider doing until you've reached a certain breaking point, and I believe I'm getting closer, and closer to that point every single day. I don't know where the line is, but I know that I'm racing toward it faster than a cheetah.

I walked into the house, instantly moving toward the stairs to hide in my bedroom, the only place I can ever express all of my emotions, where no one is there to judge me for how I feel about my life.

"Are you still bringing shame to our family's good name?" I heard Sebastian's voice ask as I got only two steps up the stairs.

"Do you think I asked to be this way? Don't you think I knew how you would react? Do you really think I chose this?" I asked, turning to face him.

I don't know if I cared about what he had to say. I don't know if I was still afraid of him, or what he might do to me. I think that I don't know anything other than how to mess things up. I probably shouldn't have responded to him at all, but if I didn't, he'd only be more angry with me, and everything would snowball into something so much worse.

"Then you pretend to be normal," He said, and quietly walked away from me.

What exactly was that supposed to mean?

Did he really care *that* much about our family image?

What was he actually mad about?

Was he mad about me, or was he using me as a distraction from his own issues?

What does he actually care about?

Or does he not really care at all, and does he only pretend like he gives a shit?

I guess it doesn't matter that much, he's never going to change, no matter how much I analyze him. I'm never going to understand him. He'll always be some unknown species that I can't comprehend, and he'll never be a different man than the awful one I know him as. It's not in his nature to ever change for the better, and become someone different than who he's always been.

I went to my room, enjoying the silence I've always enjoyed, finally feeling like the sounds in my head would quiet down, giving me a chance to feel real clarity for the first time in a long time.

I locked my door, something I've never done, something I've never had the privilege of doing, but it's not like anyone was going to bother me in here. No one cared enough to check on me. I could be dead in here right now, and no one would know until the smell of my rotting corpse began to travel through the house.

I walked into the bathroom, noticing my reflection in the mirror. Sometimes, I even felt like I was the only person I could talk to, because I was the only person who would always understand every single word I said. I didn't have to *try* to make my reflection understand what it was like to be Atticus DuVonet.

I don't think I understood every single thought I held in my head about what Alastair did to me. Even if he had a valid reason, I didn't want to hear it. I didn't want him to think there was any kind of excuse for what he did to me. I will never forgive him, and he needs to understand that.

This isn't some problem that brothers can solve by fighting it out. He made a choice, and no matter the situation, that choice has consequences. His reason doesn't matter, because there's some consequences that can't be healed with a simple apology. His actions don't exist without dangerous consequences, and I don't care if he meant to hurt me or not.

The fact of the matter is that he did. He ruined me, he ruined everything that I am, and that's not something that he can ever fix. He has to live the rest of his life knowing that he was the one who destroyed our relationship, and that he has no one to blame but himself, no matter how badly he may want to blame me.

I think part of me wanted to feel bad about how things were playing out, but I simply couldn't. I didn't have the energy to feel bad. I shouldn't *have* to feel bad, or guilty, or apologetic for any of this. I'm not the one who betrayed my only brother, and left him to die in the place that I know he hates more than anything. I'm not the one who turned my back on the one person who has always been there for me through everything. I'm not the one who backstabbed the person who saved my lifetime, and time again.

I don't know why I felt so confused by the face I saw in the mirror, almost like I didn't recognize myself. Maybe I didn't even know who I really was, and I only wanted to let myself believe that I knew what I looked like.

Actually seeing myself always seemed to throw me off, it was like looking at a stranger. It reminds me of why I never look in the mirror for too long.

I felt like every single emotion was building up inside of me, each trying to push its way through the surface, letting myself ruin the perfect image I'd been forced to keep up with my entire life. Everything within me wants to lash out at everyone, if only to get everyone to leave me alone for the rest of my life. I don't care about preserving anything anymore. Everything falls apart eventually anyway, why not expedite the process, and ruin everything on my own terms?

Why not release everything I've kept buried inside for so many years?

Is there anything that's stopping me, except for my own fear?

I think that for my entire life, I've been waiting for the right moment to finally give up on trying to be the perfect son, the perfect brother, the perfect everything. And I think now is finally the time.

What else do I honestly have left to lose?

I feel like Gabriel is already starting to slip away from me, and it's not right for me to try to keep him trapped in my life. He doesn't deserve that, and he shouldn't have to be afraid of my father coming after him. It's not like I want to let go of him, but I have to, for his own safety. I'd never be able to live with myself if anything happened to him because of Sebastian.

I hate looking in the mirror.

I hate seeing who I'm forced to be, the body I'm stuck in. I hate everything I see in my reflection, every single feature of my face, every small detail that only I ever seem to notice. I hate thinking about who I am, and how I got to this point in my life. My reflection only sends me on a spiral about who I am, and what I've become.

I don't know who I am, or who I want to be. All I know is that I don't want to be stuck living the rest of my life as the perfect Atticus DuVonet.

I can't do it anymore, it's driving me insane, destroying me from the inside out. It's ripping apart the very cells in my body, wrecking my anatomy, only making me more and more confused about my life, and the things I can never seem to escape. The things I'm forced to make myself understand, or at least pretend to understand.

Who am I really?

Who am I going to become?

Or am I going to be like this for the rest of my life, cursed to never change, never grow, never be anything more than the name I was born as?

I don't want to speak to anyone anymore.

I want to give up on myself. At this point, nothing even matters anymore. I don't think that's so wrong of me, I feel that I've more than earned the right to give up on people, to even give up on myself. I've spent so much of my life in pain, I deserve to finally give myself a chance to heal.

But I don't know that I will ever *truly* heal. I think I'm always going to be a broken shell of a person, never to be whole again. Always stuck in my own past, never letting myself really move on. Thinking about what I could have possibly changed, what could have made even the slightest difference in my life, believing that even the smallest change would have affected the entire outcome of my life.

Maybe if I was the perfect son that they always wanted me to be, my arms wouldn't be covered in scars. I wouldn't jump at the sound of a door slamming. I wouldn't plan an escape route for every single room I enter, preparing for the worst with every person I meet.

I wouldn't believe that every single person in this world is always going to be out to hurt me. Maybe I'd still believe that there is good left in the world, and that somewhere down the line in my life, I'll be able to be happy, and I won't be afraid every single time I take a step.

But that will never happen.

Because I'm always going to be stuck in this mindset, tied to this life. I'll never be able to forget about it, and pretend I didn't go through all the things I've been forced to survive.

I'm never going to live a fearless life. I'm never going to feel completely safe, because something, or someone, is always going to be playing on a loop in the back of my head, and I'll never be able to shut it off. It's always going to be a part of me, no matter how hard I fight to get away from it.

It's who I'm destined to be, and it's not something I can avoid. It's already been decided.

I watched the face in the mirror contort and change into something I couldn't even recognize as human. I don't know what it was, but it certainly wasn't me.

It had sharp, pointy teeth, and long black hair that covered its eyes, and it looked like it was a ghost. I don't know. Something about it seemed like it could have been human at one point, but it morphed into something that could only be described as a monster. Maybe it was some kind of messed-up version of myself.

"You can't blame yourself for the things out of your control," The reflection said with a gravelly voice.

Was I going insane?

Or was the mirror really talking to me?

Was this all some kind of weird dream?

Or did I really die in the garage, and all of this is some weird journey into the afterlife?

"I know you want to blame yourself for everything you've been through, or you want to blame your brother. But that's not going to make things any better. It's not your fault, but it's not Alastair's fault either," It said.

I didn't understand, I don't know if I wanted to understand.

"Ignoring Alastair and pretending he isn't your brother isn't going to fix anything. What's done is done, and there's nothing either of you can do to change that. You have to accept that you can't change what happened, and that you can't put the blame on anyone other than your father," It explained.

Have I officially lost my mind?

Why was the mirror speaking to me?

I don't know if all of this was somewhere deep in my mind, or if this was real. I don't know how to determine if anything is real, I'm not even convinced I'm real.

Was my reflection actually speaking to me? Was this even my reflection?

It doesn't look like me. At least, I don't think it does.

Is this how other people see me?

Or do I *really* not know what I really look like?

"You have to talk to people, Atticus, you can't talk to your reflection, and hope that everything will magically fix itself, and all your problems will vanish. You know that's not how things work," It said.

I couldn't feel anything but pure fear building up inside of me. I lost sight of all of the other emotions that were trying to take over my entire body not too long ago, nothing else existed beyond my fear.

I had to get away from the being I saw across from me reflected in the mirror, it was too much for me. I didn't think about it, my heart was racing too much, I was too afraid. My thoughts weren't clear enough. I wasn't stable enough.

I slammed my fist into the glass, shattering it, making the figure morph back into my reflection, a version of myself that I at least could sort of recognize. It was the only thing I could think to do, it was the only way I could make the figure disappear.

I don't know what's happening to me. I don't know how to stop myself from becoming something I don't understand, something I don't even recognize as a human being.

Was I a monster?

I know I certainly felt like one, that was my only explanation or understanding for anything that was happening to me. I had to be some kind of deranged monster, nothing else made sense to me.

I wish I could get away from myself, and be something different.

I walked out of the bathroom and sat on my bed, trying to catch my breath, feeling my heart pounding in my chest. I took a moment to look down at my fist, noticing the small amounts of blood that coated my knuckles, but I didn't care.

I didn't care about anything.

I heard a quiet knock at my door, but I didn't want to open it. I didn't want to speak to anyone. The door was locked, and I didn't have to worry about anyone coming in, when I clearly wanted to be left alone.

And then the doorknob started to jiggle.

Was someone picking the lock to my bedroom?

I heard the knob click and slowly push open, revealing Anastasia standing on the other side with a hairpin in her hand.

"Are you alright?" She asked.

I wasn't going to answer her, I didn't even think I could. I think I was in too much shock over the fact that she just broke into my bedroom.

Where the hell did she even learn how to do that?

I saw her eyes trailing to my hand, where she clearly noticed the small traces of blood on my knuckles.

"What happened to your hand?" She asked, closing the door and moving closer to me, sitting down next to me on the bed.

I never moved my eyes away from the door, I didn't bother to look at her. I felt her grab my hand, closely examining my injuries. I felt her slowly picking small shards of glass out of my hand that I didn't even know were there.

"You should talk to him, Atticus. I don't know what happened with you two, but Alastair seems pretty upset about it. He won't tell me what happened, but from what I gather, it's bad, and you're pissed off at him. I'm not saying you have to immediately forgive him, but you should still go talk to him. At least act like adults, and have a conversation, instead of punching each other every time you have a disagreement," She shrugged. I knew she didn't agree with our physical altercations, but that was what we had to do. She didn't have to understand it.

I wanted to tell her the truth about what Alastair did, I wanted to tell her that this was way beyond a simple disagreement, this was something that fucked up my entire life. Doesn't she deserve to know the truth about the man she's still willing to call her brother?

But I still didn't bother to speak. It didn't seem like it was worth it, it felt like I'd be talking to someone who would never really understand what I was trying to say. I still wouldn't even look at her, I only stared off into the distance, wishing I would disappear.

"Can you please say something instead of ignoring me like some child? I understand you're upset about everything that's happened. But that's not an excuse to ignore me, and act like I don't exist, like I'm not trying to talk to you right now. At least fucking acknowledge me," She demanded, clearly growing more and more frustrated with me.

She didn't understand. She would never understand. She has no idea what kind of pain I'm in right now. No one does, no matter how much they pretend to understand, or relate, or sympathize. No one fucking understands.

"Get the fuck out," I said in a low voice. I didn't want to direct my anger toward her, but at this point, anyone who pretends to understand the agonizing pain I've been dealing with for my entire life deserves my anger.

"You really are a selfish asshole," She scoffed as she stood up.

"Out!" I shouted. Fuck suppressing my emotions to try to spare her feelings. If she really thinks I'm selfish, then maybe I should start acting more like it.

"Fuck you, Atticus," She said, walking out of my bedroom, and slamming the door.

Everyone suddenly wants to make me seem like a villain, when all I've ever done my entire life is try to help everyone around me. All I've ever tried to do is protect the people I care about from having to face the same shit I have to face.

But if people want me to stop trying to help them, then I'm willing to give up. I'm willing to give up on everything, if that's what's finally going to make people happy with me.

I didn't sleep at all that night. Not that I ever really slept, but I didn't bother trying any methods to fall asleep. I let myself stare at the ceiling all night. I tried not to think about anything the entire night. I knew that if I let the countless thoughts have control over me, I'd never sleep again.

But I couldn't stop all of my thoughts from creeping in, and grabbing me by the throat, forcing me to acknowledge their existence.

I thought about what Annabelle would think of me, and how upset she'd be with me for how I was acting toward Alastair and Anastasia. She never liked it when I had even minor disagreements with Alastair, I knew she'd hate it that I refused to even call him my brother. She'd be disappointed in me, to say the least.

I miss having her around. I hate how everyone refuses to acknowledge her, or what happened to her. It's like everyone has forgotten about her. She was a *kid*, she had so much left to do in her life. Everything was so cruelly ripped away from her, and I wish more than anything that I could have stopped it, that I had been strong enough to keep this from happening. If I had just been a little bit stronger, she would still be alive, and she'd still have a chance to have a happy life.

But she's dead because of me, and everyone acts like she was never even real. They treat her like some urban legend, and refuse to even say her name, like saying it might awaken some ancient curse to destroy us all. They're all letting her memory fade away, because somehow, that's better than remembering who our sister was, and who she could have been if she had been given a single chance in her life.

If I had fought a little bit harder for her, who knows who she might have become. What she might have done with her life, how she might have changed the world. But now, no one knows, and no one ever will.

Annabelle was the only clear thought in my mind, and she was the only one that really mattered to me. I missed her more than anything, and I could never allow myself to forget about her like I never even met her. I didn't get to say goodbye to her, my father wouldn't even let me out of the garage for her funeral. I had to accept the fact that I would never get to see her again, and I would never have the chance to properly say goodbye to her.

I got out of bed earlier than I normally do in the morning. I didn't want to leave the house at the same time as Alastair and Anastasia, I didn't even want to associate with them. I wanted to pretend that they didn't exist. They already hated me, so I knew they would do the same thing to me.

I walked alone to the schoolyard, arriving earlier than most of the other students. I sat against a wall, watching the world continue to move around me as more, and more students arrived, each joining their own little clique of friends.

I saw Gabriel arrive, but I made no effort to go anywhere near him. I didn't want to speak to anyone, and that included him. I had to avoid him for his own safety. It's not that I want to, but I have to remove him from my life, it's the only way I can keep him safe from my father.

I hated the thought of not having Gabriel in my life, but sometimes, we have to let go of the people that we love the most so that they can have a better life than the one we can give them. It doesn't mean that we don't love them, it simply means that we know we aren't what's best for them, and we're giving them their best chance to be truly happy, and to live the life that they deserve.

"You're here early," Gabriel said, sitting down next to me. I didn't even think about it, I grabbed my things and stood up, quickly walking away from him.

I couldn't turn back to look at him, I knew that if I let myself see his face, I would cave and go right back to him, and that's not what he needs. He needs me to leave his life quickly and quietly, so he has a real chance at living a happy life with someone who has the real capability to be happy in this life.

Someone who isn't me.

Because I'm not the person who can give him the kind of life that he wants. I'm the kind of person that can only destroy his life.

"Atticus?!" He called to me, as I continued walking away. I wouldn't let myself turn around, I couldn't. I had to keep walking like I didn't hear him, like he wasn't even real to me, because I knew that was the only way I would be able to do this.

I walked into my first class of the day, noticing Gabriel already sitting in the same seats we always sit in toward the back of the classroom. I don't even know how he managed to get there before me.

I tried to walk past him, moving closer to the front of the classroom. I didn't get very far before I felt him grab onto my wrist, pulling me to my normal seat as he tried to get me to sit down, despite my attempts to pull away from him.

"Atticus, what the fuck?" He asked, clearly growing more frustrated as I kept trying to fight against him. His confusion seemed to weaken his grip, and I quickly pulled my arm away, and kept walking toward the front.

I could feel his eyes burning through the back of my head, staring me down as I continued to walk further and further away from him. I still didn't pay attention in class, I was too distracted by the feeling of Gabriel trying to stab me in the back of the head with his eyes. Not that I cared about this class anyway.

I didn't need him to understand, I needed him to *let me go*.

The first class ended, and I tried to quickly exit the classroom, and move on to my next class, but I noticed Gabriel was still waiting in the back of the classroom for me. He never knows when to give up.

I tried to quickly walk past him, but he grabbed onto my arm as I was on my way through the doorway, keeping me from walking any further without him right by my side.

"What the fuck was that about?" He asked. I tried to pull my arm away, but his grip only tightened the more I struggled against him.

"Let go," I roughly whispered.

"He speaks!" Gabriel said dramatically, as if that was going to convince me to engage with him.

I kept trying to free my arm, but every single time I tried to pull away, his grip strengthened. Either he didn't understand what I was trying to do, or he knew exactly what I was doing, and he was doing everything he possibly could to prevent me from silently pushing him out of my life.

"Why are you being an asshole?" He asked.

I didn't care if he was kidding, everyone always trying to villainize me pissed me off more, and more every single time it happened.

"Leave me the fuck alone," I said, ripping my arm away with all the strength I had, finally getting him to drop my arm. I quickly walked away, blending myself into the crowd of students walking through the hallway.

I walked into my next class, again sitting in the front of the room. Only this time, I didn't feel anyone staring at me. I could only assume Gabriel decided to skip this class, or he was hiding somewhere.

Or, worse, he decided to find Alastair, and talk to him about me. And if I know Gabriel as well as I think I do, he definitely went to find Alastair.

I didn't bother to ask for permission, I just left the classroom, making my way toward the bathroom that I knew was closest to both my classroom and Alastair's. I knew neither of them would think to go to a bathroom farther away to avoid me finding them. Maybe they wanted me to find them.

I walked in silently, immediately hearing both Gabriel and Alastair's distinct voices speaking to each other.

"What's wrong with him?" Gabriel asked.

"He's an asshole,"

"Alastair," Gabriel said firmly.

"He is," Alastair said defensively. I don't think Alastair has any right to be angry with me, he's the one who caused all of this.

"Did you talk to him?"

"He's refusing to talk to me, and everyone for that matter. Apparently he snapped at Anastasia last night. What's he doing to you?"

"He's avoiding me, and generally being a rude asshole. I know he's trying to break up with me without actually having to say it," Gabriel explained.

How the fuck does he know that that's exactly what I was trying to do? Am I really that predictable?

It doesn't matter.

"He won't even let me explain why I told our father about you two,"

"Why did you tell him? Maybe I can somehow get through to him and try to make him understand,"

"He told me that he knew Atticus was keeping secrets from him, but he didn't know what it was. And he knew that I had to know something about it. Our father also knew that even if he threatened to hurt me, I still wouldn't tell him. But he realized that if he threatened to *kill* Atticus, I would. It's not like I wanted to, but Sebastian was going to kill him if I didn't. I knew something bad was going to happen to him either way, but at least if I told our father about you, he'd live. I know he's mad at me, and that's fine, I deserve that, but I don't know why he doesn't realize that I wouldn't have said anything if I had any other option. But I didn't have a choice. Atticus would be dead right now if I didn't say something. I didn't even say you two were dating, all I said was that you were friends, and you might know something. The only reason he found out you were dating was because *Atticus* fucked up when our father questioned him about you, and our father was acting like he already knew everything, even though all he knew was your name," Alastair explained.

Fuck.

I am an asshole.

"And he keeps talking about how now you're in danger too, and he probably feels like it's his job to keep anything from happening to you. I'm sure he thinks breaking up with you is the only way, but he doesn't know how to actually do that, so he's trying to do it silently. Because he's an asshole," Alastair continued.

I hate that they both know me so well.

"It's almost kind of funny that he thinks that he gets to make that decision for me," Gabriel stated.

I definitely fucked up majorly, and I know that I did. That didn't mean I wasn't still upset, or trying to fight off every single emotion at once, but I owed my brother an apology. Of course, I was still angry with him, and I don't know that I'll ever be able to fully forgive him. But I owed him at least some kind of apology.

Chapter Fourteen

"I fucked up, and I'm sorry," I said, stepping further into the bathroom so both Alastair and Gabriel could see me. I think they might have known I was there the entire time, but decided to not mention it. It's not like there were many hiding spots in a small school bathroom.

"At least you can acknowledge it," Alastair said, walking closer to me, his steps seeming heavier than normal. I was almost kind of expecting him to hit me, I deserved it.

But he didn't.

Much to my surprise, my brother hugged me instead of hitting me.

"What's happening right now?" I asked, shocked Alastair forgave me so easily, but keeping the thought of his heavy steps tucked in the back of my head. I don't know what would have caused his heavy footing, but I knew it was going to bother me until I knew what was going on.

"It's called forgiveness, you could learn a thing or two about it," He said with a laugh as he let me go, leaning against the wall, pushing all of his weight onto his right foot.

Did something happen to him that I didn't know about?

I knew if I tried to ask, he'd only dodge the question and turn it right back onto me, so I had to keep the thought to myself until later.

I didn't think I deserved his forgiveness, not after how horribly I treated him. But by some miracle, my brother still believed I was worthy of forgiveness, despite how horrific I was to him. I guess we were kind of even for all the times he tried to fight me.

I think I regret not letting him explain himself sooner, I don't know why I wouldn't listen to him. I feel like I let all these thoughts form in my head, without actually trying to understand them. I let them take complete control of me, and I let myself go blind to what's actually happening. It's not like it's something I want to do, but something I can't seem to stop myself from doing.

"I don't know why I'm acting like this," I whispered, almost hoping they wouldn't hear me. I didn't want to seem vulnerable or weak, but that's all that I am, no matter how hard I try to hide it, no matter how many brave faces I put on. That's all I am.

I don't understand myself, and I can't make excuses for my actions. The way I was behaving was wrong, and there's no other explanation. I don't know why I'm being so awful to everyone, and I don't understand why everyone is so willing to keep giving me second chances, when I clearly don't deserve them.

I don't think I deserve forgiveness. I don't think I really deserve anything good, but for some reason, people keep forcing themselves to see some good in me. Maybe they feel bad for me, maybe they think if they

don't give me another chance, I'll disappear one of these days, and they'll

never see me again.

And I think they'd be right to believe that.

I *did* almost leave last night, and let myself disappear without another

word, because somehow, I believe that would be easier than saying goodbye.

For some reason, I believe that vanishing in the night like some sort of ghost

is better than having to face the consequences of the decisions I make.

Maybe I should find my own way out, no matter how brutal it seems,

because I don't know how much longer I can take this. I feel myself being

stretched thinner and thinner, and soon enough, there's going to be nothing

left of me but a skeleton if I keep living like this.

"Because you've been through hell, and you've never given yourself

a chance to recover. You're too busy trying to protect everyone else to

protect yourself. You think trying to prevent everyone else from facing the

same shit as you is somehow going to make you feel better, and it's not,"

Alastair said.

I seriously can't stand it when he does that. It's like he can peer into

my head and see all of my thoughts, plucking out exactly the right ones at the

right times, telling me exactly what I need to hear. It makes me feel like I can't keep anything to myself, not even the thoughts that circulated my mind that I wanted to be just mine.

"And, you think you have a responsibility to do whatever it takes to try to keep bad things from happening, even when it's out of your control," Gabriel added. I knew he was referring to Annabelle's death, because he didn't believe there was anything I could have done to help her. But I know that there was. I could have done something, I could have done *anything*. But I was too weak to help her.

I wasn't strong enough to save her.

Were they trying to call me an asshole who's obsessed with the idea of protecting people through any means possible, even when it makes me look like a controlling, and manipulative piece of shit in the nicest way they could? Or am I projecting?

I don't think they were wrong, they both understood me in a way that I didn't even understand myself. I feel like they know more about me than I know about myself, like they have to be the ones to explain to me how I feel, how I react in situations, because I certainly don't know.

I never know how I feel. I never know what to do. I never know anything about anything. I'm always trying to bullshit my way through life and hope for the best, not understanding a single thing that I'm doing, or why I'm doing it. Most of the time, I feel like I'm a puppet, forced to dance at someone else's every whim, existing only for their entertainment, not even regarding me as my own person, with my own thoughts, my own dreams, my own ambitions.

But I gave all of those up a long time ago. Back when I first realized that I'd never be truly happy in my lifetime, and that there will always be something holding me back from happiness.

"I always feel like someone else is in control of me, I can't even make decisions for myself. Every single choice is made for me, and I don't even get to think about the consequences of my actions. I have to just let things happen. I have to watch my freedom of choice be taken from me. I have to let Sebastian control everything about me. I've never made a single decision for myself, I've always had all my decisions made for me. Even when I've been given options, I've never felt like I *really* had a choice. I've never had the liberty of doing things that *I* want to do, because I've always had to think of everyone else before myself," I explained, saying a lot more than I intended to.

I don't know why I let myself say so much, but it felt like once the words started coming out, they wouldn't stop, no matter how hard I tried. It's not like I wanted to tell them everything I kept buried within my mind, but I think I couldn't handle keeping it to myself any longer.

I've already spent my entire life trying to push away these thoughts, and pretend that they don't exist, but I don't think I can pretend any longer. I think that if things don't change soon, I'm going to have to do something completely insane to feel alright in my life.

"You have more choices than you realize, Atticus. He can't stop you from doing everything," Alastair said.

"But he can stop me from doing enough. I've spent my entire life walking on eggshells around him, afraid to even speak, because from the age of five, I was convinced that even the sound of my voice would be enough to piss him off, and get me killed. I can't name a single time in my life that I've made a decision that was entirely my own, and nothing else forced me to make that decision," I explained.

I don't know if Alastair had to live life the same way I did. I don't know if he felt like he never had a choice either, or if he felt like he could actually make his own decisions without constantly having to worry about the potential outcomes, or how our father might react.

Sometimes I wonder if my brother and I are from two entirely different worlds, or if we have more in common than we might think. Maybe we are more similar than we both first thought, but maybe we're more different than we ever thought was possible.

"You can't keep letting him control your life," He said.

"I don't have any other options. Either I do everything he tells me, or he kills me. That's it, those are my only two choices. I'm not willingly letting him control my life. I'm trying to survive," I said. I don't think my brother truly understood what I was trying to tell him. I think he was convinced that I would be able to take control of my life, and go against our father, as if nothing would happen to me.

But I can't.

I wish I could, but things aren't that simple. They never have been, and they never will be, no matter how hard I try. There's nothing I can do to *actually* change things in my life. I have to deal with the fact that some things will never change, and they're always going to be a certain way.

"There has to be something else you can do," Alastair began. I think my same sense of hopelessness was finally setting in on him.

I had my own ideas of things I could do, but that didn't mean that they were good options. They were pushed to the back of my mind as desperate solutions to an even more desperate situation. I'd never do anything with any of these ideas, unless I was running out of time to do anything to save my life.

"There's not. I've accepted all of this shit already, and it's time for you to do the same. The sooner you make your peace with the things you have no control over, the better you'll be," I said, reminding my brother of what I said to him that horrible night in his room. He still refused to accept

the fact that sometimes, there's nothing you can do but accept whatever fate

is on its way to you, no matter how desperately you may want to change it.

You're not God.

You can't change fate.

Not every story has a happy ending, and I wish my brother would

realize that. Maybe he does know that, but wants to pretend that things will

be okay for a little while longer. But the longer he lives in his disbelief, the

harder it's going to be to accept the truth, and understand the reality of the

world he lives in.

"I don't understand why you're so willing to give up on yourself, and

act like there's nothing you can do to help yourself," He scoffed. I didn't

think he was going to understand, and that was fine, I didn't need him to. I

only needed him to realize that he wasn't going to ever change my mind.

"It's not giving up, Alastair. It's called being realistic. Not everything

is going to have a perfect ending, and you need to accept that," I said, as I

slowly walked out of the bathroom and back toward my class.

I didn't want to fight with him anymore, it's not something I ever

enjoyed, despite what my brother might think. I don't think he really

understands me or the things I say. He's so stuck in his own ways that he can't possibly comprehend why I've already made my peace with the life I have to live.

I heard footsteps coming up behind me, and I knew they were either Gabriel's or Alastair's, but I didn't bother to turn around. I felt like I had said everything that I needed to say to them, and if they didn't understand me, or wouldn't listen to me, there was nothing I could do about it.

"It's not your job to make decisions for everyone, you know," Gabriel said, catching up to me, and slinging his arm around my shoulder.

"But, it is my job to keep anything from happening to you all because I fucked up," I said.

"Number one, it's not. Number two, you didn't know. You thought your father knew, and you knew it would only make things worse if you lied, and he knew the truth. You did the best you could, and that's all that matters. And number three, you don't have to worry about me, I can take care of myself," He continued.

I knew Gabriel was more than capable of protecting himself, but that didn't mean this wasn't my fault. It doesn't matter how many times he tries to convince me that it isn't, or that there was nothing I could have done differently.

Whether he admits it or not, all of this is my fault.

And nothing is going to change that.

Nothing is going to take the blame off me, because nothing can fix the mess I made. I don't know why he wants to pretend that I'm innocent, or that I'm some kind of victim. The things that have happened to me are my own fault, and I have no one, and nothing to blame but myself.

I can't stop myself from thinking that if I had only been a better son, these things wouldn't be happening to me. If I had been a better brother, Annabelle would still be alive. If I had been a better boyfriend, I wouldn't have to be afraid for Gabriel's life, because every moment he spends with me, he puts his life at risk.

I want to be able to take control of my thoughts, and my life, but I don't think that's even a possibility anymore. I think I gave up the hope of ever controlling myself a long time ago. I don't know when it disappeared, but I know that it did, and I know that I'll never see it again, not really.

I reentered the classroom, this time staying hidden in the back of the room. I don't think I owe anyone an explanation for any of the things I do, and I wish people wouldn't feel so entitled to know every single detail about my life, when it's none of their business. Nothing in my life is anyone else's concern.

Still, the day pushed on, dragging me along with it, never giving me a choice in how fast the world seemed to spin around me. I guess it's because I'm not strong enough, or important enough to control the way the earth rotates, no matter how much I might want to change it. It's merely another thing I have to accept that I have no control over. I think once I finally understand that there's so little I can do in this world to impact the grand scheme of things, the easier my life will be.

Hours felt like they passed with the snap of a finger, and before I could even process a single thing that was happening, I was making my way to the schoolyard to meet my brother and sister. I don't even remember how I got there, I don't even remember ever leaving my second class. It was like I teleported to the yard, not understanding why I was there.

"Are you two finally speaking to each other?" Anastasia asked as I turned to see Alastair standing next to me.

Was he there the whole time?

"You could say that," Alastair said. Anastasia nodded, almost like she didn't believe him. I guess I understand her suspicion. A few hours ago, I was ready to rip Alastair's throat out, and she knew that.

We walked home in silence. These walks felt so empty without Annabelle. I still don't understand why everyone refuses to talk about her, like even uttering her name unlocks some kind of ancient curse. She's still our sister, no matter what happened to her. How can we be expected to pretend that we don't know who she is? Like she didn't die a tragic death?

Like our father isn't to blame for the fact that her body is buried in the ground?

Come to think of it, I don't even know where her body is buried. I don't even know if she was buried. I don't know if she's in an urn somewhere, if she's rotting in the ground, if she's in a mausoleum, or if she's somewhere else. I have no idea what happened to my sister's body. And I think that hurt me more than anything. I didn't get to say goodbye to her in any imaginable way. If she had a funeral, I didn't even get to go. I didn't get to say goodbye before her body was taken away.

And I didn't get the chance to tell her how much I loved her the night she died.

We arrived at the house, quickly walked inside, and instantly saw Sebastian and Elizabeth waiting for us. I couldn't even call Elizabeth my mother anymore, I knew the truth. I knew she wasn't. I don't know why she still bothered pretending, not when she knew that I knew the truth about my existence. About all of us.

"Where's Annabelle's body?" I blurted out, unable to stop myself. It probably wasn't a good idea to ask my father this, but I had to know. I couldn't continue on, not knowing where her final resting place was, if she could even rest peacefully now. I hope that she had her peace, whatever that means for her. I hope that wherever she is, she's happy, and she knows how much I miss her. I hope she's not angry with me for not being able to protect her that night, and I hope she understands that I would have done anything I possibly could to keep those horrible things from happening to her.

But I don't know if she knows that. I don't know if there *is* a way for her to know. I think I simply have to hold onto a feeling that she knows everything I wish I could tell her.

"Why do you care?" Sebastian asked with a sneer. He didn't care that I wanted to know, he just didn't want to tell me, that much was obvious. I've been dealing with him my entire life, I always know exactly what it is that he cares about.

"She's my sister,"

"She's dead!" Elizabeth interrupted, laughing.

What kind of sick freak laughs at something tragic like that?

"She was a human being! She was fourteen years old! And you're standing here, laughing at that? A child is dead, and you're laughing?" I spat. I didn't care about what my father was going to do to me for speaking to Elizabeth like that, it didn't matter, not really. Maybe he wouldn't even care.

"And it's your fault that she's dead. Aren't you supposed to be some kind of knight in shining armor? And you couldn't even manage to keep a child alive? What kind of protector do you think you are?" She cackled.

I hated that woman with everything in me. She wasn't our mother, all she did was pretend that she was. She probably didn't even know that I knew everything that my father tried so hard to keep hidden from me.

"Where the fuck is her body?" I pushed. I wasn't going to stop until I had my answer, and everyone in the room knew it.

"Don't speak to your mother that way, Atticus," Sebastian said. He almost looked like he wanted to hit me, but he held himself back. I think he knew exactly what was coming.

Now, this was going to be really fun.

For me at least. I can't say the same for anyone else involved.

"She's not even my fucking mother!" I shouted.

And now, let the show begin.

This was probably one of the worst ideas I've ever had, but for once, I don't think I actually cared. What was genuinely the worst that was going to happen to me? I'd get my ass beat? It's not like that's anything new. If they're going to try to scare me into submission, shouldn't they at least try to change up their tactics at least a little bit?

"How dare you!" Elizabeth said, slapping me across the face.

"How dare I? *You're* the one who married a man who violated his own sisters, and pretended to be the mother of four children born from his sick behavior!" I shouted. I didn't look at Alastair or Anastasia, but I could only imagine the expressions etched on their faces. Alastair already knew the truth about our mother, but he didn't know about Anastasia, and she didn't know anything at all.

"What the fuck?" Anastasia screeched.

I may or may not have started a fight that will rip apart this family completely, but I don't think it's right to blame me for this. I think the only person to blame is my father.

"You don't know what you're talking about! Sebastian, tell him!" Elizabeth said in a shrill voice, as if he could say anything that would change my mind. I knew the truth, and they both knew it. I saw my father glaring at me, saying everything with his eyes rather than his voice.

I was beginning to wonder if he was starting to see no point in fighting with me. By now, he has to realize that every single time he pushes me, I'm going to push back twice as hard. He doesn't scare me anymore, and I think that terrifies him more than anything.

"Downtown. D section, fourth row, third headstone back. I suggest you fall to the ground in front of her grave, and beg her for her forgiveness, because you won't find any anywhere else," He finally said, looking me up and down.

He didn't bother to discredit anything I said, he knew it was entirely the truth, and he knew I was going to stop at nothing to prove it if he tried to deny anything.

I quickly walked back out of the house, fighting the tears welling up in my eyes as I made my way toward the cemetery. I was going to say goodbye to my sister one way or another, and there was nothing anyone could do to stop me.

I still couldn't help but blame myself. I'll always think about that day, what I could have done differently, how I could have saved Annabelle. There has to have been something more I could have done for her.

I think about everything I did that day more times than I probably should, but I can't help it. I think I believe that if I revisit that night in my mind enough times, maybe I could actually go back and change what happened.

And maybe one day, I might be able to, but maybe I won't.

I walked into the silent and grim graveyard, walking past the dirty and aged headstones, wondering about all those who are underneath the ground, and have been long forgotten about. As I walk past the names, I can't help but wonder about their lives, who they were, what happened to them, and how their passing impacted those who loved them.

I wonder if anyone had the same questions when walking past Annabelle's headstone. The engraving probably stated the year she was born and when she died, making it easy for anyone to see exactly how young she was. I wonder if seeing that she was only fourteen saddened people, people who didn't even know her, and now would never have the chance.

D section. Fourth row. Third headstone back.

There it was.

Freshly engraved in words that didn't even look real to me.

Annabelle DuVonet

Born January 25th, 2007

Died September 18th, 2021.

Beloved Daughter, Sister, and Friend.

How could my father have the audacity to call her a "beloved daughter"? He didn't care about Annabelle, he didn't care about any of us. He never has, and he never will.

I sat down on the freshly covered ground in front of my little sister's headstone, almost feeling like this would bring her closer to me somehow. Part of me hoped that she would know that I was with her, but the rest of me wished that she could finally rest now.

"Hi, Annabelle. Today is October 20th, and you've been gone for about a month," I began speaking to her, hoping that by some miracle, she'd be able to hear my words.

Maybe she could hear me.

But maybe she couldn't.

"It's weird for me to think that Alastair and I turn eighteen in only a few days. I'm sorry I didn't get to come to your funeral, and that I didn't get to say goodbye to you. I'm sorry that this happened to you. I'm sorry that I couldn't save you that night. If I could go back in time and do anything differently to change what happened, I would. It's my fault that this happened, and I'm never going to be able to forgive myself for this. I hope that if you can hear me right now, that you can find it within yourself to forgive me. I don't think I deserve your forgiveness, not really, but I know how you are. I don't think you ever had the capability to hold a grudge, not against me. I guess I mainly want you to know that I miss you. And I'm sorry," I finished, tears leaking from my eyes that I didn't bother to try to hold in. I missed her, more than anything. And I hope that somehow, she knew that.

I knew she was never going to respond to me, but part of me hoped that she'd give me some kind of sign that she heard me, or even if she could forgive me.

"It isn't your fault, you know," I heard Anastasia's approaching voice say. I didn't realize she had followed me here.

"It is,"

"No, it's not. You know that. You couldn't have known what was going to happen to her, there was nothing you could have done," She stated firmly, like she actually believed it. But she wasn't with Annabelle that night. She didn't hear her screams.

"You don't understand,"

"I think I do. For some reason, you think it's your job to try to protect everyone, and you never seem to realize that you can't keep everyone safe from *everything*. That doesn't make you a bad person, and that doesn't make you the one to blame. It makes you human. I know you don't want to see anyone in pain, but you can't be the one to carry everyone's struggles for them. Have you ever even stopped to think about your own pain? About the things that you already have to carry? Do you ever actually think about yourself, or do you always focus on anyone else so you don't have to think about your issues?" Anastasia said, sitting down next to me. She was right, and I knew she was right.

I don't understand how she was able to analyze me so well, she hardly ever speaks to me. And yet, I think she knows me better than I know myself.

"Stop doing that," I laughed as I wiped my eyes.

Am I really that transparent that everyone can see right through me? Am I really a walking ghost?

"It's pretty entertaining though," She giggled as she leaned into me, surprising me with her sudden interest in having a relationship with me.

I can't remember the last time I hugged Anastasia. She's always been so against even speaking to me, which meant she never hugged me either.

But still, I held onto my sister as we sat together in front of Annabelle's grave, finding comfort in our shared silence. There was nothing either one of us had to say, not here at least, and that was okay. For once, I didn't mind my sister's quiet nature. The absence of our voices felt right for the first time in either of our lives.

"We have a lot to talk about," Anastasia whispered as the sun slowly began to set, signaling us that we had to leave sooner rather than later.

"I know," I responded. I knew she was talking about the bomb I dropped on her before I came here, but I had my own situation in mind as well. I can't let her brush past what I witnessed yesterday. I understand that she doesn't want to talk about it, but that doesn't mean she gets to pretend that it didn't happen, and furthermore, pretend that I didn't see it. Ignoring a problem doesn't make it go away. I would know that better than anyone.

"Elizabeth isn't my mother?"

"She isn't the mother of any of us. Your mother is Sebastian's sister, Michelle. Mine, Alastair's, and Annabelle's mother was Mary," I explained.

"So I'm not really your sister?"

"Biologically, you're our half-sister. You're still my sister, though. Nothing is ever going to change that," I responded.

"You mean to tell me that all four of us are products of incest?" She asked, horrified.

"Technically, yes. I didn't want to tell you the truth about our mother, but I couldn't stop myself from yelling at Elizabeth. I didn't plan for you to find out about this for a long time, not ever actually. It just sort of happened," I stated. I feel like Anastasia deserved to know, but that didn't mean she should have to be burdened with the knowledge of how she came to be.

"How long have you known?" She asked after several moments of silence, which I presume was her trying to process the information I had thrown at her.

"Since the party," I quietly said. Anastasia didn't say anything. She stayed there, leaning into me, trying to wrap her head around all of this. I couldn't tell how she was feeling, and what was going through her mind. I didn't imagine it was anything pleasant, I know it wasn't when I found out about all of this.

"I think we should go home," She eventually said.

"Do not say anything to them about this. I know how you're feeling right now, but confronting them is not the right decision. Stay quiet, and don't say anything to them. I promise you that starting a fight with them over this is going to get you nowhere, and it's not going to make you feel any better. Honestly, there's nothing that *can* make you feel better. You can either pretend you don't know the truth, or try to accept that there's nothing you can do to change things, and this was far beyond your control," I explained.

"I know you want to ask about Mr. Wilis, so just do it already," She said, quickly changing the subject. I didn't bother to question her speedy change, I knew she didn't want to think about it anymore.

"What was that about? Did you tell anyone?" I asked, trying to tread lightly on the situation.

"He's creepy, that's what it's about. I always thought the way he acted with me was weird, but I didn't think anything else of it at first. I didn't even really think about it until a month ago. And I knew it wasn't right, but I didn't care until yesterday. I knew it was wrong, but something about you seeing it made me realize that I can't keep letting this happen. I don't want you to be mad at me. I'm trying to get him to back off, but I don't know how. I don't know what to do," She said, keeping her voice low. She tends to do the same thing I do, speaking so softly in the hopes that if she keeps her tone quiet enough, she'll be able to move on from the subject with no questions asked.

I felt my rage bubbling up inside of me, but I knew I had to keep it to myself for now, for Anastasia's sake. This isn't her fault, and there's no one to blame except for the fucking pervert teacher.

"You know this isn't your fault, right? And I'm not mad at you for this, I would never be mad at you for something like this. It's not your fault at all," I said, trying to keep her calm.

"I don't know what to do,"

"From now on, I'll leave my last class a few minutes early, and I'll get Alastair and Gabriel to do the same. If he tries to pull any shit, the three of us will handle him. Avoid talking to him, but if he tries anything at all, let me or Alastair know, and we'll deal with him, okay?" I said.

The three of us would have no objections whatsoever to beating the shit out of a pedophile if we had to. I'd even be willing to do it now, and make him stop before he has the chance to even start anything.

Anastasia only nodded, she knew she didn't even have to say anything for me to understand the thoughts she held in her head. She should know by now that she has three personal bodyguards who are willing to do anything to keep her safe.

The sky continued to get darker, and we knew we had no choice but to start heading back to the house, as the night air got colder and colder, biting at our skin as we sat on the ground that only got more and more bitter with each passing moment.

"Goodbye, Annabelle," I whispered to my sister's grave as we stood up. It felt like a weight was finally lifted off of my shoulders, almost like I could actually breathe again. I finally got to say goodbye to my sister.

It was another walk filled with silence, we had both said everything we needed to say, and there was nothing left to verbalize. We knew each other's thoughts now, and we knew we had to help each other, it was the only thing we could do.

I knew Anastasia wouldn't want to explain her current situation to Alastair herself, and I knew she'd want me to do it for her. Not that he needed an explanation, if I told him we had to stand outside of a classroom to keep our sister safe, he would do it without a second thought. But he should probably be aware of what exactly is going on.

We arrived back at the house, silently entering and swiftly moving up the stairs, each going up to our respective bedrooms without another word to each other. There was nothing left to say. There were no other words left to describe what we both were feeling, and no other way left to understand our lives, and the things we had to either deal with, or pretend didn't exist.

And that was all that we could ever do, accept the things we wished we could change, or pretend they weren't real.

I could already feel like this was going to be a long and painful night. I don't think I really understood why, it was like something within me instinctively knew that tonight was going to be difficult. I didn't know what exactly would be the trigger for the wave of pain I felt rushing toward the shore, but I knew there would be no stopping it once it was on its way to me, there was nothing I could do to prevent it. It's one of those things that have become a part of my life that I can't change.

And I've finally accepted that.

Chapter Fifteen

It wasn't that late in the evening, but I knew it was going to be another sleepless night. Which seems to be every night at this point. It's simply the way things are, and there's nothing I can do about it.

I waited for everyone in the house to fall asleep, and the moment I knew I was in the clear, I quietly snuck out my window, making my way not too far down the street to the giant library that it seemed like no one ever went inside of. I knew there was a ladder in the back of the building that led straight up to the roof, I went up there all of the time when I was younger, and didn't know where else to go to get away from my life.

I sat on top of the insanely tall building, I had to be at least sixty feet off of the ground, dangling my legs over the side as I sat at the edge, staring at the ground below me. Everything looked so different from so high up.

I wondered what would happen if I pushed myself slightly forward, allowing myself to fall to the ground below. I can't say I wasn't considering it.

I don't know how much more of this life I can take. I feel like I have some sort of obligation to stick around for the people I love, but I don't know how much more torture I can subject myself to. I've been fighting myself everyday for the past ten years, trying to stay alive. Fighting every single thought that popped into my head. Trying to convince myself that it wouldn't be as easy as I thought. What seven-year-old should ever be considering taking their own life?

A seven-year-old who has had his own body *ripped* away from him, made to feel like he was never in control of himself, and someone else always owned his body. A seven-year-old who was told that he didn't get to make his own decisions, and that he had to let some older man he didn't know do whatever he wanted to do to him.

I've always known how truly terrible my father was. What they did to Annabelle the night she killed herself is the same goddamn thing they did to me every single week. We were kids. We were fucking kids. And only a truly sick man would sign away his children's bodies to strange old men for some extra cash. It's not like he even needed the money, all he wanted was to destroy us, and break us down into nothing but the shell of a person. He wanted to make us lose all sense of identity, autonomy, and free choice.

I've had to deal with so much shit in my seventeen years of life, more than any person should ever have to experience. I've been to hell and back more times than I could ever count. I've had everything ripped away from me, and I'll never get any of that back. I have to spend the rest of my life feeling like something is missing, knowing that so much of me is gone.

I've spent seven years of my life carving into my skin, hoping that would make the pain stop. Seven years never understanding why no matter how deep I went, I never felt any better. I only felt worse when looking back on the choices I've made.

I've spent ten years of my life trying to convince myself to build up the courage to finally push myself off of the building. Finally let go of my body. Finally let myself fade away, like a shadow in the night, vanishing without a single trace.

I don't know why I've always been so afraid to push myself. And I don't know if I should be afraid of the fact that the initial fear was starting to disappear, leaving nothing holding me back but my own mind, trying everything it possibly could to save myself.

If I'm even still worth saving.

Maybe I am to some, but to others, maybe I'm not even worth the oxygen that I breathe, and I'm only wasting away, trapped in my own bubble of self-righteousness, convincing myself that I deserve to be alive. Maybe I'm too far gone down my own path of self destruction, or maybe, my mind has already been destroyed beyond repair, and to end my own life would simply be a mercy killing. Like putting down a horse with a broken leg, knowing it will never heal, and it will never be able to walk again.

It's an act of mercy.

Because maybe there isn't much left for anyone to save. Maybe I'm already gone, and I've merely failed to realize why it seems like everyone can see right through me. How they can somehow know all the things about me that I've tried so hard to keep hidden for so long. Maybe I have to finally, truly give up on myself to free me from the disaster of a life I've been forced to live, and escape from the "glamorous" life of a DuVonet.

Maybe I don't know what I'm talking about.

But what I do know, is that I'm tired of being known as Sebastian DuVonet's son. I'm tired of people knowing who I am, all because I've had the great misfortune of being born his son. Of having his DNA. Of being cursed to either end up exactly like him, or die by his hand before I even have the chance to try to be anything better. Because that's the life I was born into, and that's the life I will die living.

The cold air of the October night kept slapping me across the face, but I knew it would never hurt more than anything I'd dealt with at home. I felt a million thoughts running through my head all at once, and I couldn't focus on a single one of them. It was like a hive of bees swarming around my head, buzzing into my ears, each trying to be louder than the last, trying its hardest to be the one to catch my attention.

Jump.

Don't jump.

Do it.

Don't do it.

Think about Anastasia.

Don't think about her.

What about Alastair?

Forget about him.

Gabriel?

He'll understand.

I shouldn't.

But I have to.

I can't.

But maybe then I'll be able to see Annabelle again.

But maybe I won't.

I could finally be at peace.

Or maybe I'll have to do this all over again in a new life.

Everything horrible can finally fade away.

Will this really solve anything?

Is there anything this won't solve?

Things can get better one day.

But they won't.

I don't know that for sure.

It doesn't change the fact that I believe it.

I didn't know how to push these thoughts away, if I even could. I didn't know if I was stuck with them until I finally caved, and jumped off the roof, or learned to silence the voice that screams inside my head, trying to convince me nothing is ever going to change.

I still feel like I'm going insane. I can't even remember the last time I felt truly sane, if I ever was. I don't think sane people sit on rooftops, arguing with themselves about whether or not they should jump, speeding to the ground as they hoped their problems would end when they met the concrete.

I wish I knew what the future held for me, maybe then this decision would be easier. I would know if I should stick around, and deal with the pain, as I wait for things to inevitably improve, or end my problems before they truly begin when things ultimately get a million times worse.

I can't say that I haven't thought about this a million times before, but I can say that no one ever knew about the thoughts running rampant in my head, there was no need for anyone to know. I don't want people to worry about me. Everyone has their own issues to worry about, they don't need to add mine onto their already gigantic load.

I can take care of myself. I always have, and I always will. I don't need to depend on anyone other than myself to keep me together. I can keep stitching myself back together every single day. I can keep holding onto an ounce of hope, the smallest belief that things are going to turn out alright for me.

Because I don't know what I'm going to do if I don't.

This town is always insanely quiet at night, especially at three in the morning, when not a single soul is wandering the streets other than me. Not a sound can be heard except my own breathing. It's peaceful up here, high above the ground, looking down at the insignificant world below me.

Sitting up here almost made me feel like I was something more than an ant roaming the world, trying to find its grand purpose in life, or what exactly it's meant to do. The height of this building makes me feel like I'm some sort of powerful force, who can see all forms of life below him. An overseeing force, watching people carry on in their individual lives that I know nothing about, as they all try to find the same thing everyone truly wants in life. Searching for their ability to be happy, to really have meaning, or some sort of strong purpose, or even a simple sense of identity. I think deep down, we all want to know who we are, and I don't believe a single person has any clue about who that is.

But we all pretend that we do.

No one could stop me from jumping right now. No one would even find my body splattered on the ground for at least a few more hours. No one would know anything until it was already too late.

I think I'm making this a harder decision than what it needs to be, and I'm overanalyzing everything that can happen based on the decision I make while sitting on this rooftop, kicking my feet over the edge, where exerting even the smallest increase in force will make my world go dark in a matter of seconds.

I don't have to jump. Instead, I could fake my death, and run far away from here. I could leave everything and everyone behind, and never tell anyone the truth about what happened to me. No one would ever be able to find me, and I'd never have to worry about my father coming after me. He'd be chasing after a ghost.

But I'd have to leave everyone else behind. I couldn't take Anastasia with me. I couldn't take Alastair with me. And I couldn't take Gabriel with me. None of them would know where I was, they wouldn't even know that I was still alive.

Can I really force them to mourn over me?

Believe that I'm dead?

Would this actually be for the best, or am I selfish, and think this is my only chance to get away from everything?

I feel like I have to do something, and I have to do it soon, or everything is only going to fall apart. But I don't know if I could truly handle faking my own death, and leaving everyone I love behind. This would all be so much easier if I could make them all hate me instead.

I stared into the night sky, as if the stars were going to give me some kind of answer, or some kind of justification for the different ideas I let run wild in my head. None of them seemed like good ideas the longer I thought about them, but I knew that eventually, I was going to follow through on one of them. I have a limited amount of paths left to follow in my life, and that doesn't mean that any of them are good, but they're all I have left.

I didn't stop thinking about my life, and the things I've been forced to live through. Those things never escaped my mind, they were always there, taking up space, blocking any positive thoughts from forming. I've always wondered why, of all the people in the world, I had to be the one to go through these things. Why was I the person who got so unlucky as to be the oldest son of Sebastian DuVonet?

I don't know why my father put me through the things he did, and I don't think there truly is a reason why. I believe that he's so miserable in his own life, and he feels the need to pass his pain onto everyone else, rather than deal with it on his own as a normal person would. I don't know why he turned out the way that he did, and I don't think I'll ever know. I can't keep asking his siblings, not when there are so few of them left, and not when they've all vanished at the news of three of their sibling's murders.

I don't know how I've managed to survive this long. I never thought I was going to make it to age eighteen, and that arrives in only nine short days. Maybe on that day, I'll move out. I'll find a nice, cheap apartment, and I'll take Anastasia and Alastair with me, and we'll finally be away from our father, and he'll never be able to hurt us again.

I can't help but believe that this is all wishful thinking, and I certainly can't stop myself from forcing in the thought that nothing is ever going to work out for me. I'm never going to get away, and I'll be stuck in this vicious cycle for the rest of my life, always wishing there was something more I could do to find a way out.

I think the only option I have to get away is to simply die. And that thought is only getting stronger and stronger, to the point where it's the only thing I'm ever thinking about, ever considering. It's the one thing I know for a fact would get me away from my father, no matter how horrible it may seem.

It doesn't automatically mean that this is what I want to do, but I know that it would work, and I'd finally be away from him. It was the only thing I could think to do. It wouldn't be difficult either, all I have to do is just slide forward, right over the edge of the building. It's one of the easiest things a person can do.

But I'm too weak to do it.

I can survive digging into my own skin constantly for seven straight years. I can survive having the rights to my own body taken from me on a weekly basis for five years. I can survive thinking about ending everything every single day for ten years. But I think I'm finally at my limit. I don't know how much more of this I can put up with. How many more agonizing minutes I can spend being forced to think about what's happened to me, labeling my own life a tragedy, like I'm some kind of play that people put on a stage for their own entertainment.

I want all of this to end. I don't want to have to keep waking up every time I can actually sleep at night, and think about what's going to go wrong in my life today. This isn't a way to live, and it's not fair. And I can understand that life isn't usually fair to anyone, but this isn't right.

I have to make some sort of decision about what I'm going to do, and what the rest of my life is going to look like. Does my life end with me sitting on this rooftop? Does it end seventy years down the line after living a full life with the man I love the most? Does it end in a few years by some freak accident? Is it something that I could have prevented? Or something that was destined to happen from the moment I first opened my eyes?

Is there anything that anyone can do in regards to their own deaths, or is it merely a thing that we have to learn to accept, knowing that it's coming for us one day, no matter if we're ready for it or not? It's not something we can outrun, and it will always be waiting for us behind some closed door. Waiting for the moment we finally become curious enough to peek at the world on the other side of the door, sucking us in for something we can never get away from.

I watched the sun slowly start to peek out from the horizon, I knew I had to make my decision now or never, I was running out of time. I let my mind run through every single option one more time, trying to determine the outcome for every situation.

As I felt the sun's warmth wash over my face, I knew I had finally made my decision after sitting on the rooftop all night, trying to understand a single thing that ran through my head. I didn't like any of the options that presented themselves, and I didn't even like the option I picked, but I knew it was what I *had* to do.

I don't think that I really had any other choice.

I took a deep breath, and quickly began climbing back down the side of the building. I didn't jump, I couldn't. Not this time at least. But I knew that soon enough, I would have to find a way to convince everyone that I did.

I knew actually jumping would only let my father win, and it would only make things even worse for Alastair and Anastasia. I couldn't do that to them, not now, not ever. I didn't want to keep fighting, but I don't think I really have much of a choice. I think I believe that I have a moral obligation to do what seems like the right thing.

I reached the street as the sun made itself fully known in the sky, illuminating the world around me, almost making everything seem like it had more color in it than it actually did. It made the world seem like it was happy for once, instead of looking like it was only filled with gray.

I didn't bother to walk back home that morning to walk to school with Alastair and Anastasia, I didn't have the time to go back there. I knew they would already be gone by the time I got back, and I couldn't deal with being there alone with my father and Elizabeth, I wouldn't subject myself to that kind of torment.

I walked into the schoolyard with a million thoughts in my head, but unable to focus on a single one of them, wandering around, listening to the thoughts all fighting for my attention, not really knowing where I was going, or even having any sort of plan. I simply let my feet carry me wherever they wanted.

"Atticus!" Alastair said, grabbing onto my shoulders and shaking me. I wondered how long he'd been trying to get my attention. I noticed Gabriel and Anastasia standing with him, both looking at me with concern.

"What?" I asked.

"Are you deaf or something? I've been trying to get your attention for the past five minutes," Alastair said, letting go of me.

"I didn't hear you," I said sincerely.

"Obviously," Anastasia added.

"What do you want?" I asked, sounding more rude than I meant to. I wish I knew why words flew off my tongue in such a disrespectful way sometimes, it's not even something I feel like I have control over, it just happens.

"Okay, rude. First of all, where did you go last night?" Alastair asked.

How did he know I went anywhere?

Was he looking for me?

"Don't even try to say you were with me, I already told him you weren't," Gabriel said. I really do hate that they're friends now, it makes everything that much more difficult for me.

"I was stargazing," I said. It wasn't a total lie, there was some truth to that. They didn't need to know that I was stargazing on top of a building, deciding if I should jump or not.

"Bullshit," Alastair said, crossing his arms and staring deep into my face, almost like he was trying to read my mind or something.

"The fuck do you mean? You asked where I went, I went stargazing. Is it illegal to go look at the stars now?" I asked defensively.

"See, he immediately got defensive, so he's lying," Gabriel said.

"What the fuck?" I protested, feeling like the three of them were interrogating me as if I had been accused of murder.

"Where were you really?" Gabriel asked.

"Can I ask what the fuck is going on here, and why the three of you have suddenly banded together to start grilling me on what I do when I'm alone? And why none of you believe that I spent my night looking at stars?" I asked, more and more questions forming the more that I spoke.

"Because you keep lying to us about everything. And it's time you start giving us some real answers," Anastasia added.

"I have absolutely no idea what you're talking about," I said. It was true, I didn't know what they were talking about this time, or what exactly they were accusing me of.

"Where did you go last night?" Alastair asked once again, with more force this time, like he was ready to punch me in the face, again.

"What exactly do you want me to say?" I asked.

"The truth would be nice," Gabriel said.

"I'm not lying?"

What the fuck were they talking about? There's no way any of them could have known that I was sitting on top of the roof, there wasn't a single person who could have seen me.

"Oh, so you weren't sitting on the roof of the library?" Gabriel asked.

"How the fuck do you know that?" I asked. Was someone watching me? Were they following me around or something?

"So you were lying to us?" Anastasia asked in a cocky tone, like she had caught me wrapped up in some scandal.

"No, I wasn't. I was up there looking at the fucking stars because that's the highest building in the town, and you can get the best view from there," I said. I still wasn't fully lying, the top of the library did have a nice view, and it did give you the clearest look at the sky.

No matter how hard they questioned me, I wasn't going to tell them that I considered jumping. I didn't jump, and that's all that matters. The thoughts I let run around in my mind are none of their business, they never have been, and they never will be. They don't need to know about every single detail of my life, or the thoughts I store deep in my mind.

"Why'd you go out?" Alastair asked.

"Because I like looking at the stars? When did that become a crime?" I asked, feeling my frustration grow with each passing second.

"You were gone all night," Alastair added.

"Don't you know by now that I rarely ever sleep?" I reminded him. I didn't understand what was going on, or why they were being like this. There was nothing more for me to tell them, and yet they kept insisting that there was. Almost like they were creating problems that weren't actually there, or that they didn't need to know about.

"You're the same one that always told me that I could talk to you. Don't you think you should take your own advice?" Anastasia added. It felt like they were all trying to attack me in some way, for some reason.

"There's nothing to talk about,"

"There always is," Alastair said. I could see that he and Anastasia were thinking the same things. But I could also tell that Gabriel could sense that they were all pissing me off beyond belief. And he knew that if they irritated me enough, I'd stop speaking to all of them altogether.

"If Atticus says it's nothing, then it's nothing. Just drop it," Gabriel said, never breaking eye contact with me. He knew the words to say when I didn't have the emotional control to say them myself.

"Weren't you the same one suggesting that something was wrong in the first place?" Anastasia responded. Of course he was, because who else would instantly pick up that something wasn't right, other than him?

"I was, but if Atticus is adamant about the fact that it's nothing, then drop it," He replied. The look he gave me almost said that our conversation was far from over, but he knew he had to stop things here, or they'd only get gradually worse as the morning carried on.

I made my way in the direction of my first class, knowing that Gabriel was following right behind me, leaving my brother and sister standing in the schoolyard on their own, trying to convince themselves that nothing was wrong.

"You and I both know that you weren't on that roof to *just* look at the stars," Gabriel whispered to me as soon as we were far enough away from my siblings.

"Yes, I was,"

"Atticus,"

"How did you even know I was there?" I asked, turning to face him.

"Because I went up there last night. Alastair came over, told me that you were gone, and that he didn't know where you were. So, I went to go look for you, and I knew that you'd be there. And when I saw you sitting at the edge, I knew you weren't just trying to get a good view," He said.

"If you knew that was happening, why didn't you say anything?" I asked. It didn't seem like him to ignore me in a situation like that.

"I did. You ignored me," He said.

"I never heard anything. I wasn't ignoring you," I corrected him.

"Atticus,"

"I'm faking my death," I quietly blurted out.

"What?"

"That's why I was up there. I was deciding what to do, and I finally decided. I'm faking my death, and getting as far away from here as I possibly can. I don't know when, but probably soon. Before I turn eighteen. So in about a week," I said. I didn't see a point in trying to keep this a secret from him, I knew he was going to find out one way or another eventually.

"That's not fucking funny, Atticus," He said, his voice taking on a serious tone.

"It's not a joke, Gabe. It's what I have to do," I explained.

"Why are you telling me this then?" He asked, tears forming in his eyes.

"You would have figured it out one way or another. So I might as well tell you myself. At least then you'll have some time to prepare yourself," I said. I didn't feel anything as I told him this. All I felt was a weight was being lifted off of my shoulders; like I could finally breathe for the first time in seventeen long years. It's not like I really wanted to do this, but what choice did I have?

I'm so sick of never having a choice in my life. Even when I'm trying to take control of my life, and change things for the better, I still don't even feel like I have a single choice. Like everything is so far out of my control, and there's nothing I can do about it.

"You're fucking with me, right? You're not *actually* doing this, are you?" Gabriel asked.

I'm not surprised that he was so taken aback at this, it's not something that anyone wants to hear. I only hope he can understand that this is what I have to do, it's the only way I'm ever going to be okay. This is the only way I can get away from my father, and finally make my life my own, and do whatever I want, whatever is going to make *me* happy for once.

"I have to,"

"No, you fucking don't," He interrupted.

"This is the only way I'm ever going to get away from my father. I'm not asking you to be okay with it, I'm asking you to understand. I need you to realize that for once, I'm finally trying to do what's best for me, no matter how extreme it seems. I'm out of options, Gabe. I can't do this anymore, and there's nothing else I can do to get out of here alive. I can't keep hanging on, hoping that one day this will all stop, it's never going to. I can't do this anymore. I found a way out, and I have to take it, you're the same one that tried to get me to leave a month ago. I can't sit in that house and suffer anymore, it's driving me insane," I explained, finally walking into the classroom and taking my seat in the back of the room.

Gabriel sat there in silence. I don't think there was anything for him to say, I don't think there was anything anyone could say. There are no words to form a perfect response to this kind of situation, and there isn't a perfect response. There isn't a good reaction to being told your boyfriend is going to fake his death, and you'll never be able to see him again.

I didn't want to have to leave everyone behind, not like this, but I didn't know what else to do. I've come to some of the most important realizations and decisions on that rooftop, and if being up there told me that I had to fake my death, then that's what I have to do. There hasn't been a single thought I've had up there that has been wrong, and I'm not going to start doubting the power that rooftop holds now. Part of me felt like that roof could simply peel back my skin and peer into my brain, poking around at all the thoughts I didn't understand, and somehow make sense of them all, giving me some sort of clarity, even if the answers still did seem kind of fuzzy sometimes.

But for the most part, everything seemed to make sense up there. It felt like all of my problems faded away, like they didn't exist; like they were never even real in the first place. Like they only had power buried deep in my mind, because I was too weak to stop them from taking control of me, and I always let them run around, messing everything up.

But the rooftop took that power away from my problems, and took control of my life for me. Everything was always easier up there somehow. I've never understood why, but the rooftop feels like a place where things work differently, like nothing is real up there except for me, and the conversations I have between the cold roof and I, even allowing the stars to join the conversation sometimes, because they were the only other thing that listened to me. Maybe things have been so difficult lately because I haven't gotten a chance to sit up there, and watch the stars for hours in so long.

I don't know where I'm going, but I know I can't go anywhere as Atticus DuVonet, I need a new name. Maybe I'd even take a name from the stars. Orion has always been my favorite constellation. I've never really understood why I felt so attached to that particular clump of stars, maybe it's because deep down, something within me knew that was going to become my name one day. Or maybe it was because the rooftop knew. I don't think I'd even be surprised if the rooftop knew exactly how the rest of my life was going to go.

Gabriel and I both sat through our class in complete silence, hardly even acknowledging each other's presence. He didn't even turn to look at me, and I didn't bother to say a word to him. He was angry with me, that much I knew. I didn't think it was right for him to be angry, I was only trying to do what was best for me, it didn't matter if he agreed with me or not. But that didn't mean that it didn't hurt that he was angry with me. I don't know if he was mad that I told him, mad that I was doing this, or mad that I was willing to leave everyone and everything behind to try to feel safe for once in my life.

I don't think this makes me selfish, I don't think a person can be selfish for trying to take care of themselves. I think this makes me someone who's spent his entire life living in fear of the people who were supposed to love him more than anything; and doesn't know any other way to get away from the life he's been trapped in. Trapped, feeling hopeless for so long, always thinking every moment is going to be his last.

We moved on to our next class, still not speaking to each other. I had already said everything I felt I needed to say, and Gabriel clearly hadn't seen a need to say anything else to me. So we didn't speak. It's not that I didn't *want* to talk to him, it's that he didn't want to talk to me. And I couldn't force him to do anything, I couldn't make him understand, I couldn't make him be okay with this, and I couldn't make him talk to me. I had to sit there silently, hoping that he would understand, and that he wouldn't be mad at me for prioritizing myself for once in my life. I guess people aren't used to me putting myself first.

I don't think he understood, and I honestly don't know that he ever will. He ignored me for the entire rest of the day, he wouldn't even look at me. It was like I was a ghost to him. Maybe he was simply trying to prepare himself for what life is going to be like for him in about a week.

"What's going on with you?" Alastair asked as I sat down next to him in the back of the room.

"What is it with you always thinking that something's wrong?" I asked, trying to dismiss my brother's question.

"Don't you dare answer my question with another question," He responded. I should have known he wasn't going to drop it.

"Were you looking for me last night, or something?"

"Yeah, actually, I was,"

"Why?"

"Well it doesn't matter now, it mattered last night," He scoffed.

"Then why are you being such an asshole about last night?"

"It's nothing,"

"Obviously it's something if you're that hung up on it," I persisted.

"Atticus, shut the fuck up," Alastair pushed, turning to look at me.

It seems like lately, everyone suddenly has a problem with me. I don't know why, or what I recently changed to make everyone so angry all of the time, but it doesn't matter. I'll be gone soon enough anyway, and I won't be anyone's problem anymore. No one will have to think about me anymore, and I'll be able to vanish like a cloud of smoke, thinning out in the air, gone without a trace.

Part of me believes that this is going to be a peaceful disappearance, but the rest of me feels like I'm never going to actually get away. I don't think it's as simple as leaving the house, leaving the town, or even leaving the state. No matter how far away I go, I think there's always going to be some part of me that's stuck here. Unable to leave, like a ghost chained to a house, forced to let their spirit wander, looking for any kind of resolution, knowing it's never going to arrive, eventually accepting they'll always be a piece of the house they could never quite escape, haunting everyone who's left behind in a place that left them in so much pain. Maybe I already am a ghost, and I'm only trying to hold on to the things I'm afraid to let go of, because I don't know what waits for me in the beyond.

I can't say I'm not afraid of what's going to come next for me, I don't even know what to expect. I know I have to hope it's for the best; because I don't know what I'm going to do if things only get worse from here. I don't think it's even possible for things to get even worse. I believe that at this point in my life, I've already faced the worst things I will ever be forced to survive. And I think that through all these horrible things, I've only become stronger, and I've finally gained the strength to get out of here.

The day was reaching its end, and I left my final class five minutes earlier than I was supposed to. I had forgotten to say anything to Alastair and Gabriel about Anastasia's classroom, but I didn't need to. They were already waiting outside the door as I walked up to it. She must have told them herself. I don't know what they knew, and I certainly wasn't going to ask, it wasn't my place.

None of us spoke, we simply stood at the open door, watching the pervert standing at the front of the classroom, never taking our eyes off him for a moment. I don't think he even bothered to notice that we were standing there, waiting for him.

"Anastasia, please stay back for a few moments," He said with a wicked grin. The three of us looked at each other, it was clear we all had the same thought in mind. I led us into the classroom, and we stood together at the back of the room as the other students slowly started exiting the class, leaving only my sister and the pedophile in the room.

The three of us walked closer to the front of the room as the creep inched closer to my sister, and we formed a line right behind her. I knew that I'd have absolutely no protests against slamming that freak's head into a desk if he took even one step closer.

"Let's go, Ana," Alastair said, grabbing her bag for her, and beginning to usher her out of the door.

"I need to speak with Miss DuVonet," The disgusting excuse for a man said, looking like he was sweating bullets.

"So speak," I said, never taking my eyes off of him.

"Privately," He gulped. There's no possible way he's stupid enough to think that's going to work.

"Not happening," Gabriel added.

"We're her brothers, you can say whatever it is you have to say to her in front of us," Alastair said.

"Well, I can't," He said nervously.

"Alright, here are your options. You shut the fuck up and leave my sister alone, or I bash your fucking skull in. That's it. Those are your only options. Make your choice now, or I make it for you," I said. I didn't care about anything he could possibly threaten me with, it didn't matter anyway.

"I suggest you go with the first option," Alastair said.

"You're threatening a teacher, I'll,"

"Shut the fuck up. Option one, or option two?" I interrupted, rolling my sleeves up.

The little coward nodded, agreeing to take the first choice. I still wanted to crack his skull open, but today wasn't the day. He'll get what's coming to him soon enough. My only hope is that I'm still here to see it when it finally arrives for him.

The four of us walked out of the classroom, with Anastasia exiting first, and quickly walked out to the schoolyard, Gabriel quietly going his separate way only moments after exiting the building.

I wish he wasn't angry with me, but I can't change that. He's going to feel how he wants to feel, and there's nothing I can do about it. If he doesn't understand why this is something I have to do, I can't force him to understand. He either gets it, or he doesn't. And I don't have the time to make him understand. But, I have to hope that one of these days, he can forgive me. And maybe he will.

But there's always a chance that he'll never be able to forgive me for vanishing, leaving nothing behind but memories that are only going to fade over time.

"You're both weirdly quiet," Anastasia said as we were almost halfway home.

"There's nothing to say," Alastair and I said in unison, turning to look at each other in disgust.

"Stop doing that," We said together, again.

"Stop!" Once again, prompting laughter from Anastasia. It was nice hearing her laugh. It's become almost like a foreign sound, only existing in memories that I flip back to when I don't know what else to do, or where else to let my mind wander.

I think that's one of the things I'm going to miss the most, hearing her laugh, and as much as we both hate it, being so in sync with Alastair. I don't want to mourn for myself as if I'm already gone, but it's something that I can't help. It's like I've never seen the good things in my life until I'm preparing to say goodbye to them. I think I've always looked at my life like a gray area, and I've never bothered to take a moment to realize that not everything is awful.

But that's not going to change my mind. I've made my decision, and I've accepted what I have to do, no matter how much I'm going to miss, or how painful it's going to be. For once in my life, I finally made a decision that's going to make my life better, and I can't go back on that. Not now, not ever.

Chapter Sixteen

We walked into the house together, still hushing our laughter. It was never often that we had these kinds of moments together, filled with pure joy and happiness. We lived in our moments when we could, and then we'd store them in our minds, going back to them whenever we needed something to lift our spirits, which, in this house, was constantly.

"Stop laughing," Sebastian said to the three of us as he came down the stairs, instantly silencing us. I've never understood why our father was so against the sound of his children being happy, and I don't think I really care to understand anymore. He's a bitter man, and he doesn't believe that anyone deserves to be happy. All because *he* can't even manage to be happy. I did still wonder how he turned out this way, but I don't think there is an explanation for something like that. I believe there's simply something fundamentally wrong with him, and nothing is ever going to change that.

"There's nothing for any of you to be laughing at," Elizabeth said from the top of the stairs. I didn't know what their problem was today, and quite honestly, it didn't matter to me. They're terrible people with terrible morals, the fact that we even breathe their air is a problem to them.

"In case you were not aware, my three siblings are back in town for whatever reason. You are to not engage with them in any way, or there will be severe consequences, am I understood?" He asked, walking closer to the three of us, eyeing me up and down as he delivered his threat, almost as if he already knew I had no intentions of following his demand.

"Yes, Sir," Alastair and Anastasia said.

"Atticus, answer your father," Elizabeth barked down at me.

"I'm not going to make promises I can't keep, Elizabeth," I said with the same tone she gave to me.

"Be respectful!" Sebastian said, slapping me.

"You first,"

"You don't deserve my respect," He said, looking down at me.

"And neither do you," I laughed. I knew he was going to do whatever he wanted to do to me, and I didn't care. Things were going to change soon enough, and nothing that he could do to me was ever going to matter ever again.

"Garage, now!" He shouted, instantly wiping the smirk off of my face.

Fuck.

I should have known this was coming. This is what he always does. I can't even try to fight him this time, he'll leave me in there for another month again, and I can't go through that again. That's the only thing I can't do. If I'm left in there for more than one night, I know with absolute certainty that I won't be alive when he finally opens the door.

I didn't say anything in protest. I silently walked to the garage, heading inside, allowing my father to shut the door behind me, locking me in the darkness once again. At least in here, maybe I could think about what I was going to do when I finally left here. Where I was going to go, what my plans were, and who I'd become.

I wanted to go somewhere where the weather was nice, and where I could do a million things I've always wanted to do. Anywhere is better than here, and at least somewhere else, I'd finally get to make all the decisions in my life, and no one would be able to tell me what I can and can't do.

I can become the person I've always wanted to be, and finally have the happiness I've spent seventeen years searching for. At least thinking about the life I have ahead of me kept my mind off of the fact that I was still locked inside the cold garage.

I think I'm going to leave in two days, exactly a week before I turn eighteen. It almost feels metaphorical, like I'm leaving the life of my youth behind, and trading it in for a new existence as an adult. It's a way of saying goodbye to so many things, and it allows me to make room for something new in my life. It allows me to finally be able to heal, and move on from what I was *forced* to be, giving me the space to become who I'm *meant* to be. Giving me a life where I don't have to hide who I am, and what I want from life.

For the first time in my entire life, I think I felt calm in the garage. I didn't feel like I couldn't breathe, my heart wasn't pounding out of my chest, and I wasn't panicking. I felt a type of numbing calm I don't think I've ever experienced before. It was a kind of floating sensation, like none of my problems were real, and they all materialized themselves in my head. It felt like things might actually be okay.

Time seemed to pass by quickly. It felt like I'd only been in here for a few minutes, maybe an hour at most. And before I knew it, the door slowly opened, pushing light into the dark garage, blinding me with the sheer intensity of the light seeping in.

"Out. Go to school," Sebastian said plainly, quickly urging me out of the garage. I didn't speak, I only did what he told me. I went upstairs, quickly changing my clothes, throwing on an old dark blue sweater and black sweatpants. I grabbed my things, and quickly moved down the stairs, meeting Alastair and Anastasia outside.

"You didn't have to wait for me," I said, beginning to walk to school.

"We figured we'd be nice," Alastair said, nudging me. He seemed happier than he was yesterday. I still don't know what he wanted from me the other night, and it didn't feel right to ask. If he wanted to tell me, he would. It didn't really matter, if he was happy now, then the events of yesterday didn't matter.

"Today's the twenty-second, right?" I asked.

"Yes, it was only one night," Alastair said, instantly understanding the point of my question.

We carried on in silence, only sparing glances at each other every few moments, almost as if we were asserting that our siblings were still beside us, and didn't fade away into the darkness of our lives.

Despite the fact that they were both right next to me, I don't think I've ever felt more alone in my life. I have to say goodbye to the people I loved the most my entire life in less than two days, and I don't even get to actually say goodbye. I simply have to leave. I can't even tell them where I'm going, or the truth about what's going to happen to me.

I don't know if they're going to miss me. I know that I'll miss them. There won't be a single day that they aren't taking up space in my mind, I know I'm going to be thinking about them in everything I do. Part of me hopes they'll miss me, but at the same time, I hope they don't. If they don't, maybe that would make it easier on them.

I've never been good at goodbyes, and I know that's not going to change now. It almost doesn't even feel real, like it's all some wild dream in my head, or like I've been asleep for years, and this is all some insane idea that's been planted in my thoughts, as some kind of solution to my problems.

The three of us walked into the schoolyard, but didn't move away from each other. It was like we were all frozen in this single moment, afraid to let go of it.

"Is it just me or does something seem off to you guys too?" Anastasia asked, looking at me, as if she knew what I was going to do, or like she could see into my mind. I don't think I'm even convinced that she can't read my thoughts, she always seems to know somehow.

"I think it's just you," Alastair said.

"Off how?" I asked.

"I don't know, but I have a weird feeling. It's probably nothing, I just didn't know if it was a me-thing," She elaborated.

"Nope, it's all you," Alastair said, walking toward his group of friends. I stayed with Anastasia for a few moments, it didn't feel right to walk away from her.

"You're going to be eighteen soon," She began.

"What about it?" I asked, turning to look at my sister who only stared straight ahead. It was like she was afraid to look at me.

"Are you leaving? You know, you'll be an adult, you could walk away and live on your own. So I'm asking if you *are* doing that, or if you're going to stick around with me for a little bit longer?" She asked, still never turning to look at me.

I didn't have an answer for her. I didn't want to lie to her, but that didn't mean that I could tell her the truth either. No one can know what I have planned for myself, if anyone else knows, then my plan won't work, and I'll only increase the chance that my father finds out what I'm doing, and tries to stop me.

"I don't know," Was all I managed to say.

"I think somewhere within you, you know. You don't have to lie to me. If you want to leave, I get it, I'm not going to ask you to stay. You deserve to get out of here as soon as you can, you don't need to stick around for my sake," She said. I feel like Anastasia might know what I'm planning to do, even though I never said a word about it to her. I think she somehow understands me on a level I never knew, and she knows exactly what I want to do.

"But I want you to know that whatever happens, I love you," I said, fighting to keep my eyes from filling with tears.

"I love you too," She said, still refusing to look at me. I didn't need to see her face to know that she was crying, I know her well enough to know how she was reacting. I can't be convinced that Anastasia doesn't have at least some sort of idea of what I have planned for the rest of my life. But even if she knows, she's not going to say it out loud.

I watched my sister walk away from me, noticing her hands move to her eyes to wipe her tears away. I felt guilty about leaving her behind, but I knew she would understand. Better than anyone, I think.

I had to collect myself before I could even move from where I was standing. It hurt me to think about how Anastasia would react to the statement that I was dead, even though it was false. She can put up a tough front all that she wants, but I don't think she'll accept it for a long time, if she ever does. I think she'll be able to see right through it, and she'll never buy into the lie that I'm dead, not really. Sure, she'll pretend that she believes it in front of our father, but I don't think she'll ever truly accept it.

I finally walked further into the yard, eventually spotting Gabriel, leaning against the same wall as always. I noticed him looking at me with anger in his eyes. He still hasn't accepted that he's not going to change my mind, and he's running out of time.

I walked up to him, prepared for him to start screaming at me, but much to my surprise, he didn't say anything to me. He only stared at me, waiting for me to say something.

"Gabriel,"

"I fucking hate you, you selfish prick," He said with fury, shoving me, and quickly walking away.

Did he really mean that?

Did he really hate me?

Was telling him what I was going to do a mistake?

Do I seriously have to spend the last few days I have here with the love of my life hating me?

It felt like my entire spirit was thrown off of a building, falling, and eventually thudding on the ground, breaking everything it held in it. Never to be whole again, never being able to be fixed. If Gabriel truly hated me, then there was nothing I could do to change that. That didn't mean it didn't still feel like there was a serrated knife lodged in my heart, twisting and turning, ripping me apart from the inside out every single time I took a breath, causing my lungs to fill up with blood, my own body drowning itself in its sorrow and pain.

I slowly made my way to my class, I didn't care if I was late. I needed to take the little time I had to think about what I was doing, and if it was too late to change my mind. But I can't change my mind, I won't. I have to do what's best for me, even if no one agrees with me, or if I'm suddenly selfish for trying to prioritize myself for once.

I walked into the classroom, noticing Gabriel sitting in the front of the room, rather than the back. He didn't want to speak to me, that much was clear. But not speaking to me isn't going to change anything. His silence isn't going to persuade me to stay here, and keep taking my father's abuse. I don't know why he can't understand that, or why it seems like he thinks I'm leaving simply because I can, or as if I don't have a valid reason.

He's the same one who tried to get me to leave when he first learned what really went on in the DuVonet house. I don't understand why he suddenly is so against me trying to safely escape.

I don't feel like I have to explain the thousands of thoughts and ideas that circulated in my head before I decided on this one to him. He doesn't need to know about every little detail or idea that forms in my mind, and to feel as if I owe him an explanation for anything is simply wrong. I don't think I have to give anyone an explanation for anything, and yet, I still think Gabriel is trying to silently demand one. But if he can't speak to me without insulting me, or even trying to understand where I'm coming from, why should I even bother speaking to him at all?

That doesn't mean it didn't still break my heart to not speak to him, or to realize that I may never speak to him again, and the last thing he said to me is that he hates me. I don't know if I believe that's true. I certainly hope it's not, I don't want to believe that all the time we've spent together was permanently tainted by one decision.

But I can't force him to understand. I can't make anyone do anything. If he doesn't want to listen to me, then there's nothing I can do about that. I can only accept that I'm never going to see him again, and this is where our paths diverge. I want him to be able to be happy without me, and if his happiness begins with hating me, then I can learn to live with that. That doesn't mean that I'm okay with it, but it's something that I have to deal with.

Every single class that I had with Gabriel was the exact same. He sat as far away from me as possible, and he wouldn't even look in my direction. He treated me like I was a ghost, like I didn't matter to him, like all the years we've spent together didn't mean anything to him. I won't pretend that I understand why he's being like this, because I don't. He's never been one to avoid problems instead of dealing with them, that's always been me.

I think his silence might be an attempt at trying to convince me to stick around, and if it is, I don't think he realizes that this isn't going to get him anywhere. There's nothing that he can say, or do to get me to change my mind, and I wish he would understand that.

The day was half over before I saw my brother again. For once, I couldn't get a read on how he was feeling. He didn't seem quiet, but he didn't seem particularly talkative either.

"What's up with you?" I asked Alastair after ten minutes of sitting in silence.

"I'm just thinking about what Anastasia said this morning, about how something feels off to her," He explained.

"Why? Are you getting that same feeling?"

"I don't know if it's the same, but it's definitely a feeling. I don't know, I can't explain it, but I feel weird. It's probably because she's getting in my head about it, I'm sure it's nothing," He said, shrugging it off. I didn't understand the feelings that my siblings had, all I knew was that I didn't have that same instinctive thought. If anything, I think the world felt blank to me, like nothing around me was even real, and it was all a part of some wild story running around in my brain.

Maybe I'm overthinking things, and I'm trying to find problems where they don't exist, or where nothing is really wrong, all because I don't know how to live a life where there are moments when everything is quiet, and peaceful.

To me, the moments where peace prevails seem like giant lies, all as a means of trying to convince me that maybe, things can change. Maybe things can be better, and I won't have to take such extreme measures to feel safe in this world. Maybe I won't have to run away from everything I've ever known, and everyone I've ever loved, if only to have a place where I feel like I truly belong, and where I don't have to be afraid of every single noise I hear.

Where the sound of a piano can bring me some amount of relaxation, as it does for everyone else.

Where children don't have to be afraid of their parents, and what might be waiting for them when they come home from school every day, expecting some form of punishment for breathing air, and trying to live their lives.

"Are you okay?" Alastair asked, lightly elbowing me.

Had he been speaking to me this entire time, but I was too lost deep within my own mind to even hear the words he was saying, or acknowledge that he was sitting right next to me?

"I'm completely fine, why do you ask?"

"You seem more quiet than normal. Like, weirdly quiet," He said.

"I'm just thinking," I quietly said. It wasn't a lie, I was buried somewhere deep within my mind as I tried to understand anything about my life, about my future even.

"About?" He asked. I could tell he was bored, and Alastair always seemed to find great enjoyment in picking apart my thoughts, trying to understand the way that my brain worked, and why I did the things I did.

"Everything, I think," I said thoughtfully. I couldn't exactly pinpoint my thoughts to a single topic, they were all over the place, and about things I don't think I could ever really explain. I've never been able to explain the things that go on in my head, but Alastair always seems to understand what I mean.

"You can't possibly be thinking about everything," He laughed.

"Maybe you don't have the mental capacity for such a feat," I said in a cocky tone.

"Oh, and you do?"

"I do, actually. It's this thing called being the better twin," I said, leaving Alastair's mouth hanging open in pure shock.

"You know what," He began.

"Atticus and Alastair DuVonet!" Our teacher called to us from the front of the room, motioning us toward her, cutting off Alastair's sentence.

"What'd you do?" Alastair asked as we moved to the front of the room.

"Me?" I asked as we reached the teacher's desk. I didn't even know her name, I don't think I even knew half of my teacher's names.

"Your father is having you both return home early today. You're leaving after this class," She said.

"What about our sister?" Alastair asked.

"No, just you boys," She explained, shrugging, dismissing us back to our seats.

What could our father possibly want from us that required pulling us out of school early, and that didn't include Anastasia? I didn't imagine that it was going to be anything good, but I couldn't think of a single thing that he could have wanted us for.

"Any ideas?" I asked Alastair as we sat back down.

"I was going to ask you the same thing," He said, looking at me with confusion written all over his face.

"Did we fuck anything up before we left for school this morning? I know there's nothing I fucked up last night, I was in the garage all night," I said.

"No, you came out of the garage, changed, and then we left. What could we have possibly done in that literal ten-minute span of time?" He asked.

"I have no idea, that's why I asked if you had any ideas,"

"Well, I don't have shit, so I don't know what to tell you," He shrugged.

I tried running through everything I could have possibly done in my mind, and I couldn't think of a single thing that could have pissed my father off so much that he deemed it necessary to bring Alastair and I home early.

We both watched the clock anxiously, fearing the moment that we would be sent home. We didn't have enough time to prepare ourselves for whatever we were about to deal with from our father. Maybe this was proving Anastasia's feeling from this morning right.

Our class ended, and Alastair and I were dismissed to go home. We didn't get a chance to find Anastasia and tell her what was going on, we had to leave right away, and we knew we'd only make things even worse if we didn't get there as quickly as we possibly could.

Alastair and I exited the school, and I felt my heart pounding in my chest, like it was going to explode inside my body, threatening to kill me in the middle of the schoolyard.

"Are you ready?" Alastair asked, his voice slightly shaking as we stood in the yard, trying to prepare ourselves to make our way home.

"Not really, but what choice do we have?" I asked. My brother nodded, and we began walking in the direction of our house.

I felt my legs shaking underneath me, panic rushing through my entire body, it was like every single system in my body was sending a warning sign, like everything within me knew that there was no possible way this could end well.

"Breathe," Alastair said as we were halfway home.

"What?"

"If you're not going to talk, at least remember to breathe. I haven't heard you take a single breath this entire time," He said. How have I never realized that my brother literally studies my breathing?

"What do you want me to say?" I asked.

"Anything at all. The silence is only making both of us panic even more, and you know that. And when *you* panic, you forget to breathe, which never fucking ends well, and usually ends up with you on the ground, and me having to carry you again. And when *you* panic, *I* panic, and when *I* panic, *you* panic, and it's an extremely vicious cycle, so please, say anything at all," He said in a rushed tone.

"I'm not panicking," I said, trying to keep my voice level.

"You're also a shit liar,"

"Stop analyzing me,"

"I'm not analyzing you, it's basic observations,"

"Who observes that kind of thing?" I asked, almost feeling like my nerves were slowly fading away.

"I do," He said sheepishly.

"What the fuck is wrong with you?" I laughed, prompting the same reaction from my brother, who finally started to slow his voice down.

"We don't have the time to dive into that, and you know that," He said as we were only moments away from reaching our house, which was our signal to stop laughing, and mentally prepare ourselves to deal with whatever our father wanted from us that he decided was important enough to pull us out of our classes for the rest of the day.

I led us to the door, slowly opening it, taking as much time as I possibly could to allow my mind to calm down, so I could react rationally to whatever Sebastian was going to throw at us. I knew I couldn't let my emotions take over, not this time.

We quietly walked into the house, not trying to draw too much attention to ourselves, hoping that the less known we made ourselves, the less irritated our father would be with the fact that we were alive.

"Boys!" Sebastian shouted as he came down the stairs, coming face to face with Alastair and I, causing my heart to beat even faster with each passing millisecond.

"Sir," Alastair said.

"Do you have any idea what exactly you've done?" He shouted. Of course, we didn't know. We never knew exactly what had set our father off at any given moment. He was always angry about something, for no reason other than the fact that he always found it justifiable.

"No, Sir," Alastair said.

"Of course, you don't, because you two never think of anyone but yourselves!" He screamed, slapping Alastair.

"What the fuck are you talking about now?!" I yelled. I never cared when my father hit me, but the moment he touched anyone else, I didn't give a shit about what he would do to me. He could kill me for all I care if it meant he wouldn't hurt anyone else ever again.

"Don't play dumb!" He said, slapping me.

"We don't know what you're talking about! We never know what you're talking about!" I screamed. I don't know why I had some moments where I suddenly was no longer afraid of my father, or what he might do to me, but if it discouraged him even the smallest amount, I'd take those moments at any chance I could get.

"You idiotic boy! Did you really think I wouldn't find out that you spread your lies to people all over this town?!" He shouted, shoving me.

"I don't know what you're talking about!" I yelled back.

"You lied to everyone, you told them that I abuse you! You thought you were doing some kind of noble work, claiming that I'm some kind of monster!" He screamed.

None of that is a lie, but I never told anyone. In my seventeen years, I've only ever told one person about the things that happen here.

No.

There's no fucking way he told anyone about this.

He couldn't have.

He wouldn't have.

"You claimed to be telling everyone the truth about me, and all you told were lies!" Sebastian shouted, pushing me, his words hitting me in the face all right after each other.

I let myself get so caught up in my own mind that I didn't hear anything around me. I couldn't hear what my father was saying, I couldn't hear if Alastair was saying anything. Everything around me felt quiet.

I suppose that my father used my distracted state to his advantage, and took the few moments that I was lost somewhere that I couldn't even find to do what he'd been trying to do for so long.

The feeling of a cold metal blade piercing through my stomach was enough to snap me back to reality, forcing me to realize the knife that my father had shoved into my body, which he quickly removed moments later.

I felt my blood quickly start oozing out of my body, and all my strength vanished from my body, I couldn't keep myself standing.

So I didn't bother to try.

I let myself begin to fall, Alastair catching me before I could hit the ground. I could hardly see him, he looked like some kind of blurry mess that didn't even seem real.

"Atticus, hold on, please," Alastair said, pressing his hand to the gaping wound that continued to leak without any mercy. I felt drops of water begin to poke at the corners of my eyes.

"Alastair," Was the last word I could choke out as blood poured into my lungs, making it difficult to breathe.

"Stay with me," He said as I tried to fight my eyes from closing, hoping for the impossible.

I knew I was going to die, it was only a matter of time now. Nothing was going to save me, my life was fading away faster than I would have ever thought was possible. This was the end of the road for me. This was what I always expected from my life, but what I always hoped I'd be able to avoid.

But I guess it was ridiculous of me to believe that I could dodge what I always knew was meant for me.

I felt all of my senses slowly fading away from me. Alastair's loud pleading turned into mumbling, his tears falling onto my face, matching my own silent cries that I had no control over.

The world around me went dark, and all I heard were footsteps. I couldn't quite figure out who they were, but I guess it didn't really matter anyway. There was nothing I could do about them, but try to listen as my hearing slowly slipped away from me. It was all that was left, and I knew it would be gone soon too.

Everything seemed to get quiet, and I thought I was finally gone, until I heard the ear-splitting scream that I recognized instantly as Anastasia's voice ringing in my ears, slowly growing quieter and quieter, until no sound remained, and the world was only an empty void that I was floating in, nothing tying me down except my own desires to try to cheat fate.

I don't know what I feel. I don't know if I feel peace or pain, I'm not even sure I feel anything at all. Despite all my desires to die, I guess I never really imagined what it felt like, or what would happen to me after I took my final breath and my heart stopped beating.

I don't know if there's anything beyond this, I don't know if I want there to be anything beyond this. I'm not sure I could go through this all again. Maybe there's something waiting for me in the beyond, but maybe there isn't.

It's hard to allow myself to let go, but I know my fight is over. There's nothing more for me to do. I'm not strong enough to keep fighting this war that I know will never end.

So I have to let myself go, and I have to hope that Alastair and Anastasia can continue to survive without me. I wish I could have done more for them, but I've done all that I can do. I protected them for seventeen years, and I hope that it was enough. I hope that one day, Gabriel can move on, and live a peaceful, happy life without me, like he's always deserved.

And maybe now, I'll finally be able to see Annabelle again.

www.ingramcontent.com/pod-product-compliance
Lightning Source LLC
Chambersburg PA
CBHW080716020726

47501CB00010B/2447

* 9 7 9 8 2 1 8 6 2 4 8 5 9 *